D0064844

THE TREE STILL STANDS

ALSO BY MAE BRISKIN:

A Boy Like Astrid's Mother

THE TREE STILL STANDS

MAE BRISKIN

W. W. Norton & Company
New York • London

Printed in the United States of America.

The text of this book is composed in Meridien,
with the display set in Bauer Text Initials.
Composition and manufacturing by Maple-Vail Book Manufacturing Group.
Book design by Charlotte Staub.

First edition.

Library of Congress Cataloging-in-Publication Data

Briskin, Mae, 1924–
The tree still stands / Mae Briskin.
p. cm.
I. title.
PS3552.R492L4 1990
813'.54—dc20 90-31463

ISBN 0-393-02894-1
W.W. Norton & Company, Inc.
500 Fifth Avenue, New York, N.Y. 10110
W.W. Norton & Company, Ltd.
10 Coptic Street, London WC1A 1PU

1 2 3 4 5 6 7 8 9 0

Dedicated to
Monsignor Leto Casini and
Matilde Cassin Vardi,

to the memory of
Rabbi Nathan Cassuto
Padre Cipriano Ricotti
Raffaele Cantoni and
Mario Finzi,

and to the memory of
my husband, Herbert B. Briskin,
without whom I could not have
gone on the journey
into the past

My Sincere Thanks
for sharing their memories:

above all, to Hulda Cassuto Campagnano,

and to
Monsignor Leto Casini
Matilde Cassin Vardi
Susanna Cassuto Evron
Ada Algranati Bolotin
Natalia and Dan Hochman
Basia and Herman Wisniewski
Odette Meyers
Rubin Pick   Sonia Pick
Raffaello Fellah and
John L'Heureux

THE TREE STILL STANDS

PROLOGUE

WE WERE LIVING IN WARSAW THEN, IN A HOME that is still the setting for some of my dreams. It had crystal chandeliers, a gleaming mahogany table where thirty could sit, and huge armoires as black as onyx—all imported from France. And yet, on Friday nights, my father, as if he were still in a shtetl, blessed us each in turn according to age—my sister Eva first, and then Nathan, Aaron, and Joel, my brothers. I, Ruth, was last.

Once as he ended my blessing he said, "You're seven years old. You can understand."

I'd heard those words in the past, when I was four and Joel seven, and my father had said them to him. Joel recalls that my father had said them to Aaron, as Aaron recalls he had said them to Nathan, though he spoke to us each in a matter-of-fact tone, with no hint of danger in what followed. "As long as you and Nathan live," he'd said to Eva, "you're responsible for Nathan." Later, to Nathan, "You're responsible for Aaron." In time, Aaron became responsible for Joel and Joel for me.

We all accepted those words as fact. I remember Joel as he was at seven—turning, searching my eyes as if seeing me, discovering me, for the first time, and in utter silence taking on himself to be my guardian, from that time on and for life.

And now that I, in turn, was seven, my father continued, "Ruth, you're now the weaker of the two, but in time this'll change. For as long as she lives, you're responsible for Imma."

I should have laughed, because Imma, my grandmother—tall for a woman, and sturdy—didn't think of herself as needing protection. Her very name—meaning "Mother"—was one she had chosen when Eva was born, a substitute for "Grandma," a denial that a generation separated them. But try as I may to recall how she looked when I faced her, I remember nothing—neither surprise, nor indignation, nor even amusement.

What I see instead is Imma's older self. Her face, ancient beyond her years, is hardly visible between a pillow and a cover pulled to her eyes, and her voice is begging a distant God for a quick and merciful death. And then a door opens, and a young Dominican priest, tall, slender, in white robes, enters the squalid attic room where Imma is huddled in bed. He calls her name, and she ignores his call. He comes to the bed, calls her again, and slowly she turns to the sound. Her eyes are without expression at first, and then disbelieving, but at last a light is kindled, followed by tears of joy.

This was in Florence, Italy, in 1944. I don't, of course, remember all that occurred, but even events I don't recall by myself, or didn't witness, are vivid in my memory, as vivid as numbers branded on flesh. I hear them as told in my family's voices, later, when we reunited—those of us who survived.

I

IN 1908, WHEN MY FATHER WAS TEN, THREE POLISH peasants, drunk and celebrating, came to the shtetl and banged on the door to his father's house. They had known my grandfather well, had been having him make their boots, and had always been on cordial terms.

Now, they said, they needed a Jew for another and more festive purpose. They didn't come into the house, but—gently, good-naturedly—pulled him outdoors by his shirt. Imma told her daughters not to move, but she and my father followed. Suddenly, one of the peasants lifted a gun, and my father's father was dead.

The peasants, including the three, found another Jew to make their boots. Imma and the family, having no alternative, adapted too, and as the years passed, and despite the problem of dowries, first one and then another of the four daughters married. Two remained in the shtetl, while the others left to join their husbands in another one nearby.

After the war, when my father was twenty, Imma's parents died, her mother shortly after her father. At the end of the month of mourning, Imma declared that now that nobody needed her, she and my father were going to Warsaw, where somebody owed her a debt.

Long before—even before my father was born—a distant cousin named Abner, whose family had not been on the best of terms with hers, had settled in Warsaw. Later, prosperous and self-assured, he returned to the shtetl to ask for a favor. His daughter, sixteen, was pregnant by a Polish man, and he wanted her hidden from sight till the baby was born.

"One thing more," he said. "Whether you believe me or not, I really don't care anymore how the child was conceived. We want it, and we want it cared for well. You're nursing a child of your own, but surely just for a short time more, so when hers is born, I'd like you to nurse it yourself." He offered to pay her well.

"I'll do it," she said, "not for money, but because I should. On my own terms. I'll take some money for her food, but she'll live as my daughters live, as if she were my widowed child, and I'll never let her put on airs. But I'm giving you something important, and if ever I have to I'll ask for something important from you. If you agree, it's settled."

Though her terms were terribly vague, Abner agreed.

The girl, Imma discovered, was helpful, grateful, suddenly mature through need. Imma, in turn, was as good as her word. She nursed the newborn boy, and when his mother and grandparents found a believable story for Warsaw, they took him home.

"So," Imma concluded, "they owe me a favor—to start with, a job in their home."

My father said no. Among Jews, then, nothing was lower in status than being a servant.

"I don't care," Imma said. "We'll have a home, and the rest of what I want is help for you."

In Warsaw, even in the chaos that followed the First World War, and even for Jews, there was a way of life that dazzled them. Abner was a better friend than Imma had expected. He persuaded a man he dealt with, a watchmaker, to hire my father to be his apprentice, and while my father learned the trade, Abner paid for tutors, so that my father studied the history, Latin, and German that others were taught at school. By the time he was twenty-two, the shtetl-bred boy had become a presentable man, handsome, educated, and with polished manners.

It was then that my mother—as wealthy as my father had once been poor—came to the shop with a broken watch. She was nineteen, of medium height, full-figured, blue-eyed, blond, the opposite of my father, who was tall, slim, angular, dark.

Their story is an old one: they fell in love, met secretly, and when her parents learned of him, they were enraged. Magda, their cherished only child, would lose the status to which she'd been born. But for all their vehemence, they relented. My grandfather took my father into his business, and if my mother's social position was lowered, and it probably was, I don't believe it mattered greatly to her.

It was my father who paid the higher price. The memory of his father's death was never far from his thoughts, and, early in their marriage, when he talked of leaving Poland for America or western Europe, my mother dismissed the idea with a laugh.

She had never known anguish or fear. Imma, though hoping the same would be true for us children, had a bit of contempt for people who never had suffered, but she happily managed the newlyweds' household, and my mother could in many ways continue in her husband's house as she and her mother had lived in her father's.

Unlike the wealthy women of Warsaw, she had five children. Unlike Imma, however, she had wet nurses and governesses to take care of us. She served on the board of an orphanage, went out for tea with her friends, took lessons in the latest Latin dances from America, skied in the Tatra Mountains, and in summer went off by herself, as women then did, to the Sopoty spa. And was always aware she was very much loved.

After 1933, when indignities against the Jews in Germany began, my father again was talking of leaving Poland. Jews, my mother's parents answered, were fleeing to Poland from Germany. Surely it showed that Poland was safe. When my father said that the Poles, envying the Germans their sadistic pleasures, would look to them for new ideas, my mother replied that surely the civilized Germans soon would get rid of the madman, and when Poland's economy strengthened, the Poles would be nicer, and Warsaw's Jews would be safe. My father yielded.

Then, in mid-March 1936, on a market day in Przytyk, near Warsaw, some peasants marched on the village with clubs and stones. They overturned carts in the village square, descended on Jewish homes, killed a man and his wife, and brutally beat their children. Out in the square, the Jews resisted, and one of them, twenty years old, fired a revolver, killing a peasant.

That evening, Imma, my father, and I were alone in the parlor. My father sat at his desk reading a German paper, Imma sat in a chair nearby, and I was off in a corner, drawing as usual. They had forgotten, or hadn't noticed, that I was there.

When I looked up, I saw my father's face in the light of the lamp. He had set the paper aside, and he was staring down at nothing, rubbing his chin.

Imma was watching him too. "What is it, child?" she said.

He looked up in surprise. "Yes. Child. That boy in Przytyk, with his sidecurls and revolver, is more of a man than I."

"Joseph, don't," she said.

"Why not? I wanted to leave the shtetl when Papa was killed, but did I say so? I waited till *you* decided. Who decided we'd stay in Poland? Magda. And whom does she follow? Her parents. We follow our parents, and nobody learns."

"Maybe the parents are right. You don't like this . . . what you call 'resignation,' but maybe it's part of being a Jew."

"An *avoidable* part."

"I don't think so. This doesn't happen only in Poland or Germany—this is the price of being a Jew. And anyway, Joseph," she added, *"your* children don't follow."

"Of course they do. How is Eva different from Magda? And Nathan! He thinks whatever his *sister* thinks."

"You've encouraged it, you've tied them one to the other, and I understand—a fatherless boy, what else would you do? *I* believe it's good. Besides, since when are you dissatisfied with Magda?"

"I've never been dissatisfied. Who but Magda would have agreed to so many children? But I want my daughters different. Independent, strong."

"Jealous father," she said with a smile, leaning over to pat his hand. "You want no other man to replace you. No other man to have them completely."

"I don't know where you get such ideas. Anyway, Nathan worries me more. He's a follower. Born that way."

Nathan was then thirteen, a pupil at the middle school. He was the only one of the five of us brothers and sisters who, in all ways, resembled our mother. He was blond and handsome—with large, innocent, deep-blue eyes, with fine features in an oval face—and always cheerful. But though my father worshiped my mother, he was often impatient with Nathan. When a story of Nathan's would get a bit long, my father would cut him short, but he'd listen with close attention to boring details of my mother's "amusing" days with her friends.

"Aaron," my father continued, "is only eleven, but already he's different. If we were in Przytyk, and Aaron were twenty, it would have been he who was firing that gun."

I knew even then why he'd said it. Only days before, Aaron had been in a fight. It had started with a taunt, a nickname invented by one of the boys—"ear-and-a-half," a name inspired by a minor deformity Aaron was born with. The lower part of his left ear, where there should have been an earlobe, was missing entirely. So far as we knew, this didn't disturb him at all, and when the boys began to taunt him and push him around, his response, I think, was less to the sense of being insulted than just to thinking they *meant* to insult him. He fought them savagely, and when he got home, his dark hair stuck to his forehead with sweat, his dark skin flushed, and his eyes flashing with pleasure, his head was high.

"I'm not even hurt," he said, his split lip wet with blood.

That picture of Aaron came back to me late in the week. The seamstress was with us, kneeling, pinning the hem of a violet gown that revealed my mother's shoulders and arms. My mother turned white. The door was ajar, and as I went to it, trying to see what had frightened her, there was our maid, Krystyna, saying firmly, "Don't cry." Beside her was Nathan, not crying but dazed, the blue sweater of his school uniform torn, his hair disheveled, his face scraped, a bloodstained handkerchief held to his nose.

"Oh, my darling, how?" my mother said.

"Even Marek," he answered.

Imma ordered him quiet until she had treated his injuries.

It had been a commonplace—boring, I'm sure, to many by now. Nathan was coming from school when some of his classmates stopped him, accusing him and us of using Polish children's blood in making the Passover matzo. What was so different now was that Marek, his closest friend, had been one of these boys.

When my father got home and looked at my brother, he knew what had happened. He came to him slowly, put his arms about him, and buried his lips in his hair.

Soon, Krystyna came in to say that Marek had come, but Nathan refused to see him.

My father protested. "Why not hear what he says?"

Marek came in, a short, heavy boy, quiet and sensitive, a boy we had liked, whom we had seen countless times and were seeing now in a different way.

He nodded to my parents, and to Nathan he said, "It was a trick on me too. They asked me to walk with them, that's all, and it was only later, when they caught you, that they said they'd you-know-what. I was afraid. I couldn't think. But I'd *never* do it again."

Nathan looked down, and Marek approached my mother. "Do *you* forgive me?" he asked.

"You need *his* forgiveness," she said, "not mine."

"My mother won't forgive me either, unless *you* will."

My mother looked puzzled. "Is *that* why you're here?"

"I'd have come anyway."

"Are you saying your mother feels bad?"

"Yes."

Nathan looked up at my father for what he should do.

"You were beaten," my father said. *"You* decide."

Nathan shrugged. Formally, in a way that would have made us laugh at any other time, he said, "Marek, I forgive you. For your mother's sake."

"Then I do too," my mother said.

When Marek had left, my father said, "All of you, listen. Remember Marek's mother. She's a Pole you can trust."

That evening at dinner, watching Nathan, we were subdued. Some of his teeth had been loosened, and he was cautiously eating peas and potatoes Imma had told Krystyna to mash.

"Nathan," my father said, "would you like to go to Paris?"

My mother's fork clattered onto her plate and down to the floor.

His eyes on my mother, my father said, "Just for the time being, Magda, for a vacation. You'll finally meet your Paris cousins, Nathan—how does it sound?"

"By myself?"

"No, of course not. All of us."

"But you're letting *me* decide?"

"Yes."

"When would we go?"

"Not right now. We've lots of arrangements to make, and the little French you've learned at school is not enough. We'd all have to learn it."

Joel, always the laziest, asked, "All of us?"

"If Imma wants to be exempt," my father said, "that's fine. Anyone over forty can be exempt."

"Oh, Nathan," Eva said, "it'll be so much fun."

And at once Nathan said yes.

My mother, however, was not taken in. She too had learned some French at school. Like almost everyone else in Poland, she revered Napoleon and everything French, but she knew what my father was thinking.

"Joseph," she said, quietly, seriously, "let's not discuss it now. You're confusing the children."

"Magda," he answered, just as quietly, and as if she didn't already know, "French is an international language. Paris is a center of culture. I can afford to show it to them, and they have a right to be shown."

"They're too young to appreciate it. I'm sorry, Eva darling, even you—you're hardly fifteen—you're more wrapped up in movie stars than in art or anything else. You have time. I've never seen Paris myself."

"Neither have I," my father said, "and we should. We'll meet interesting people. Our lives will all be enriched."

There was a moment's silence, and then, still softly, as if she weren't arguing, my mother said, "Joseph, all I'm saying is that you and I, alone, should talk about it later."

"Magda," he said, "there is no later. Look at your son."

It was the first quarrel between our parents that we had ever seen. It was not at all like the screaming we heard at a later date, and if my mother said anything more when they were alone, I doubt it was much. Just as Nathan, with his usual good nature, forgave Marek the next day, not only for his mother's sake but also for his own, my mother forgave, or seemed to have forgiven, my father.

The following Monday, my father hired the young man who'd be teaching us French. His name was Piotr. He was a student at the university, short, wiry, and aloof. He had studied in France, and though his French had a Polish accent, it was otherwise good. He came in the evenings, always on time, and he didn't say a word that was not connected to what we were learning.

But if it seemed my father had won, the impression was wrong. When a month had passed, and Nathan's face had healed, my mother, daunted by French pronunciation, said she already knew more than she needed. She had studied both French and Latin, remembered enough, and was dropping the lessons, though, by the rules my father had made, she was far too young to claim an exemption. She was thirty-five, so she announced that she had borrowed five of Imma's years, was therefore forty, two years older than he, and she and Imma together were still a hundred and four.

My mother's attempt at humor lasted till August. Then the Polish government decreed that the sign on every shop must have the owner's name. My grandfather's name was Stein, ours Levy. Again my father spoke of the west.

"Joseph," my mother said, patiently, indulgently, "it's twenty-eight *years* since your father was killed."

"Magda," he said, "I'm putting our assets into diamonds."

My mother abruptly left the room, and my father followed her out.

Aaron turned to Nathan. "I don't understand. Why are diamonds better than money?"

Nathan, who along with Eva had learned from my father some things that Aaron hadn't yet heard, explained inflation and told the story of Russia's worthless paper ruble. "Most times," he summarized, "you're better off with diamonds."

Eva said, "Look. To buy a loaf of bread, you want money. To escape from a country and not have to carry kilos of money, you want diamonds."

"So it's *not* a vacation," Aaron answered. He turned to Joel and me. "Papa was saying we'd better get out."

But, because leaving would make my mother unhappy, we stayed, despite assaults on Polish Jews, despite reports of hideous atrocities in Austria—long before Kristallnacht—and nothing happened to us or the family's store. Then, in early November, my mother's mother was stricken with cancer, and my father agreed we could not abandon her now.

We stayed, doing our lessons with Piotr and seeing my grandmother every day, and we were still there in the middle of March 1939, when Czechoslovakia was dismembered, and Jews were fleeing to Poland from Prague.

That month, however, was the turning point. One day, as Aaron was leaving for school, he found on the door a message painted in red. It said, JEWS! OUT OF POLAND NOW. On the floor at his feet was a bird, its neck wrung.

At my father's store, a message painted in black covered the window. JEW LEVY. JEW STEIN. OUT OF POLAND NOW.

By evening, the messages were painted over. Only Krystyna, my mother, and I were still in the dining room. Suddenly, my mother started to cry. Until then, I had seen some tears in her eyes on occasion, but nothing more.

Krystyna looked up. She was my mother's age and had been living with us since my parents had been married. She was therefore more than just another servant, and especially in our house, managed as it was by Imma, who felt a bond of sympathy with servants, Krystyna spoke her mind with much more freedom than she would have done had she been working elsewhere.

"Who could have done it, Krystyna? Who?" my mother asked.

"Don't cry," Krystyna said, as she'd said to Nathan the day he was hurt. "What does it matter? You have to expect it."

Like a child, my mother asked, "But why? *Why?*"

And Krystyna said, "Because you killed God."

I did not understand the shock, or the pain, that came in quick succession to my mother's face. I went up to her and put my hand on her cheek. "You see?" she said. "Papa was right."

The next morning, my father went off to my grandparents' house. He had prepared for this day, had made arrangements for the trip to France, which now, he told them, he wouldn't postpone. He urged them to think it over again and join us in Paris as soon as they could. My grandfather, with a glance at his invalid wife, said there was nothing to fear. From there, my father went on to arrange for our absence from school.

When I got home, my mother, with Krystyna's help, was sorting our clothes, and in the evening, my father repeated to us what he'd said at our schools—and what *we* were to say to our friends: we were going to France for several months. He, without us, would be back on occasion on matters of business.

Shortly before we left, we spent an emotional evening with Abner, during which Imma thanked him, for the last time, for all he had done for her son.

But the day and night I remember best are our last ones in Warsaw. We had gone to my grandparents' home. My grandmother, frail, in a purple velvet gown, was on a sofa, drinking her tea from a delicate cup and doing her best to be cheerful. After a while, my grandfather called us to look at some pictures he'd put on his desk, and my grandmother sat by herself. Nathan looked up and, seeing her alone, walked to the sofa. He sat down, and as he put his arm about her, she said, "Oh, Nathan, do be careful. You don't protect yourself as you should."

Later, at around midnight, I awoke from a dream. I was in a funeral procession like some I had heard about but never seen. We were on Gęsia Street, where I had been with Imma once—in the slums near the Jewish cemetery. In the dream, I was with a crowd of Jewish children, paid mourners, recruited to swell the number of actual mourners, and I was as poor as these children.

Far ahead were beautiful horses drawing the hearse, and the horses and hearse were draped in black and adorned with silver. In carriages following them were the relatives of the deceased, people who'd pay us the single roll—or the candy—with which children mourners were paid. Around us, as far as I could see, were the dilapidated wooden houses occupied by Warsaw's Jewish poor.

"Where do you live?" asked the girl at my left. "On Pawia?"

"No."

"On Gliniana?"

I didn't answer, but when we reached Okopowa Street, and the cemetery stretched before us, I turned to her and asked, "Who was it who died?"

Now it was she who refused to talk. Even her clothes had changed. She was wearing the uniform of middle school, a white blouse with blue piping, and the piping was ripped and hanging, as if she had just been attacked. I asked again, again she didn't answer, and I turned to my right. I didn't see a child, but the bodice of my mother's violet gown. It wasn't my mother wearing the gown but Krystyna, smiling, her head held high.

"Who died?" I asked.

"Don't you know?" she said with satisfaction. "It's your brother Nathan."

I awoke. On the wall near my bed were photos of stars of American films. One was of Loretta Young. For a second or two it puzzled me, distracted me, blurring the dream. Then, sharply, the outline of the dream returned. I wanted to run to Nathan but didn't want to tell him the dream, so I hurried to Joel. He was sitting on his bed, fully dressed but barefoot and shivering.

Miserably, he said, "We never went to Czestochowa."

His words were senseless to me, but his sorrow was so real that it displaced my nightmare.

Sitting down beside him, I said, "So?"

"I wanted to see it. They say it has streets like Paris, but that Czestochowa is better, because the Black Madonna's there. There's a shiny mountain, and a monastery, and a wall so wide you can walk on the top. And her."

"Who?"

"The Black Madonna."

"You really want to see her?"

"Yes, don't *you?* The boys all say we should."

"I *suppose* Papa would let us," I said, "but later, when we come back. Because we will—Papa told them at school that it's just a vacation." He didn't answer. "Besides," I said, "Papa said we'll meet lots of interesting people."

"I don't care about lots of people. We'll never remember them."

"We will," I said. "Ask Imma. She remembers from when she was young even better than she can remember from now."

His continued shivering, and now his silence, worried me. "Joel? Do you want some bread and jam?"

He stood up and took my hand and, carefully, as if only he were sighted and I blind, led me toward the kitchen. When we got to the parlor, we stopped to look in at our parents. My father, at his desk, was staring at nothing, as he'd done on the day of the Przytyk pogrom. My mother was moving about, slowly, touching things, dreamily, lightly, storing them up in her fingertips—the heavy brocaded draperies, the hand-carved credenza imported from France, the bindings of books.

I called out, "Papa?"and he almost leapt from his chair. "Who will take care of our things?"

"Oh, Ruthie," he said sadly. "Don't worry, darling—I've seen to everything. Krystyna will stay. And Grandpa and Abner will come. And if they can't, Marek's mother will come."

II

IN PARIS, HOWEVER, EXCITED AND BUSY, WE CHILDREN didn't think about Krystyna, or Marek's mother, or even my mother's parents.

One Sunday, I was sitting on the parlor floor buckling my shoes. There were boxes and trunks scattered about, making the room an obstacle course, and Eva, happily rushing away, bumped into one of the boxes, toppling a tall one on me and making me yelp. My mother and Imma, coming toward me from different directions, collided and stood there, immobile. Nathan laughed, an infectious laugh I instantly caught. My mother rubbed her brow in exactly the spot where my own had been hit, and my laughter got out of control. It spread to Eva, to my mother, and then to Imma, who laughed until she cried. Clutching her sides, she said, *"Oy veh,"* and our laughter got louder. Suddenly, Imma bent over, her hands clutching her head. She sobbed, not from laughter, as I thought, but from grief, which my mother understood.

"Oh, Mama," she said. "Mama, don't cry. Maybe Joseph is wrong. Maybe they'll be all right."

Imma straightened up, wiped her eyes, and composed her face. She turned to Eva. "Where were you rushing? Again to museums?"

"Oh, Mama, why not?" my mother said. "This is what Joseph *hoped* would happen."

"All right," she conceded, "she's a girl, but must Nathan go too? A war is coming—he should be doing something else."

"Go, children, go," my mother said, and Eva and Nathan, allies as always, left.

"Mama, darling, what should Nathan do?" my mother asked. "Practice shooting? Please don't you start doing this. It's bad enough that Joseph does it."

"Joseph? What did Joseph ever do to Nathan?"

"All right, he doesn't do, he just thinks, but Nathan knows."

For a while, Imma was silent. Then, "Magda," she said, "I don't begrudge them their pleasure, or you yours."

"Mine?"

"Oh, Magda dear. Always buying clothes. We aren't in Warsaw, where a man's success is judged by his wife's clothes. Nobody knows him in Paris—or even knows *you*—so why do you care what anyone thinks?"

"I won't protect the Jews by looking frumpy, Mama. Do you think that if *we* have pleasure in Paris, they in the shtetl and Warsaw will pay?"

Imma didn't answer, and that was enough to tell me that that was exactly what she was afraid of.

Gently again, my mother went on, "Mama, even if trouble is coming, Joseph is happy in France. Don't make him worry. Let him do whatever he wants."

Even if Imma had not looked hurt I'd have known my mother

was being unfair. My grandmother didn't begrudge my father his pleasure in Paris or try to tell him what he should do.

Part of his day he spent on "business," but before that, in the early morning, he'd leave for Place de l'Étoile, to explore its broad, tree-lined avenues, or to walk on the Champs-Élysées and across the Seine to Montparnasse. Late in the day, he'd go walking again with Joel and me, and often with Aaron. Since our stride was shorter than his, he'd stroll. He'd stop to buy us some chocolate or pastry, or to point—silently, as though a word would intrude—at a scene we shouldn't forget. Paris moved him profoundly, and I'm not sure why—whether because of its beauty or merely because of the way in which he was seeing it, through a haze of France's history, and of all it had promised to Western man.

I remember a day when Joel was sick, and my father and I were alone. We had reached the Arc du Carrousel, where, for the fourth or fifth time, we stopped. He was holding my hand, and he turned us around to absorb the scene. When at last we were facing the way we had come, the Arc de Triomphe was far in the distance, framed by trees and the darkening sky. I was bored, ready to hurry him on, until I saw tears on his face.

But for Imma, Paris meant her friendship with our cousins, an intimate friendship that I, who knew her only since late in her life, had never known her to have. Gershon, her brother's son, four years older than my father, was someone my father rarely had seen. He had lived in a distant village and after the war had settled in Paris, as my father and Imma had settled in Warsaw. Now a citizen of France, he spoke French when he had to, but the times when he had to were rare. He worked in a factory owned by immigrant Jews, and there and at home his language was Yiddish, which we children hardly knew, and which my mother understood but didn't speak.

Chatting in Yiddish with Imma, Gershon was always at ease, expansive, entertaining, but in French he became inhibited, as if he saw us as the other kind of Jew, the French acculturated one, whose concerns were different from his own, which were the socialist politics and class allegiances brought from his native Poland. He was right. It was the upper-class Jews with whom my mother would have felt at home, and whom my father would have chosen too.

Gershon's wife was Esther. She was about my mother's age but seemed to be fifty or more. She was bland-looking, quiet, and kind, but easily ignored, eclipsed by her charming, more talkative husband. They had a daughter, Nicole, who had gone to Italy to study art, had married a student, and had settled in Rome. When the Fascists passed the racial laws, many Italian Jews went off to France, but Nicole had remained where she was.

Imma, fond of Gershon and his wife, was especially drawn to Theo, their son, a shy, intelligent boy of twenty, with a rigid left leg and a marked limp. Often when I was alone outdoors, I'd mimic his walk—quick, energetic, as if he could make up in speed what he had lost in grace. I would lock my left knee, swing my leg around in an arc, making my body tip toward the rear from my waist, looking for the sympathy of passersby.

One evening at dinner, my father said, "I have to get help with some business affairs. I'd want to give Eva or Nathan the job, but I have to have someone who really knows France, so I'm planning to give it to Theo and ask him to live with us. What do you think?"

"He has a family!" Imma said. "What is he? A servant?"

"Will his father let him?" Aaron said. "They're such dogmatic socialists—they'll think we'll lead him astray."

Furious, as if chopping off words with a knife, Imma answered, "Don't . . . make . . . fun!"

My father was taken aback. "Not as a servant, Mama. As one of the family. Besides, you were once a servant yourself."

"I *had* to be a servant—what did I know? Theo is French. He has an education, a government job, and you and your son don't even respect him. You want to use him. You'll give him a lovely home, but for how long? And he's in love with Eva, but she's not in love with him, so how will he feel? Don't forget who we are—we aren't better than Gershon and Theo."

Offended, my father said, "I know *exactly* who I am—a Jew, vulnerable, even though I have some money. And I'm not an exploiter. I'll pay him more than he gets from the Paris bureaucracy. Teach him a business, as Magda's father taught me his. And give him a home where we *all* will give him respect. In return I want him to teach me my way around France, tell me to whom I must go for a favor or papers or anything else, turn this Polish-speaking house to one where *French* is spoken, and without an accent! So that Ruth and Joel, and maybe Aaron, will pass for French. But to speak Yiddish to you, and be your friend, and call you Imma, as if he were one of my children."

Imma was silent.

"As for his interest in Eva," he said, "I can't protect him, and neither can you, but I'll make it clear that she isn't part of the bargain." He turned to Aaron. "They're socialists, yes, but sincere—they don't deserve contempt—and in spite of their rhetoric, they respect a wealthy man."

A chill had fallen, and even my mother, who'd normally waft it away, couldn't rise to the challenge of this.

It was Eva who answered. "Papa, are you worried even here? Don't you feel safe?"

"With that madman in power over the border, *should* I?"

The pause seemed endless.

"But look what you're doing to us," she said. "To the little ones especially."

"And what do *you* know about the pain of little ones?"

"But *we* have to pass for French?" Aaron asked. "Because *you're* still afraid?"

"Aaron, that's enough," my father said.

"You said you wanted our opinion."

"I've heard as much as I need from you both."

Imma, as if the disagreement over Theo had unhinged her,

said, "They're right! 'Passing for French'—I didn't notice it. This *isn't* Poland. This is what you wanted. You're making the children afraid to live!"

I had never heard anyone insult my father, nor ever seen him appear so hurt. It was the first of many days in which we felt ourselves suddenly, painfully, separate, as my father withdrew from us, and as Eva and Aaron, seeing him alone, avoided each other entirely, afraid that if he should see them together he'd think that they had conspired.

Only when Theo accepted the offer and came to our house with his clothing and books did the atmosphere change. He probably never surmised that the warmth we offered to him that evening was really meant for each other—for my father, whose touch we craved, as he craved ours, for Imma, who had spoken on our behalf, who wouldn't retract her words and couldn't conceal her anguish at being cut off from her son, and for Eva and Aaron, who had assigned the blame to themselves.

But that evening, Imma, taking the place of the cook, baked my father's favorite cake—a *lekakh,* our first since leaving Warsaw. Cinnamon, honey, and cloves scented the air. As my father savored the cake, Nathan delivered a long but inspired welcoming speech, and Theo became, in Aaron's fewer words, our "honorary brother and our friend." Some foolishness from Joel made my father laugh, and the rift between us was healed.

It was late in August 1939, a few days after Hitler signed the pact with Stalin, and on September 1, German troops marched on Poland. My father's semi-vacation in Paris came to an end.

But for Aaron, something had just begun. He was now fifteen, tall, thin, angular, and with a somewhat aquiline nose. He was not especially handsome, and appeared even less so compared with Nathan. As addicted to bookstores as Eva was to museums, he had met a girl in one of them, had taken her out to La Coupole, and by evening had fallen in love. Two weeks later, he wanted to bring her to dinner.

"She isn't Jewish," he told my mother.

She shrugged. "Bring her. Nobody marries the first girl he meets." Then, with a smile, "Is she pretty?"

As if he hadn't thought about it, but with his usual self-confidence, Aaron said, "Oh? I guess she is. She looks a lot like me."

She did, but I would not have called her pretty. She was bony and dark, and tall, almost taller than he, but proud of her height, and even her aquiline nose was like his.

On meeting her, Joel said, "If you and Aaron shaved your heads, you'd look like twins."

Ondine moved closer to Aaron, touched him with her elbow, and smiled. "But Aaron has only an ear and a half."

A year older than he, she seemed even older. She was an only child, but she was not intimidated there among the eight of us. She guided the talk, and all during dinner my parents, amused by her self-assurance, let her lead.

"Aaron told me you're Jewish," she said. "In the convent school, all we ever met were other Catholics. But at a party I met an Egyptian. He said that before his sisters could marry, he'd have to approve. His father would ask him, because he, being closer in age to the man, could judge. And the women—such useless lives! He said they mostly play tennis. Eva, what about you? After university, what'll you do?"

"I don't even know where we'll be. What will *you* do?"

"I'll be a journalist." She turned to my father. "Aaron is brilliant—he ought to be a writer."

"Oh? I never knew that that's what he wanted."

"I'm not quite sure he knows it himself."

I listened, entranced. She seemed worldly, different from Eva's friends in Warsaw, and she was what my father wanted me to be—independent, opinionated, strong. I pictured myself grown-up, saying what she was saying, and I liked what I saw.

Later, as she was leaving, my eyes were drawn to two little gold-colored brooches pinned to her coat. They were a pair of leaves, not like any particular leaf, but rather the essence of leafness in fall—thin, curled, torn. I scrutinized them, memorizing jagged breaks, planning to draw the leaves as soon as she'd left, and then I noticed they weren't perfectly matched. They had surely been made by hand, and they were torn and curled in different places.

"What is it?" she asked.

"Nothing," I said. "Just your leaves."

"Do you like them?"

"They're not the same."

"Of course not." She quickly unpinned one, and before I knew it she'd started to pin the leaf to my blouse.

"Oh, I can't," I said.

"Of course you can—it's not real gold," and with a gentle pat she settled the leaf on my blouse. "Now," she said, "we each have one."

The following week, as she and Aaron approached her house, she said, "I haven't told my parents you're Jewish. My father might guess, but you're free to say whatever you like."

Though forewarned, Aaron was unprepared.

Ondine's father studied his face. "There's an accent. Where are you from?"

"Poland. But I'm not a Pole, monsieur, I'm a Jew."

"I thought so. Can you tell me," he asked, "how a rational man can continue being a Jew?"

"If *you* can tell *me* how a rational man can be a Catholic."

"I can tell you easily. I'm an atheist, and a Catholic for convenience. If I lived in London, I would be an Anglican."

"No matter where," Aaron said, "I would be a Jew."

"But you haven't answered my question. For clinging to an out-of-date idea of God, Jews are paying a price. How can a rational man believe there's a God?"

"That's a different question, monsieur. The answer to this one is that not all things are knowable by reason. The answer to the other is that that's what I want to be."

"You're clever," he said. "That's what Ondine must see in

you. But tell me, do you think in France you'll be safe? That France gives a damn about Jews?"

"I think you'll consider us human, like you."

"You've come too late. The French hate foreigners almost by instinct. And the most hated of all are the Jews. Now especially. France has problems, and like everywhere else when times get bad, it's worst for the Jews."

"France," Aaron said, "is not Poland."

"France," the other answered, "is two distinct kinds of people. Half would consider you equals and act with honor, and half would be glad to see you in hell."

"And to which half, monsieur, do *you* belong?"

Pointing a finger, "Watch! Your tongue'll get you into trouble." Then, calmly, "I wouldn't want to see you in hell, but I want Ondine to be safe, so you're not to see her again."

"Papa!" she said.

"You didn't say he's a Jew!"

"I didn't lie!"

"Neither did I!"

Aaron turned to leave, and Ondine said, "Wait. I'll settle this later. I'm going with you." As they left the building, minutes after they'd come, she said, "My father was a Jew."

Aaron stopped. "I don't find that funny."

"Neither do I. My mother loved him. He converted, but even if he hadn't she'd have married him."

"Why are you telling me this?"

"So that you won't blame him. He was tired of paying for being a Jew and didn't want *me* to pay. But just as my mother accepted a Jew, so can I."

"But *I* would not convert."

"I wouldn't *expect* you to."

He started to walk. Coming along beside him, she said, "Aaron, he told you the truth. France is afraid you'll swamp our culture. Corrupt the language. And these last years—they've been afraid of everything, mostly of war. It's something you and your father should know."

"What should we do? Go back to Poland? Give ourselves up to the Germans?"

"No, but be realistic. Don't be angry at *us.*"

"And stop seeing you?"

"Of course not."

"You should have told me all about him in advance."

"No. Not at all. I didn't tell either of you in advance."

They walked for a while, and Aaron said, "I don't ever want to see your father again."

"You don't have to, but I can be as stubborn as he, and I want to see yours."

And she did. It was she who reported the meeting to us. I was eight years old, and as the weeks went by I listened in awe, and in fact with love, to this girl of sixteen who had chosen my brother, and who was so independent and so grown-up.

Two days later, France and Britain declared themselves at war on Poland's side, but before they did any more, Poland fell.

It had taken less than a month. At first, my father made countless inquiries—about my mother's parents, about his sisters and their families, and about Abner and his—but he couldn't get news. Then all communication stopped.

In the next six months of military inactivity, whenever my father and Theo traveled, it was not for reasons of business as they would pretend, but rather to see what the people were like in the cities and towns, and where you could go and hardly be noticed, and where there were Christian friends of the Jews.

And when they were with us in Paris, I watched Theo. His lameness opened my eyes to the differences among the rest of us. In the past, when I felt like drawing a face, it was likely to be the face of an actor or actress. I hadn't been drawing the family. Now I was drawing Aaron, emphasizing his peculiar ear, and Nathan, with his chiseled features, and Eva, as dark as my father, but otherwise so like my mother.

The one I never drew was Joel. He was a part of me. He was to be my guardian, but he was more. He completed me, and I him. He was three years older, but short, whereas I, for my age, was tall, so that our height that year was the same. And because he was small, he could be childish without becoming offensive. More often than not, when he spoke for himself he spoke for us both, so, just as I never drew myself, I never thought of drawing Joel.

And as carefully as I was now observing us, Theo was doing the same. He admired us and called us "strong." He persisted in saying "strong," even when Aaron challenged him. "Strong? You mean rich? *Aware* of our strength *because* of our wealth?" If Aaron, by showing how well he could argue, ever embarrassed him, I never saw Theo reveal it.

What I saw was his growing love for Eva. Whenever she entered a room he was in, he would turn himself into a statue. It seemed, even to me, as if he thought that if she didn't see him move, he could keep his lameness a secret. Had Eva meant to enslave him, Theo would not have protested.

What she did was avoid him. If she was not in her room, she was with one or another of us. And though she was always polite, she was never especially warm.

One evening, Theo said, "Five of you, and only Nathan is blond." Eva nodded. "And you, you have your father's coloring, but your mother's lovely face."

"Thank you."

"I don't mean your father isn't handsome. But it's so interesting. You're the only one who's like them both."

"Theo, please, I know all this."

"I'm sorry. I'm boring you. I just want you to know I wasn't born lame. I only had polio."

"I know."

"Eva, do you like me at all?"

"Theo, you're my cousin."

"Your *second* cousin."

"Facts don't help. I *feel* you're my cousin. I like you, but I feel you're like—I don't know—like Nathan, I guess."

"And you *love* Nathan."

"As a brother."

"Eva," he begged, "just don't close your mind."

"Theo, I've never been in love. I don't think I'll *ever* be in love."

"How can you say that?"

"I'm eighteen! Aaron is fifteen, and Aaron's in love."

"But you're a girl."

"So I should have been in love at twelve."

But Theo didn't give up.

Whatever innocence we might have had about our safety ended in April of 1940, when German troops turned toward the west. All our thoughts were now on the war, our eyes on the map. Denmark fell in a day, Norway in two months, Luxembourg in a day, Holland in five days, and Belgium in eighteen. France, of course, would be next, and however good the Germans might decide to be to others, we didn't expect any kindness toward Jews.

As June began, they breached the borders of France. At once there were Jews on the run going south, many toward Nice. That's where my mother wanted to go, but my father refused. If everyone went toward Nice, *we* had to go somewhere else.

He and Theo hurried to Gershon's apartment to ask him to go to Lyons with us. He refused—he couldn't accept "charity," and he couldn't desert his working-class friends.

Theo said that money was coming to France from abroad, that the friends could go too. "We'll wait in Lyons. If Germany occupies France, we'll go south and cross into Spain."

"Fascist Spain? How long do you think it will be till Franco is siding with Hitler?" To my father, Gershon said, "Maybe *you* have to go, but *I* have a country. I'm French."

My father had lost all patience. "What's wrong with you?" He turned to Esther. "Talk to him. Please!"

Gershon thrust the palm of his hand toward his wife, shutting her out. "There are not enough Germans to victimize all of us French."

Cruelly, my father said, "Us French? You live in your own little world, speaking Yiddish. *We* are leaving. Let Esther come with us. If later it's safe in Paris, she can come back."

"Don't you have enough?" Gershon asked. "You've already stolen my son."

My father and Theo were silent, stricken.

At last my father said, "The offer stands. If you decide to go, you'll always be able to find me. Wherever there's a group of Jews, someone will know."

When they got home, it was from Theo we learned what had happened. "I ought to go home," he said. "I owe it. But I don't want to." Softly, ashamed, he added, "Joseph, I'm going with you."

For the first time, I saw some compassion for Theo in Eva. She was sitting near him, and she touched his arm.

Miserably, he said, "You think I'm terrible, don't you? None of *you* would have made that choice."

"It's just for a while," Eva said. "Then you'll be back."

"And maybe I won't. Coming home, I thought about Nicole in Italy. My mother worries about her, and my sister knows she does but stays, for herself, for what she sees as her own future—with her husband and *his* family—whether she's right or not. Is it wrong for me to be doing the same?"

"Theo," she said, "don't. We've talked about this. I told you—I like you, I like you very much, but that's all."

"I know," he said, "but I want to go with you anyway." He turned to my father. "I know how much you value family loyalty, so I hope you can still respect me."

"Theo," my mother said, "you're not abandoning them. You're only going to Lyons."

But Theo was right. Aaron had chosen a title for him—he had called him our honorary brother—and Theo had taken the title to heart.

He turned to Aaron. "Have you told Ondine we're leaving?"
"Yes, I met her while you and Papa were out."
And what my mother told my father, later that night, was that she was again carrying a child.

III

THE LAST PREGNANCY, OF COURSE, HAD NOT BEEN planned, and though in Paris my mother was well, in Lyons she was ill and depressed. My father, trying to make our money last, had taken a smaller, shabbier apartment than any my mother had ever set foot in. She was also, for the first time, living without any servants. She understood the need, but the hard life joined a difficult pregnancy, the news from Poland, and events in France, and together they drained her spirit and strength.

France had surrendered. The Germans had taken the north, including Paris, and the western coast to the border with Spain. They had left the rest of the country "free," to be governed by the French collaborationists installed at Vichy.

Then, in September, in the occupied zone, the Germans proclaimed the first of the racial laws. All Jews—even the native French—were to register. We, in the other zone, had our own surprises in early October, when Vichy established racial laws of its own. Not only were we to register, but prefects—heads of the *départements*—could, on a mere whim, deliver the Jews like us, foreign ones, to camps.

We didn't register. We were hardly known in Lyons, and the people who knew we were foreign Jews were people my father could trust. For dealing with anyone else, he had bought us identity papers that said we were French.

It was then only late 1940, and plans for the "final solution" hadn't been made. In Alsace-Lorraine, the Germans had been expelling—not exterminating—Jews. They rounded them up, took them on trains and trucks to the border, and dumped them out on the roads near Lyons. Later, when they delivered the ones from Baden and the Saar, the local French officials shipped them off to "shelter" camps in southern France.

In our area, there were people helping these refugee Jews, and my father, Theo, and Nathan were spending their days with one of the groups, while Aaron stayed in the house. With Theo's relentless drilling, he had lost the last of his Polish accent. He could pass for French as surely as I and could therefore become a protector of sorts to those remaining at home.

After a while, Aaron got bored and wanted Theo to spell him. Eva, who hated the chores of the kitchen, wanted to go with my father too. One day, while Theo and Nathan stayed in the house, my father took Eva and Aaron. Soon they were back, with Eva in shock and wrapped in my father's muffler and coat. She had seen an unloading of Jews.

On a truck was a boy of seven or eight, clinging to the rim, afraid to jump down. His mother called, encouraged him, but the boy hung back. One of the Germans approached him, and lifting a crowbar high in the air, crashed it down on the hands of the child. The boy cried out and fell to the ground. His mother shrieked, threw her body across him, and lifted him up and away from the truck. Another German came over, and the two of them fought her, prying the boy from her arms. One of them gripped the child by the elbows and pressed his hands to the side of the truck, while the other one smashed them again and again, destroying them.

Eva fainted. When Aaron and my father brought her home, my mother and Imma wrapped her in blankets and spooned some brandy into her mouth. My father said that a shipment of Jews had arrived and that Eva had gotten upset. My mother sent Joel and me from the room, and my father revealed the details to the rest. Before bedtime, Aaron decided to tell those details to Joel and me, and forever afterward, when the day was referred to at all, it was called "the day of the truck."

That night, my mother sat in the room I shared with Eva and Joel. I lay awake, conscious of my hands, picturing crowbars, while Eva, as if drugged, slept. My mother watched.

My father came in, and in a gesture I had never seen him make, he put his hand on her abdomen, lightly, his eyes shut.

"Let me watch for a while," he said. "You need to sleep."

She shook her head. "You're not to take them again."

"I won't take Eva."

"You're not to take any of them. I'm afraid."

"It didn't hurt Aaron—Aaron was fine."

She raised her voice. "None of them. Not even Nathan."

"I have to. He needs to be tough."

"You're not to take him! And *you're* not to go either."

"Magda, listen," he said. "When I left the shtetl, I thought that safety was everything. But I was wrong. It's something, but it's not everything. I'm not poor, I'm not ignorant, and I can't run away anymore."

"I need you at home."

"Magda, don't. Someday we'll be old. What will matter then is whether we have the children's respect. You're their mother, and all that's expected of you is to keep them living and well. But a man can't stay at home. What will the children say of me later, when they remember their father did nothing but hide?"

"Protecting your own isn't nothing—especially now with another one coming."

My father began to protest, but then, his lips in a tight white line, he turned and went out of the room.

Toward morning, my mother went off to their bed, and she was asleep when the rest of us sat in the kitchen at breakfast.

"Theo," my father said, "Magda's uneasy. She'll feel safer if you're here with her, so today I'll only take Nathan."

Aaron asked to be taken too.

"Not yet," my father said. "When your mother calms down."

"Joseph," Imma said, "don't take Nathan either."

"I have to have someone," he said.

"Take Theo. He's older."

He refused, and though Imma argued, it didn't help. He took Nathan, and when my mother awoke and heard, she sat by herself in a corner, and for a long time no one disturbed her.

That evening, she ignored my father entirely. Later, Joel, Eva, and I were wakened from sleep by her voice. If she and my father had quarreled before, in spacious surroundings, we must not have heard, but now, through a single wall, her voice was a strange one, loud and harsh. She was shouting in Polish.

Eva, to protect us, started to babble, but Joel, frantic, jumped from his cot and screamed, "Eva, shut up!" The apartment got quiet, but soon my mother was shouting again, with words that are still in my ears.

"I will not be hushed! I said I was afraid, and you took him—out of spite!"

We couldn't hear my father. We heard my mother, then silences, and then my mother again.

"*Let* them hear. If I'm living like a peasant I can *act* like one."

"You will *not* decide. It was *you* who wanted so many children—*you* who thought it would keep them safe—but *I* carried them, and *I* won't let you harm them."

And then, even louder, "Joseph!"

There was a terrifying silence. Then, softly, incredulously, she said, "You raise your hand? Against *me?*"

We had never seen my father raise his hand against anyone. Now, from him we heard a rush of muted sounds, but we couldn't make out the words.

We heard my mother's. "I don't care. You raised your hand. From this moment, I'm no longer your wife."

Eva seized Joel and held him, murmuring his name, but from my parents' room there wasn't a sound, and after a while we fell asleep.

The sounds began again, a woman's moans, and right after sunrise Daniel was born, tiny, furious, strong.

Imma had been the midwife. We others had all been waiting, my father a little apart from us, his head in his hands, and audibly praying. At the sound of Daniel's cry, his murmuring stopped, but he didn't look up.

Imma came in, and in a worried tone she said, "Magda's fine. Another son, and I think he's sturdy, Joseph dear, but I'm not sure. He's small—he's terribly small."

Looking up, he said, "He'll live, Mama, you'll see. Magda needs him."

When we entered, my mother was absorbed, peering at the squalling child in wide-eyed wonder.

Touching my father's hand, she said, "Listen to him, listen!"

"I hear him, darling. What shall we call him?"

"Daniel," she answered.

"Good."

So far as we know, it was in that simple, brief exchange that my parents made up.

My father had been right. Daniel lived, and he forced from my mother an animal strength she never had shown. In the weeks that followed she nursed him, rested, nursed him again, held him close in the warmth of her body, and was, in the process, nourished and healed.

Then, almost two months after Daniel was born, as Eva and I got back from a long line at the baker's, a man emerged from the flat adjacent to ours and stood in our path, serious, bent over us. He was my father's height but twice as broad. His sudden appearance, his closeness, and his skin—so white it was almost green—almost buckled my knees.

To Eva, he said, "*Bonjour*. But you are not the one who was screaming in Russian."

Except at home, I did most of the talking for Eva, as Theo and Aaron did for my father. Without thinking, I said, "*Non.*"

Turning to me, sharply: "The young lady is mute?"

"The young lady," Eva said, with a momentary tremor in her voice, "does not speak Russian."

"But has a foreign accent."

"Nevertheless, monsieur, I'm French."

"So it was your mother shouting?"

Calmly, Eva said, "Monsieur, there's nothing to discuss."

"With anyone?"

"With anyone."

Letting us pass, he said, "You'll change your mind."

When my mother had heard, she said, "If he didn't know it was Polish, he didn't understand a word."

"But, Mama," Eva said, "he knows we're foreigners."

My mother hesitated. "Maybe all he was doing was flirting."

"I don't think so."

"Neither do I," my mother admitted. "God knows what harm I've done to you all."

We said she hadn't meant to, and besides, others were not as careful as we, and still, not a single Jew we knew had been arrested.

"What matters is law," she said. "If officials can put you in prison for nothing, how can you ever be sure you're safe? Whatever he's thinking, it's better to know than to wonder." She handed Daniel to Imma, hesitated over who should go along with her, and decided at last on Eva rather than me.

Our neighbor made a sarcastic, elaborate bow, let them in, and said, "I wondered how long it would take."

In Polish, my mother said, "I apparently disturbed you, so I've come to apologize." Eva translated.

Pointing to some chairs, he said, "Wasn't that Russian?"

"Polish," my mother said. "I know French, as you see, but my accent is bad, so, to the French, I'd rather not speak it." Eva translated.

"Your daughter's is bad too. You've just arrived from Poland?"

"No, we've been back for years."

He smiled. "You didn't arrive with the rest of the Jews?"

"I'm a Pole, monsieur, not a Jew."

"Is your husband the Jew?"

Indignantly, my mother said, "He's Catholic—French by birth." Then, agreeably, "But of Polish descent. As a child he was raised in Poland, by his grandparents, landed aristocrats. Later he lived in France, until, as a young man, he revisited Poland, and we met and married."

"And he stayed?"

"He was a journalist, covering Warsaw. That's where we raised this girl and a son."

"Such a complicated story," he said. "And that's why your daughter speaks French like a Pole." To Eva he said, "Why did your father come back?"

"Why are you questioning us?" my mother asked. "And why—since I came with an apology—why in that offensive tone?"

"I thought you wanted to talk," he said. "*I* talk. Always. It's useful. Other things are useful too, don't you agree?"

She stood up. "I don't know what you mean, but I've apologized, and now I'm going. I have an infant."

"I know. That's why I waited till now."

"Waited?"

"Two months. I can still be patient a little while longer. Shall we say three days?"

My mother, repeating all this, was livid. "That he would *dare* to talk to us like that. And that *I* had to hold my tongue."

"Thank God you did," Imma said. "Who knows who he is or whom he knows."

When my father and Theo got home, the discussion was just as brief. We'd have to pay blackmail forever, perhaps both to him and the prefect himself.

The next day, when we knew our neighbor had left for work, we packed—an easy matter, since now we were living with very few things. Theo and Nathan went off to a man who could help, and he found us another apartment, even smaller and shabbier than the first. By nightfall, we were gone.

During that winter, hundreds of Jews from the Saar, in vermin-infested camps to which they'd been sent from Lyons, already had died from the cold, malnutrition, and disease.

Then, on a rainy night as winter was ending, my father was out with Aaron, who had persuaded my mother to say he could go. When they got home, there was a large irregular bulge in my father's coat, under his chin. Slowly he opened his coat and, looking in, whispered, "Good little darling. Good Marianne."

She was no more than a year and a half. She looked at us, curiously, but without any fear.

"She's from the Saar," my father said. "We have her just for the night."

"The concierge!" my mother said. "Did she see?"

"Yes, of course, but I'm sure we can trust her."

Nathan held out his arms. The little girl hesitated, but then she leaned toward him, and he took her.

"Before her parents were shipped to the camp," my father explained, "they handed her off to a farmer."

My mother, holding Daniel, held him tighter. "Oh, my God."

"This man and his wife have had her since then, but he's quarreled with one of his neighbors, and now he's afraid."

"Of what?" I asked.

"That someone'll take her away."

"And after tonight?" my mother asked.

"Somebody's out, looking to find her a place."

"She trusts us," Aaron said. "Why don't we keep her?"

"And if we leave?" my father asked. "How will her parents know where she is?"

Aaron became impatient. "How do you know they're alive?"

"I don't. I assume it. After all they've been through, should they lose her?"

"No! But you don't know who'll get her next!"

"Shhh," Nathan said, softly, looking at the little girl. "Let's be quiet, Aaron, all right? You'll get her upset."

While Imma heated some milk and diced some bread, Nathan sat with the child, reassuring her with smiles and silly faces. "See, Marianne?" he said. "You're safe with me. My hair is blond, like yours, like your papa's and mama's, no?"

As the evening wore on, my mother put Daniel to sleep, but the little girl, restless, clung to Imma, who walked with her, softly singing a lullaby: "On the hearth a little fire is burning, and the room is warm, and the little children . . ."

The child became even more alert, but as Imma sang the lullaby over and over, she relaxed and fell asleep, and Imma put her down. She slept in the narrow bed between Eva and me, and the following morning she left with my father and Aaron, in my father's arms, like his own child.

When they got back, my father was greatly relieved. "It was easy," he said. "Easier than with some other children. She was marvelous. She didn't cry once."

Aaron stared at my father a moment, ripped off his coat, and started to pace. After a while, he took himself off to a side of the room, where he sat with his back to us, brooding, his head bent down and his arms across his chest.

"Aaron," my father said. "They're nice people—we can trust them. You saw—she didn't even cry."

Aaron swung around, upsetting his chair. He came to the table, where the rest of us were, and, glaring at my father, he lifted his fist in the air and slammed it down on the table, bringing us all to our feet.

His voice was quiet. "When is enough? You've forgotten the day of the truck? Now a baby. Too innocent to know she ought to cry. Like a puppy, she's abandoned once and twice and again, and still she trusts."

He snatched his coat and rushed to the door as Imma and my mother shouted, "Aaron!"

Nathan could have stopped him, but didn't, and as the door slammed, my mother said, "Nathan, quick, bring him back."

"Nathan, don't," my father said. "Magda, darling, don't. Let him go out for a walk. This place is a cage."

Mildly, with resignation, Nathan said, "Stupid kid. He always gets so upset."

"He's not stupid," my father said. "He has much more sense than you and I together."

"Why? Because he says whatever comes into his head?"

"Because he doesn't wait to be told what to do."

It was a statement my father would later regret.

Except for Imma, who took Daniel from my mother's arms and walked with him, we sat, hardly moving, silent, waiting for Aaron. When at last he got back, he went to my father.

"I'm sorry," he said. "But I want you to buy me a gun."

He was then seventeen.

Groups of resisters, scattered about, had been forming since shortly after the French surrender. They were in both of the zones, and Theo and Aaron had joined one as soon as we'd moved to our second Lyons apartment.

They'd started an underground paper, an innocuous thing it might seem, but very important in launching the groups and keeping them active. My mother wanted to know why they needed a gun for newspaper work, and Aaron, hinting at things he couldn't disclose, insisted he did. My father, who didn't seem very reluctant, gave in. He bought the gun, and then books on guns, which Aaron all but memorized.

One evening, as Theo was taking his turn at assembling the

gun, he said, "Around Paris, they're doing more than putting out a paper. They're taunting—infuriating—the Germans."

The word he had used for taunt was *narguer,* a slang word we didn't know. My mother asked what it meant, and when he explained she shrugged.

"They don't do *childish* things," he said. "They're acts of sabotage. If ever we do them here, who'll care that I'm lame?" He looked toward Eva.

"Theo," she said, "nobody cares even now."

"No," Imma said, "we have to be honest. Theo, forgive me. It doesn't matter to *us,* but if you use a gun the way you mean to use it, even with twenty other boys, it's you the witnesses won't forget. They'll *remember* a boy with a limp."

"Don't worry, Imma," Aaron said, "Theo and I will always be in it together, and neither of us will be caught."

My mother's hand flew to her chest.

That night, alone with Joel and Eva, I said, "Will anything happen to Theo and Aaron?"

"No," Eva said. "They're not doing anything dangerous yet, and no one's been caught. Besides, Theo's a man, even if Imma calls him a boy. He'll always keep Aaron in check."

"Eva?" I asked. "Do you like Theo better now?"

She hesitated. Carefully, she said, "I *always* liked him."

A little while later, she raised her head from the mattress and, seeing Joel asleep, she said, "Ruth? Yes, I do."

"Why? He was *always* nice."

"He was *too* nice. I think I like men who are . . . I don't know . . . more forceful—even angry, I think—better than I like quiet men."

"But Nathan is quiet, and still you love him better than you love Aaron."

"I don't. Why do you say that?"

"You do. You love Nathan better than anyone." She didn't answer. "I'm the one who draws," I said, "but in Paris, you never took *me* to museums. Only Papa ever took me."

"You never asked me to."

"Did Nathan have to ask you?"

"Oh, Ruth," she said, "you read too much into everything. Forget what I said about Theo. Go to sleep."

I didn't forget, and now, as if the work of the resisters' group had changed, or at any moment would, we watched and listened to Aaron and Theo as never before. The one whom no one, not even my mother or Eva, seemed aware of now was Nathan.

Then, on the 14th of May, 1941, in Paris, almost four thousand Polish Jewish men who were citizens of France were told to appear. It had been easy to find them. At the time they had registered, index cards were filed with the Paris police, informing whoever might later be looking for Jews—as the Germans were finally doing—where all of them lived and all had been born.

Theo announced he was leaving Lyons, returning to Paris.

"Please," Imma begged. "How do you know your father was taken?"

He turned on her, shocked and angry, a Theo we had never seen. "Now you're optimistic. When it was your own—your daughters in Poland—you were afraid."

For a moment, Imma was silenced.

"And if he wasn't taken," Theo said, "I'll get him out of Paris."

"And if he was?"

"I'm French by birth. I could go to him, try to get him released, bring him food, take my mother away." He turned to my father. "Joseph, I'd bring her to you if you'd let me."

"Of course I'd let you, but do you think you can do it?"

"Yes! But then, afterward, I don't think I'll stay. I *know* I won't stay. There are resisters in Paris. Here in Lyons, safe from the Germans, it's hardly better than hiding."

"But you *can't* go back to Paris," Imma said. "Even to get your mother. There's a law—it forbids your coming back—you told me. They'll arrest you the minute you get to the line."

"No," he said, "they won't. They'd have to catch me first."

"Oh, Theo," she said, shaking her head, refraining from saying the obvious. "All right, child, let's say you don't get caught. You get to Paris, and—just for the sake of argument, Theo—what if your mother refuses to leave?"

"My mother does what my father wants. And now he'll want her going with me."

"With *us*, Imma," Aaron said. "I'm going too."

"No, you won't," my mother said. "I'm your mother, and I say you won't. Theo is French. He has *that* to protect him."

"For the time being! His father's a citizen, isn't he? What good did it do? The police who do the arresting, *they* aren't German, they're French."

"We don't even know he was arrested!" my mother said. "Maybe he didn't turn himself in. Maybe by now they've left and they're somewhere in hiding. And if he *was* taken, will it help if *you* get taken too? After all we've done to get to where we're safer, you'll go back?"

"Yes! Mama, *I* don't *have* a country. If I did, I'd be in the army, so if Theo's finally ready, I'm making the French resisters my army."

Calmly, it seemed, my father said, "This is just romantic talk. As a practical matter, how will you not get caught at the border?"

"We'll figure it out. While you were traveling, Theo met plenty of people. In Paris we'll go to Ondine's."

This had been said in the mixture of Polish and French with which we had lived for the past two years. Imma could follow enough, but on hearing the name "Ondine," she turned to my father.

"Ondine?"

His faced had turned white. *"That's* where they'll go. To Ondine's! *That's* where they think they'll be safe."

Imma said, "Aaron! You trust that apostate, her father?"

Impatiently, my father said, "It's not her father, it's Ondine he trusts."

"But Aaron," she said, "she's not your wife. She might have someone else by now."

"She doesn't, any more than *I* would have someone else."

"But all those years in a convent school, hearing what they hear from nuns and priests—how can you trust her?"

"I do, Imma. I trust her father too, because I know his secret. If he betrays me to the French police, I'll do the same to him."

My father was appalled. "You'd endanger the girl?"

"It'll never come to that. Her father's a practical man, an apostate, yes, but not a monster. He wouldn't betray me."

"But what your group is doing here, putting out that paper—it has value—in Paris they're getting arrested for that. And what we've done together, the four of us, for the refugees." Aaron was shaking his head. "With the *children?*" my father asked. "Has our work for the *children* been useless?"

"Not when *you* do it, but it's not enough for *me.* Why do you think I wanted a gun? And how can I fight from here when the Germans are there?"

Eva turned to Theo. "Don't do this," she begged. "I think I know how you feel, but don't take Aaron."

"I'm not taking him," he said, "It's his own decision—he doesn't have to come."

"I do," Aaron said, facing Eva. "I was ready to go the day we gave the little girl away. I was ready before that—the day of the truck. It was Theo who wasn't—he wouldn't leave *you.*"

"Theo," she begged, "tell him to wait. Give my parents a little more time."

"I can't. What he said is true, and he's safer going with me than going alone. *I'm* the one who knows where to go."

"But you're bringing back your mother—he can wait."

Aaron got furious. "Eva! Stop running my life."

She turned away. "Nathan!" she said. *"Say* something."

I doubt that anyone had looked at Nathan until she called his name, but now, there he was, leaning back in a chair with his arms on his chest, as if none of this mattered to him.

"If I do," he said, "will they listen? When did Aaron tell me he would go wherever Theo goes? And *when*ever Theo goes. *I* am his brother. *Joel* is his brother. I don't have any quarrel with Theo—he doesn't owe us a thing. He *should* go back to Gershon and Esther; *they* are his family. If I argued at all, I'd argue with Aaron. Everyone thinks he's a god, and for me you have only contempt, so why should I bother to argue?"

I turned to my father. He was looking from Nathan to Aaron and back, seeing at last that the bond so important to him had been broken. He took my mother's hand, led her to a chair, and sat beside her in another one. No one spoke, and Theo and Aaron gathered some things and carefully placed them in canvas bags. The gun was in Aaron's.

When it seemed they had finished, my father said, "I need Ondine's address. And your sister's, Theo, in Rome."

Papers were passed back and forth, and my father took out of his pocket some packets of money. Aaron accepted, but Theo refused, and my father insisted. When Theo at last accepted the money, my father added, "Bring us your parents, and take care of my son."

He stood up and embraced Aaron, a long embrace, and then Theo. My mother and Imma did the same, and Eva was next. I watched her carefully. As she drew away from Theo, she lifted her hand and touched his cheek. Joel and I were last. Nathan remained by himself, off to a side, and when Aaron, hesitant, turned to him and extended his arms, Nathan drew back.

"I wish you well, Aaron," he said, "both Theo and you. But anything more will have to wait."

I looked at my father. I had seen him hurt by Imma the night he had talked of our passing for French, but this was worse. My mother put her arms about him, and they clung to each other silently, in this first long embrace of theirs I had ever seen, a fierce one, as if by their ferocity they could inhibit in each other the tears that rose in everyone else.

IV

WHEN THEY HAD LEFT, MY FATHER APPROACHED Nathan. "I don't know why you think we have contempt for you, but if you do, the fault must be mine, and I'm sorry. But what you did to Aaron and Theo was wrong."

With what I think was both regret and bitterness, Nathan said, "I'm always wrong. Aaron is always right."

"That's not what I said."

"It's what you mean."

"No, it isn't," Imma said. "Think about *him* for a change. Part of him wished he were going with them."

A shiver of fear rippled my skin. I wanted my father to say

she was wrong, that he never would leave us, but instead he was silent, pacing the room. After a while he turned to my mother.

"I'll do as you wanted—leave the committee. We have to get out of the country."

Shocked, my mother almost shouted, "*Now* you say it? Why didn't you say it while they were here?"

"It wasn't as clear when they were."

"But how will we find each other?"

"Someone will figure out ways."

"But you told Theo to bring us his parents."

"You really believe Gershon can come? And will Esther come without him? If not for these children, would *you* leave *me* in prison in Paris and go?"

"Do you really think he's in prison?"

My father, impatient, didn't answer. "With Theo and Aaron," he said, "there were ten of us, and eight even now—it's like smuggling an army over the border. But now that they're gone, and with only the little ones passing for French, we have to get out."

He glanced around, as if counting, and Joel and I, in our unspoken language, reached toward each other, as if we were guilty, as if our presence in the world had made the danger greater for the others.

From then on, my father worked at getting us out of the country. He had chosen Lyons partly because it was close to the border with Switzerland, but—even after our neighbor's threat—Lyons had appeared to be safe, and my father's attention to getting to Switzerland waned. It was now revived.

One day, in a bizarre event we'd thought could never occur, Eva and I, on a crowded street, were suddenly facing our former neighbor. He loomed above us, as close and large and green as on the day he had blocked our way in the hall.

Turning, convinced he was following, we ran to a maze of

alleys and steps that later became an escape route for many resisters. We, however, became confused, and went cautiously back to where we had been, Eva berating herself for not keeping track of the names of the streets.

The man was nowhere about, but we couldn't get free of the fear that he was. We ran to the alleys again, but afraid of asking directions and being remembered, we finally found our way by ourselves, thinking he'd followed us back.

Again my family left, but now to the countryside right outside of Lyons. At least a hundred thousand Jews had sought asylum in the Vichy zone, and most were going from place to place.

Later, as German barbarity grew and—everywhere—French police were rounding up Jews, people started to show some compassion. But now, they blamed us for the shortages of food and the thriving black market. Only in areas inhabited by Protestants—outsiders in France like ourselves—were we offered some friendship and help.

We moved from village to village, from one *département* to another. We had a new prefect and a new commissariat of police, and our emigration documents, painfully gotten, were void, and had to be gotten all over again.

I was nine at the time, and Joel twelve, and only Joel was aware that I was obsessed with my hands. I saw any metal bar, any club, as a tool to crush them. Joel would see me clenching my fists, and he would touch my arm to stop me.

I was drawing pictures constantly—if not of hands, then of faces of people who helped us. And always, no matter what I might draw from experience, I drew the stars of American films. Their photos, from which I copied, were with me still—they and some clothes were my only possessions remaining from Warsaw.

Deportations from occupied France had started in March. By August, to meet the quota for Auschwitz, the Germans increased their pressure on Vichy, and though Vichy refused to deliver the

Jews who were French, they didn't have qualms about foreigners.

Again we had to go back to Lyons, and what I remember best was the week it seemed we were entering Switzerland. It was late September 1942. My father had given up trying to emigrate legally, and had arranged with a man called Étienne to smuggle us over the border. We'd leave as a group, we and a family of four—Rudy, a tall, athletic-looking man, Liesel, his little, fragile wife, their infant daughter, and a boy of five.

On almost the last day, as final plans were made, Étienne increased his fee, and Rudy was short some hundreds of francs. My father, despite his previous scrimping, supplied them. That day, Joel, prone to bronchitis, developed a raging fever that nothing would lower, and my parents decided to stay. They pleaded with Imma, Eva, and Nathan to take me and leave, but no one would go till we all could go.

My father went off to explain to Étienne and to pay the final installment, as if we were going. Étienne, in turn, said he would take us when Joel was well, but again he'd be taking the risks, so again he would have to be paid. My father agreed.

Rudy pleaded with my father: he had to repay him, he would carry Joel. My father refused, but Liesel begged, and my father at last accepted.

It was Étienne who wouldn't hear of it. "What do you think this is? A stroll? An old woman, a small boy, two babes in arms, and now you'll carry a boy that big? It's too much risk."

My father understood, or said he did, embraced Liesel, and promised that after the war he'd find them.

On the fifth day, when Joel was better, my father went back to Étienne. The man was cordial and matter-of-fact.

He'd been caught. The border police—honorable men, he said—had let him get off with only a warning, but he wouldn't be able to do this again. As for this Rudy and his family, the border police had turned them in. "They were sent to the east," he said. "Be glad your son got sick."

By fall, the British and Americans had landed in North Africa. To prevent their going through France, the Germans took over the Vichy zone, except for eight southeastern departments taken by Italy, Germany's partner.

We fled from the Nazis and toward the Fascists, whose racial laws and violent past convinced us that they—even more than the French collaborationists—would welcome seeing us dead.

But as we moved toward the south, we met a physician named Hartman, a Belgian Jew about my father's age, whose wife and son had died in a column of refugees strafed by German planes. He was left with only his daughter, Yvette, a scrawny young woman of twenty, silent, with strawlike hair and eyes that darted about in fear. Hartman kept watching her, urging her to speak, as if she were mute from some physical trauma and needed retraining.

With them was Bernard, somewhat older than Yvette, solemn-faced, with lifeless eyes and kinky orange hair. He had a peculiar walk. He was long-legged, lanky, and his stride began at the shoulders as he thrust a side of his body forward onto a long, inflexible leg and then, with a bounce, onto the other.

"There's a reception center in Nice," Hartman said. "Isn't that so, Yvette?" She nodded. "It's run by Jews, but under Italian protection. They won't allow the Germans to take us."

My mother looked at my father in triumph. She had wanted to go from Paris to Nice.

To Hartman my father said, "Forgive me, but I think you're deluding yourself. Italy is Germany's ally. If they protect us from the Germans now, it's only to get us together, all in a single place."

Yvette, her eyes wide, drew back, pressing herself against Bernard.

"No, no," Hartman said, looking toward Yvette, touching her, but addressing my father. "You're mistaken, monsieur."

"The Italian army failed," my father said, "both in Greece and

Africa, and the Germans came to their rescue. Italy owes them a favor, and the favor, you'll see, will be us."

"Monsieur," Yvette said, leaning forward. Her posture and that single word were a plea.

"A time comes, Monsieur Levy," Hartman said, "when people come into your life whom you know you can trust." He turned to Bernard. "Why don't you and Yvette go back to our room?"

Bernard didn't answer. He took Yvette's hand and stood up. In the days we later traveled together, I remember him always beside her, taking one long step to two of hers, holding her hand, as on the night before our departure from Warsaw Joel had held mine.

When they had gone, my father said, "I'm sorry. With my own children I became impatient, but I shouldn't upset someone else's. Monsieur Hartman, I'm not optimistic."

In anguish, Hartman said, "Why not? *Look* at you. You have a family left. A whole family."

I thought he would never forgive us for having each other, but the following day we left together with no resentment, and without a clue as to why my father had changed his mind and chosen to go with the Hartmans to Nice.

And there, on Rue Dubouchage, was what Hartman had said we would find. There was also a synagogue. *Carabinieri* were out in the street, protecting both the synagogue and the reception center, and with the power, if necessary, to arrest the Vichy police. And inside the center, a white-haired Jew gave us our papers.

Nice would be hard to forget—the Alps as a backdrop, the sea to the south, white hotels along the waterfront, a wide boulevard bordered by palm trees and curving around the bay, pastel villas, and sunny outdoor cafés where people appeared not even to know or to care what was happening anywhere else. But much more vivid even today are that elderly man, his face florid and lined, and the giddiness with which I touched the documents issued by Jews—authorized by Italians—to legalize our status there and in all of Italian-occupied France.

We would be in *résidence forcée*. Those with means, like us, would support themselves, and Jewish community funds would support the others. We'd be in nearby villages, many of them vacation resorts, where the Italians had requisitioned houses and hotels for us, where we'd be allowed to organize schools, clubs, lectures, where we could go to cafés and restaurants—and all they were asking of us was to stay in the villages, abide by a nine-o'clock curfew, and, twice a day, report to the local police. Even my father began to feel we were safe.

I never saw the other villages—Barcelonnette, Mégève, St. Gervais, and others, which must have been equal to ours—but ours, St. Martin-Vésubie, which took a few hundred of us, was a taste of heaven itself.

It was sixty kilometers from Nice and close to the border with Italy, an enchanting roller-coaster town of narrow winding streets at the juncture of two little valleys high in the mountains. Whenever we lifted our eyes from Rue Centrale, or Place de la Marché, or anywhere else in this village of refuge, where at last we believed that no one would seize us or plan to denounce us, where Imma was openly speaking in Yiddish, and Jews in side-curls and caftans could meet in the streets serenely while *carabinieri* and *bersaglieri* strolled among them—whenever, that is, we remembered that living like this was allowed, that we could take our eyes from all the evidence and it wouldn't disappear—we would look up and away to marvel at other wonders, the towering snow-capped peaks.

A time was to come when the Germans, for so long thwarted and enraged by the audacity of these Italians who so brazenly protected us, took their revenge on Jews. In a manhunt more ruthless than any seen in western Europe, they combed St. Martin-Vésubie and Nice, and all the other towns and villages like ours, searching every room in every house and hotel, forcing the men to drop their pants, arresting every circumcised male and every woman and child in his household and sending them off to the Drancy camp near Paris, until a trainload was assembled and the records written up, and then to their death in the east.

But that came later. In Italy's zone there were no arrests of Jews. Those the French police had arrested but not deported were now released—suddenly—on orders of Italy's High Command.

For ten months, my family lived in a nice little house near a fine hotel, the Châlet Ferrix. My father and Hartman were on a committee that spoke for the Jews before the Italian officials.

"Another committee," my mother said, but now she was proud and didn't disguise her pride.

All that we missed was a sign that Aaron and Theo were safe. Often we spoke of Gershon and Esther and hoped they were free, but about my mother's parents, or Abner, or my father's sisters and their families in Poland, we never said a word.

Vittorio entered our life, as does so much else, by chance.

In the lobby of the Châlet Ferrix, the Jews had formed a synagogue, and there, on a morning in spring of '43, Yvette married Bernard.

Since Bernard's father was dead, my father was chosen to act in his place. The rest of our family sat in a row, Joel and Nathan on my left, Eva, Imma, and my mother on my right, and Daniel, who was two years old, on my mother's lap.

I was greatly amused as Bernard, on his way to the marriage canopy—his arm linked with my father's—tried to suppress his peculiar bounce. I wasn't amused when I looked at Yvette. That morning, I had said that only a boy as clumsy as he would marry a girl as ugly as she.

"Shah!" Imma had said. "Heartless child! Have pity!"

Neither my mother nor my father had tried to defend me, but Joel had said, "Imma, please," and to me, "When she's happy, she'll eat, and then she'll be prettier."

Watching Yvette, I felt that Imma was right in calling me heartless, but, remembering my parents' silence, I ached for myself. Joel, with his uncanny instinct for my thoughts, nudged me with his elbow, and when I looked at him, he winked.

I tried to forget. I concentrated, but I found the rabbi boring and finally looked away from the canopy out toward the guests. As I scanned the rows before us, I saw an Italian officer, in his late twenties, only two rows in front of us and off a bit to the side. He appeared to be staring at me.

His hair—what one could see of it from under his cap—was dark. His face was broad and square, and his eyebrows heavy. He had a blunt nose, which I didn't think attractive, but full lips and a cleft chin, which I did. I smiled, but he didn't respond, and I finally knew he'd been looking at Eva.

Just then, she saw him. She moved forward in her chair, staring, with a kind of interest she had never shown in Theo. The officer nodded, and she nodded to him in return.

When we left the hotel, I asked, "Do you know him?"

"Who?"

"You know who."

"Of course not."

Later that day, when my father went out, he met Dr. Hartman.

"Levy, forgive me," he said, "but . . . the Italians . . . have you ever invited them into your home?"

"My wife would like to," he answered, "but the thought of it frightens my mother. It even intimidates *me.*"

"You ought to," Hartman said. "We're indebted. There's a lieutenant, from a patrician family in Florence—nobility, I've heard, though he didn't say so. He asked about you. He's very proper, or he'd have approached you himself."

"What does he want?"

"He asked if you speak either French or Italian."

"Why?"

Hartman was hesitant. "Levy, he wants to meet Eva."

"Hartman, listen. I'm grateful for all they've done, but my daughter must marry a Jew."

"My daughter *did.* Bernard is from Antwerp, like us. His family died in a heap on the road, near mine. He and Yvette aren't in love—as *I* remember love. They cling to each other. Out of place with anyone who hasn't had a loss like theirs."

"Forgive me," my father said. "It sounds callous, but what has this to do with Eva and this Gentile boy?"

"Life is what it has to do with. How much life is left to our children? If only a little, let them have *something* that's good. My son was a child. Yvette is hardly more. A loveless marriage is not what I wanted for her."

"I can't believe so little is left. If Eva waits, there'll be a Jew she can love."

"Ha! Now you're optimistic. Well, if there is, you'll probably have a Gentile to thank."

My father, though dubious, finally yielded.

"He's Vittorio Bellini," Hartman said, "and he's coming to lunch tomorrow. Would you and your family join us?"

My father thanked him. "Not tomorrow. I need to prepare my mother. Invite him to *my* house, on my behalf. Say I'll be happy to have him call whenever he likes."

My father invited Hartman to join us, but he declined, and that evening, my father reported what he and Hartman had said.

Imma's answer was firm. "I'll *never* be prepared. I'll have no part of it."

"Mama!" my mother said. "We're only inviting the boy to a meal."

"You know what he wants, and you're making it easy, the way you did for Aaron and Ondine, when you welcomed her, thinking that just because they were children nothing would come of it."

Eva's face was as blank as if she were deaf.

"Mama, I understand," my father said. "I have doubts of my own. Not about Eva, but about the Fascists."

Appalled, she said, "You're bartering Eva for our safety?"

My father was at first confused and then bitterly offended.

"No! And I'll expect you to stay when he comes, and to be cordial, as someone to whom we're indebted deserves."

Imma was silent. Not since they'd argued over Theo had they been at odds, and never had my father been so harsh to her.

Eva, in an offhand way, asked, "Papa? Did you really say, 'My daughter must marry a Jew'?"

"That, Eva," he answered, "is exactly what I said."

He didn't ask her opinion, and she didn't give one, but when dinner was finished and dishes were cleared, she buried her face in a book whose pages she didn't remember to turn, and all evening, whenever anyone spoke to her she answered, "What?"

Vittorio got in touch with us through Hartman, but four days were to pass before he appeared at our door. During all that time, my father and Imma ignored each other as well as they could.

On one of those evenings, my father reminded us, "Italy's Germany's ally, so be careful. Don't mention Aaron. We mustn't let on why Aaron left."

Imma answered, "Why don't you tell him that you, Nathan, and Eva speak German? *That'll* appease him."

Before he could answer, Eva said, "I'll never speak German again."

She had turned quiet and restless. She was doing some work for a school, but when she was finished she kept to herself, avoiding even Nathan. In the past, on Friday evenings, she'd been taking me with her, first to observe some Hasidic Jews who'd be singing and dancing in whirling, exuberant circles. Their children, speaking Yiddish, sounded as charming as Daniel speaking French. Later we'd walk to the outskirts of town where one of the houses had a piano. We'd stand a little way off, hoping to hear it played.

On this particular Friday, when I went with her to the door, she told me she wanted to go by herself.

"Eva," I asked, "what will you do if you like him?"

Coldly, as my father had spoken to Imma, she said, "We'll have to wait and see, won't we?"

Her tone stung me, but I went on. "But what do you *want* from him? Do you want him to help you pass for a Gentile?"

"No! Play with Daniel or Joel, why don't you. You never play with Daniel—will you ever grow into a woman? Why don't all of you leave me alone?"

I didn't understand until later. She wanted to know that Hartman was right—that the yearning she felt for this handsome young man was good, that there were Gentiles we still could trust, and that she, unlike Yvette, could expect to be in love.

My parents, despite the warning from Imma, made it as easy for Vittorio as they had done for Ondine. Since he, unlike Ondine, didn't seize the lead, they asked him about the treasures of Renaissance art in Florence, about Italian education and the landscape of the Tuscan countryside—nothing that really revealed him to us or us to him—while Eva, who was visibly tense, merely listened and every so often managed to smile.

We weren't aware of all that she felt until, at a pause, she said, "Perhaps this is rude, Lieutenant. Maybe I oughtn't to ask, but why is your army helping us Jews?"

My father's hand flew forward to tell her to stop.

"Because you need the help," Vittorio said. "And because *we* are the occupiers here, not Germany, and we won't be lackeys to them. Besides, mademoiselle, it hasn't been only the army."

"And it can't be the whole explanation."

"Why not? In Nice, *your* people are giving money for the victims in our cities bombed by England and America—*your* allies. We could question *your* motives. We could say you're trying to bribe us. Or, on the other hand, we could say you're too intelligent to think you can buy us off so cheaply. That since you show compassion for Italians, it's a sign of your honor, as what *we* have been doing for *you* is a sign of ours."

"Here! But in your own country you've been putting Jews like us in concentration camps."

He looked away for a moment. "Foreign Jews, yes. To Italy's shame."

"Then why haven't your people protected us there? You've been living for years with racial laws."

"Fear," he said. "Of Mussolini. But yes, you're right."

Gathering courage, she said, "Lieutenant, your country had something to gain, and you wanted Hitler's support."

"Our government, yes."

"And now, to *keep* his support, and when we're not expecting it, you'll give us to him as a gift."

"No!"

My father gasped.

"No," Vittorio repeated, quietly. "Is that what you think?"

Eva could not have expected the hurt we saw in his face. As if pleading, she said, "It's not what I *want* to think."

"Mademoiselle," he said, "I've spoken frankly, so you ought to trust me. Italy took away the jobs of Italian Jews, their careers, their civil rights, and the freedom of the foreign ones. That was evil enough, and we weren't *all* indifferent—don't assume it. But—" and now, for the rest of the sentence, he raised his voice—"the Germans are taking your *lives!*"

He paused. "There are certain Fascists who will help them—we *know.* But until now, unlike the Vichy French, *we* have not surrendered any Jews to them, anywhere, despite their requests. Not in Italy, nor in Greece, nor in Croatia, nor here in France. Nor would our Foreign Ministry approve it. Nor would our army ever agree to it—on that I would stake my honor and life."

Eva covered her face and rocked with silent sobs. Vittorio moved forward and, on one knee, as if this were a fairy tale, he knelt on the floor, putting his hand on her arm.

"I understand, mademoiselle," he said. "I do."

When she had composed herself, she said, "No matter where it leads, no matter who demands I change, I'll remain a Jew."

"As you should," he answered. "I'll remember. And you'll always have my respect."

When Vittorio had left, Imma said—sadly, despairingly—"Eva, you encouraged him. Why? What have you done?"

"I know what I've done," she said. "For me it was right."

Afterward, I never heard a word of opposition, even from Imma, to Vittorio's visits, perhaps because he had moved them deeply, and surely because it wouldn't have helped. This was a new Eva. She had found her strength, as my mother had when Daniel was born. She became my mother's peer.

One night, she sat on my bed and took my hand.

"When we met Ondine, she asked what I'd do when the war was over, remember?" I nodded. "What about *you?*" she asked. "For a girl not even eleven, you're so grown up."

"I'll be a journalist. Like Ondine."

"Really? I thought you would say an artist."

"I've changed my mind."

"Why?"

"It depends so much on your hands."

She drew a quick breath. "The day of the truck?"

"Let's not," I said. "Besides, it's more than that."

"You really like Ondine, don't you?"

There was a note of regret in her tone, but I answered, "Yes."

"It's all right," she said. "You're entitled to like her. I haven't always been nice."

"I didn't say I like her better. I haven't been angry."

"But you're always wearing the leaf."

I didn't want to have to defend my wearing the leaf. "But what about you?" I asked. "After the war, what will you do?"

She yielded. "Now more than ever," she said, "I just don't know. I try to picture myself, married, living in Florence, but it doesn't seem real. All I know is what's here and now, and how good it is now."

In all the following months, we never saw Vittorio touch her, or saw Eva touch *him,* except in taking his arm in the street, but indoors, as their eyes followed each other about, or fastened upon each other while one of the rest of us talked, we could feel the force of their union filling the air.

She, who'd helped with the cooking only because we had needed her, now was obsessed with it. She was feeding Vittorio, not only with food, but with her eyes, as she silently urged him to eat, and with her smile as he did, as if he were not only lover but child. And though Joel and I did not understand that he was indeed her lover, our parents did.

Out of gratitude to Hartman, Eva turned to Yvette, offering friendship, gingerly, so as not to frighten her off, trying to help her recover something at least of what she had lost. The girl was always afraid, and most of all of the French militia, known for hideous tortures, and for hunting resisters and Jews.

One evening, Hartman told us she'd sung in a choir, so Eva and Nathan begged her to sing. Soon she was singing us Belgian songs, coming alive at applause, and bringing Bernard to life as well. Or it might have been just the reverse—that he, gentle and dull, had given her reason to live.

We'd have stayed together forever, I'm sure, but in late July 1943, fate interceded. For Italy, the war was going badly, and the king, together with the Fascist Grand Council, overthrew the bumbling Mussolini. In August, under Badoglio now, Italy said it was taking its troops from France, except for a minuscule zone that included Nice. The Germans would finally take the rest, and we, of course, would again have to run, and we didn't know where. By the end of the month there was marvelous news: Rome would allow us to follow its troops to the fragment of France they intended to keep.

Then, another and more brilliant bolt of hope illumined our lives. There was an influential Jew, Angelo Donati, a banker, who, with the help of Father Benoît-Marie, a Capuchin monk, submitted a plan that would lead to our ultimate rescue.

All the Jews near Nice—some twenty or thirty thousand of us—would go into Italy. There we would board the ships Donati had chartered with money sent by American Jews, and we'd go to the part of North Africa recently freed by Allied troops.

As this news was spread, Jews went streaming toward Nice. We were packed and ready to leave when my father announced he had changed his mind. By the time the Hartmans arrived, he was adamant.

"No!" he said, his arm slashing the air in a long diagonal line. "The plan is Donati's—a Jew's. The support's from Benoît-Marie—a powerless priest. Badoglio hasn't approved it. Neither have the Allies. It's far too early to go."

Hartman sat down and patiently tried to persuade him. My mother tried too, and then Yvette came forward.

"*We* can't wait," she said. "We have to find a place before the rooms fill up. Mr. Levy, I'm pregnant."

"Fine," he said, with no ceremony, no congratulations. "You above all must have a bed. I promise I'll find you one, later, no matter how crowded the city's become. But not now."

Hartman said we had better be ready in Nice when the order to enter Italy came. My father said we should wait for the order before we abandoned the safety we had. Neither could change the other one's mind. The Hartmans left. We stayed.

None of us knew that the rescue planned by Donati was part of a larger plan. An armistice was near—between the Allies and Italy—and on September 3 it was signed. The signing was secret and was to remain so until October, to give the Italians the time to prepare an attack on the Germans at just the moment the Allies would land in Italy's north. And while the Italians were moving their forces into position, Donati would summon the ships for the Jews.

On the morning of September 8, Donati's plan was fully agreed to by all of the parties—Badoglio and the Allies—but early on the evening of that very day, without explanation, Eisenhower's High Command announced the armistice. The Germans moved south, the Italians and Donati were caught unprepared, and all of the plans—the Italians' and Donati's—fell through.

Less than a week had passed since the Hartmans had left.

My father went out to look for the rest of the Jewish committee, and when he got back he was calm and resigned. "So much for the rescue," he said.

My mother turned white. "The people in Nice? Trapped?"

"I don't know, and we can't go looking. It won't help Hartman if we're trapped too." He started to gather some things. "Nothing makes sense. Mama, get ready. The Italian army's leaving for home."

"And we?" Imma asked.

"We're going with them."

"To Italy? How?"

"On foot. There are two passes through the Alps."

"And what if the Germans come down and follow us in? I'm staying—I'd slow you down. I'll go to the Home for the Aged."

"That's suicide," he said. "There's no guarantee even in Italy. There are Germans all over the country, from before, but if the Allies get to *them* before *they* get to *us*, we'll be safe. And everyone's going, including you."

Some minutes went by. Vittorio arrived, still in uniform, though others had abandoned theirs. When he saw my father preparing to leave, he said, "Good. I think it's safe to leave in the morning, but don't pack much, and above all, sleep."

He went to the door and returned with another young man, a tall Florentine named Enzo.

"He speaks nothing but Italian," Vittorio said, "but you'll manage. We're going through Entraque, and Enzo will take you all, except for your mother, who's coming with me."

My father looked stunned. "But why?"

Vittorio said she would slow us down. My father protested—if we were leaving Entraque together we might as well *get* there together. Vittorio said that getting there early would give us some time for gathering news. Now it was Eva who argued—we had never accepted safety apart from each other. And Vittorio said it was time she discovered people could part.

Nathan came forward. "If we separate, *I'll* take Imma. She hardly knows French. You won't know what she needs."

"Needs?" Vittorio said. "*Time* is what we need."

"Then she and I will *both* go with you."

"No, you will not," Vittorio said. "You're going with Eva and Enzo. The climb is hazardous—maybe not for you, but for your mother and the children. They'll need you to help."

Nathan turned to my father, and my father, in an about-face, and in a peremptory tone, said, "Do as Vittorio says."

We packed and then slept, or—in the case of some of the adults—merely tried to sleep. In the morning we gathered in one of the streets of the village, each with a rucksack strapped to the back and a suitcase in one hand.

I was greatly excited and eager to start, but without intending to do so, I memorized that narrow, cobbled street—its downward slope and curve to the west, its scent of porridge in some ancient pot. To those I added the sound I'd heard in the past and can hear even now, of the piano on the edge of town, playing "Clair de Lune."

At last we started, Nathan—with a face as immobile as stone—at my side, ignoring Enzo. Another young soldier, short and square, went to Eva and offered to carry her bags. Enzo, intent on keeping men away from her, shooed him away, explaining to us, "a Roman," as if Romans deserved his contempt. Nathan looked from one to the other and smiled. The Roman returned and stayed, alongside Nathan, glancing at Eva from time to time.

Nathan pointed to himself and said, "Nathan."

The other, his hand on his chest, answered, "Flavio." He pointed to Eva and asked, *"Sua sorella?"*

Nathan, guessing correctly, answered. *"Oui. Ma soeur."*

Flavio offered him cheese. *"Formaggio,"* he said.

Nathan refused. *"Fromage. Merci."*

Flavio marched beside us into the mountains, through the Colle Finestre, and down to Entraque, exchanging words of Nathan's in French for words of his own in Italian, lending a hand to whoever appeared to need one, carrying a bag, playing with Daniel, and cheering up Nathan, who needed a friend.

I know that for others that trek through the Alps was a nightmare. A middle-aged Jew in front of us lifted his arms to heaven and pleaded, "Punish us but not our children, who have done no wrong." What my own father was thinking, I didn't know until later. He didn't fully trust Vittorio. He was afraid he would lead my grandmother off the trail and into the woods, to leave her, so that the others of us would be safe.

I, however, could only detect that my father was tense. He had seized my hand, and for ages, it seemed, he was silent. As the hours went by, we discarded our bags, first one and then another. It hurt me when mine disappeared in a gorge. It had the pictures of my movie stars, of Loretta Young and the others—some of them like those I saw in Amsterdam, years later, on a wall of the attic that had sheltered Anne Frank. We kept a single bag, which the men kept passing from one to the other.

As we neared the pass, there was a tiny sanctuary, and near it an Italian army outpost. They gave us food, and we spent the night in the barracks. In the morning, as we started to leave, we were stopped. The army headquarters down in the valley knew we were coming, and they didn't know what they would do with so many Jews if they let us come through.

Someone envisioned a trap. The army, he said, was holding us hostage, planning to bribe the Germans. Somebody else disagreed. The army was fair—they wanted their soldiers, and then they would let us go on.

My father, in a tone that implied he was curious rather than worried, asked, "And where is Vittorio?"

"Coming," Eva said, firmly, confidently, seeing through his tone. "Slowly, because that's what Imma needs."

After a long wait, they let us go on. During that time, however, Nathan begged my father to let him stay on with the troops of the garrison, to fight against the Germans if they did arrive, and if Italy told them to fight.

My father, exasperated, said, "And what if they don't? Why must you be such a fool?"

And yet, though others were fighting their private wars, Joel and I were not. I was almost eleven, and he, though small for his age, almost fourteen. The ten months' respite in St. Martin-Vésubie had made us strong and, perhaps as important, sure of ourselves. I was seized by a wild, irrational joy, and Joel, as if joy were a virus, caught it from me. We joked and laughed as we climbed.

My mother, seeing us happy, said that perhaps we ought to be quiet, but in her voice there was the pleasure I had heard in Paris long before, when Eva and Nathan had gone to museums. She was struggling along at my father's side, but Joel and I, absorbed in ourselves, regarded the trek as a great adventure. We were as innocent as Daniel, who rode on my father's shoulders, then on Nathan's, Enzo's, and Flavio's, oblivious to danger, fast asleep or cheerfully babbling most of the time.

Eva, like my father, was silent until, impatiently, she said, "Ruth, do be quiet, won't you? You ought to listen and remember. A time will come when you'll write of this march."

And now as I do, I remember best the starless night, its blackness thrilling, flickering matches here and there lighting the trail for a second or two before going out, a wind I persuaded myself was bracing rather than bitterly cold, and the delicious joy of walking a ribbon of ledge above what appeared to be a bottomless gorge. I don't believe I thought of the Hartmans once.

Nor indeed, except when my father mentioned her name, of Imma. She had been right. The Germans had reached St. Martin-Vésubie and soon would be coming for us. We heard the rumors when we reached Entraque, almost two days after we had left.

Some of the refugees, earlier arrivals, who had fled the Vésubie Valley as soon as they'd heard of the armistice, now were fleeing again, into the mountains of Italy, some without having rested so much as an hour. Most, however, did not, because the Italians offered us shelter, and with the generosity that they had shown toward us in France.

We were given a room, and Joel and I were asleep at once. My father went out with Flavio, Enzo, and Nathan to learn what they could in the town, and to make our presence known to anyone to whom Vittorio might go for news of us.

Early the next morning, Vittorio arrived, half-carrying Imma. Eva and Nathan took her from him, and my father threw his arms about him in the kind of fierce embrace in which he had held my mother when Nathan had broken with Aaron, a silent embrace that allowed him to stifle his guilt and tears.

"Vittorio," he said at last, "forgive me. I've been keeping a secret. We have another son."

"He knows," Eva said. "I trusted him long ago."

And I, only then, recognized that our positions—Imma's and mine—really had changed, as my father a lifetime ago had said that they would, and that now I was stronger than Imma.

Vittorio went to the room that Enzo and Flavio had shared, and after he'd gotten some sleep all five of the men went out. Imma slept on, oblivious to Eva and my mother, who bathed and bandaged her legs. When my father returned, only Enzo and Vittorio were with him.

"Where is Nathan?" my father said. "He said he was coming right back."

My mother's hand flew up to her throat. "He doesn't know the language here. You let him go off by himself?"

"With an Italian!"

If Vittorio was irritated too, he hid it from us and left with Enzo, telling us all to get ready to leave. When he returned, he had in his hand a letter from Nathan.

Dear Papa,

You have Vittorio now, so I'm going with Flavio. We'll meet

the Allied troops, somehow, and after the war I'll find you. I know where Vittorio lives.

Imma, don't give up. Ever. If *you* give up, *they* will have won.

Mama, forgive me. No son ever received more. This is something I have to do.

And Vittorio. Thank you. Long ago, someone named our cousin Theo "honorary brother," but it's you who's been our brother. No one I know could better deserve my cherished Eva. Give Enzo my thanks.

And you, Eva. Be happy. Be for Joel what you've been for me.

Joel and Ruthie. The war can't last, and then the world will be good. We won't forget each other. Still, think of me—every day—as I'll think of you.

And of you all.

Kiss Daniel.

Your devoted,
Nathan

NATHAN HAD LEFT THE NOTE WITH THE MAN WHO HAD taken us in.

Bewildered, my mother said, "He didn't even talk to us."

She took the note from my father's hands, and he, in either disgust or despair, sat down on one of the beds. The midday sunlight lit his hair, which was showing some silver strands.

"Because of me," he said, "that's why. Because he thinks I treated Aaron with more respect."

"You did," my mother said.

"I didn't!" He looked at Vittorio and Enzo, embarrassed, and asked them to give us some time alone.

"A half hour," Vittorio said. "Please, no more."

Eva took Imma to rest in the room the men had been using, and when they all had left, my parents moved to opposite sides of the room.

"We'll have to talk about Nathan," my father said, "but not now. Now we'll talk about us."

Coldly, unconvincingly, my mother said, "I'm sorry. With Vittorio here, I shouldn't have said what I did."

"I don't care," he answered, equally coldly. "What matters now is that it's just as well that Nathan's gone. We'll have to separate anyway—there are simply too many of us. The Germans aren't only behind us—they're all over Italy."

In town he had heard that Badoglio, who should have closed the borders when he'd come to power, hadn't done so. A hundred thousand Germans or more had come in.

"When we have to hide," he said, "because we will, it'll be harder for us if we stay as a group."

"What are you preparing me for?" she asked. "Which of our children is going next?"

"I don't know, but whoever it is, we have to be ready."

"I'm *not* ready. I'm tired of running."

"Magda!" he shouted. "You're worse than a child!"

"*Which* child? Nathan?"

He clasped his hands to his ears and bowed his head.

At last he said, "What do you expect here? What kind of haven? This isn't France—the Italian army's not in control. Here the foreign Jews have been in camps since '39."

There was a knock at the door, and my father said, "No! They only just left!"

When he opened the door, instead of Vittorio there stood Aaron, bearded, unsmiling, gaunt.

They fell into each other's arms amid a confusion of voices shouting "Aaron," amid a jumble of hands trying to pry my father from him, and surely half a minute went by before we noticed Ondine. She was even thinner than in Paris, and her hair had been cut so short that she looked like a boy.

We pulled them into the room and sat them down on a bed.

Wearily, Aaron asked, "Where are Nathan and Eva?"

"Eva's with Imma," my father said, "three doors down, and Nathan . . .'

"Imma? Oh, thank God! I heard she didn't make it."

"From whom?"

"Papa, just listen, we're tired. We got worried about you, so we looked in Nice. They sent us to St. Martin, but by then you'd left, and the pass we took was into Valdieri. Some people who knew you said you'd be here, and here in Entraque somebody found an Italian who'd seen you. But he said there was no old woman."

Ondine's eyes were closing, and my mother took her hand. "Where are your parents?" she asked.

"In Paris. No one knows my father was ever a Jew."

"I'm glad," my mother said. "And I thank God that you and Aaron never got caught."

Ondine glanced at Aaron. "He did—he was put in a camp."

My parents were silent with shock.

"I'm fine," Aaron said. "It was harder on her than on me."

"How did you get out?" my father asked.

Aaron was tired, reluctant to talk. "On a truck," he said. "Every day a convoy left, loaded up, and in the morning it was back, empty. The same truck would always be last, so one day I stretched myself across the differential, and when it left, I rode out."

"How long were you on it?" my father asked.

"Hours."

"My God," he said, but my mother and I, who thought the differential was a platform he could lie across in comfort, sighed with relief.

"Go for the others," my mother said, but my father, hoping Imma was sleeping, stopped me.

Aaron turned to Daniel, who was on Joel's lap, watching.

"How handsome he is. Would he be afraid of me?"

"He's not afraid of anyone," my mother said. "If Hitler came to claim him, he would go with Hitler."

"But I'm so tired, I don't even feel like taking him now." He turned to Ondine. "Please go to sleep."

She faced me and, without a word, lifted her collar. There was the matching leaf. She lay down, and the rest of us moved to another bed.

"We'll have to wake her," I said. "He said to be ready."

Aaron asked me who was the "he."

"Vittorio. The officer who brought us Imma."

"He's a Gentile," my father said, "but betrothed to Eva."

"Oh, God. Poor Theo."

"Where *is* Theo?" my father asked.

"It's a long story," Aaron said. "When we left you, Theo was right—Gershon was interned. He was at Pithiviers. But when Theo wanted Esther to go to Lyons, she refused. She was working in a factory, a knit-goods place, and she could visit Gershon, bring him packages, and, believe it or not, she'd become a collector, going from factory to factory, gathering money."

My father asked him for whom.

"The Resistance. For guns."

"Esther?" my mother asked.

"Esther," he said. "Only Imma could see how terrific she was. Theo asked her what she would do if on one of her visits to Gershon she couldn't get out, and she said, 'So I'll stay,' "

"From whom did she collect?" my father asked.

"Jews! Workers, bosses, everyone gave. Anyway, she and Theo went to the camp—one of those barracks arrangements—and Gershon said the decision had to be hers. She was still young, she was doing something useful—her collecting was helping de Gaulle—so how could he honestly say she should leave?"

"She's still in Paris?" my mother asked.

"Wait. It was Theo that Gershon said should go back—he was afraid they'd take even native-born Jews. Esther insisted on staying, so Theo and I got into a group nearby, socialists, putting out a paper, making counterfeit documents, finding hiding places, getting railway workers to help us get people into the south—that kind of stuff."

He stopped, picked up a sweater, and laid it across Ondine.

"But then, in '42—my God, last year, it seems so much longer—in March, Gershon was transferred to Drancy."

My mother gasped.

"Then, in July, Esther was put in the Vel d'Hiv."

My father stood up abruptly, paced back and forth, too agitated to sit down, and Aaron waited. At last he went on.

"Theo was losing his mind. Ondine suggested we get him away from Paris, so we went to Lyons. Joined our old group. We expected an Allied invasion. They'd been dropping us arms and explosives, but they didn't invade, and we couldn't use the stuff—by ourselves we'd have been wiped out. The waiting was awful, and Theo took it the worst. We thought he would do something wild and that innocent people would pay."

He stood up and went to the window, his back toward us.

"Then one day he said that since Vichy was handing over the foreign-born Jews, he didn't feel French anymore. He was going away to an all-Jewish group, and he asked us to join him. Ondine said no, she wasn't a Jew and didn't belong in the Jewish Resistance." He turned to our father. "I thought he was unfair—don't you? What's the difference which group?"

He left the window and sat on the bed near Ondine.

"So Theo said, 'Your father was a Jew, so for practical purposes now you're a Jew.' Ondine said her mother was a Catholic, so for practical purposes she was a Catholic. Theo exploded. He said, 'You can't sit forever on two stools with one ass. Pick a stool, and let your lover pick the one that's his.' So I exploded too and told him to leave."

"When did this happen?" my father asked.

"Seven, eight months ago."

"Where did he go?"

"Southwest France. By now he's probably headed for Rome."

"Rome?" my mother asked.

"What difference does it make?" he answered. "There'll be a Resistance in Italy too, so he might as well be near his sister—she's probably all he has left."

"But Nathan is *also* headed for Rome. With a soldier, going toward the Allies, trying to join them."

"Nathan? Damn. Damn. I wanted to tell him I'm sorry."

"He's not as resourceful as you," my father said. "And he doesn't even have Nicole's address."

"He's not a fool," Aaron said. "He'll find her if he wants to. He'll do what's right—that's how he is. You ought to be proud."

"Of what?" my father said. "I don't know what I value anymore. I don't know the worth of anything but time."

"You do know. You'd have done the same as Nathan if you had been young and didn't have Mama and Imma and kids." My father was silent. "Papa? Remember the little girl in Lyons?"

"Marianne?"

"That's what the farmer called her, but it probably wasn't her name. I think she stood for the France he loved, the France betrayed. Or maybe not she, but he and his wife were the symbols, doing for France what France itself should have done—protect the victims. But whatever her name, she was with us for so little time that I never even got to hold her. You carried her home and carried her back, and Nathan held her, and Imma did, and I don't know who else, but *I* never did. So I had to hold her somewhere else." My father buried his head in his hands. "Papa," Aaron said, "it's worth it."

It was less than half an hour since Enzo and Vittorio had left, and Aaron lay down on the bed, pressed against Ondine. He was asleep in seconds, and my mother sat at his side, stroking his hair. My father stood over her, his hand on her shoulder.

"Gershon in Drancy," he said, "and Esther in the Vel d'Hiv."

With her free hand, my mother reached toward her shoulder and laid her hand on his. "Why?" she said, knowing there would never be an answer.

Drancy, close to Paris, was a group of concrete buildings, never completely finished, their windows covered with bars but not with glass. It was the transfer camp for Auschwitz.

The Vel d'Hiv—Vélodrome d'Hiver—was an indoor sports stadium. There, nine thousand Jews—half of them children and most of the others women—were penned up for five days, with no food, with water from a single hydrant, with people dying, with others going mad, and with here and there a woman giving birth. On the fifth day, the adults were taken to Drancy, the children to the camps at Beaune-la-Rolande and Pithiviers, until all could be fitted into the schedule. We knew of it, and the image of children torn from their mothers rose before me.

At the sight of Aaron, Imma said his name aloud, and he and Ondine awoke. There again was a joyous reunion, but a quick one, as Vittorio came to the business at hand.

"There's more news. The Germans have all of northern Italy, including Rome, and Badoglio and the king have fled to Sicily. The Germans control the trains, and on the roads they're taking the cars." He turned to Aaron and asked if he and Ondine were coming to Florence.

"Are there other choices?" Aaron asked.

"Some of the Jews are climbing the mountains to hide in the caves. It's impossible for children or the old—soon the cold will be brutal—but possible for you. There are Partisan bands forming there now. Other Jews will hide with peasants, some will try for Switzerland, and some are going toward Rome."

Aaron asked if he planned to take us to Florence on German-held trains.

"We're going by wagon. We've gotten a farmer who's sure there are people in Florence who'll want him to take them to Switzerland."

Aaron turned to Ondine and asked what she wanted to do.

"What do *you* want to do?" she asked.

"Look for Nathan."

"Nathan?" my father said.

As if he hadn't heard, Aaron said, "I'm sure there'll be Partisan groups near Rome."

"I'm sure too," she said. "Let's go to Rome."

"Aaron, how *can* you?" my father said. "You're clever, but please, there's more than cleverness to this—there's luck. And Ondine is not even Jewish—you don't have a right to do this to her."

"But Rome is where I want to go," she said.

"Aaron, tell her," my father insisted. "Even if *you* go, *she* should come with *us*—we have Vittorio—she'll be safe."

"Papa, almost everything I've done Ondine has also done, so I don't tell her. She decides for herself."

I was looking only at my father, seeing his puzzlement at hearing such an answer.

"If you go by yourselves," Vittorio said, "you'll need some help. To rest, you can stay right here, and for any other help you'll find a priest in Borgo San Dalmazzo. Enzo will draw you some maps."

He spoke in Italian to Enzo, and then again in French to Aaron. "From day to day, as you see which roads are safe you'll change your course."

"But they don't speak the language," my mother said.

"There'll be others like them everywhere—prisoners of war, Allied soldiers who've made their escape. Aaron, say you're that—a prisoner of war—it's safer than being a Jew. There must be French among them, or French Canadians—maybe you can join them. And your girl could come with us."

Ondine refused, and Vittorio shrugged. As Enzo drew the maps, Vittorio wrote some notes.

"Here's my address in Florence," he said, "where we'll reunite. And the phone. Both my parents speak French. This," copying slowly from a scrap of paper, "is the address of a Jewish girl in Florence. A Jew from Grosseto just gave it to me. He had friends from Poland in one of our camps, and other Jews, Italians like this girl, brought them food and clothes and for the children even birthday gifts."

"Matilde Cassin," Aaron read, pronouncing the name as if it were French.

"The name is Italian," Vittorio said, "pronounced 'Cassine,' to rhyme with 'Ondine.' And let me teach you some words."

Writing a list, first in French and alongside in Italian, Vittorio spoke slowly, repeating each Italian word.

" 'Partisans' is *partigiani,* 'Allies' is *alleati,* and 'Germans' is *tedeschi.*" He added the words for "French," "Jew," "soldier," "road," "Florence," and "Rome." "For food, water, and sleep, you can speak in gestures. For understanding others, knowing some Latin you'll figure things out."

With that vocabulary, Ondine and Aaron were supposed to find their way. I thought of how long we'd studied with Piotr in Warsaw, and of how badly, for four years, we had needed French. Even today, though I know how often we can read our children's thoughts, I'm amazed that my mother read mine.

"Don't worry, Ruth," she said. "Even *I've* learned to get along in French, so for Aaron and Ondine, and for you too, Italian won't be hard."

With Enzo beside our wagon, riding a mule, we left the mountains, and when we reached the boring Italian plain, the joy I had felt as we crossed the Alps was gone. Even when we reached the Apennines and rode among the rolling hills, with their rows of vines and gray-green olive trees, my spirits were low. I couldn't forget the Vel d'Hiv—children torn from their parents, left by themselves. I was afraid for myself—and guilty for how I had started to feel toward the others.

My mother had asked my father which of the children was next to go. If she didn't think it was Eva, who had Vittorio, it had to be Joel or me.

I remembered the climb through the Alps, and I knew that I had appeared to be stronger than Joel in every way—not only healthier, as I had always been, but less afraid. Joel, whom I'd loved above all of my brothers, seemed vulnerable, not to be abandoned, just as no one would have thought of leaving Daniel, or of sending him off to fend for himself. My mother hadn't said Italian "won't be hard for Joel and you." She had said "for Aaron and Ondine, and for you."

Her words echoed. Adding to my worries was the fact that I had recently begun to menstruate, and I thought my parents saw it as proof that I was no longer a child.

At sunset of the second day, in a sudden panic, I pulled my feet from my ragged shoes and tore off my jacket.

"What are you doing?" Imma asked. "It's cold! Do you want to make yourself sick?"

"I'm hot."

"It's cold!" She grabbed my jacket and forced my arms back into the sleeves. She put her lips to my forehead and said, "You aren't feverish, you can't be hot. Put your shoes back on, or you *will* get sick and give it to Joel."

But sick was just what I wanted to be. When Joel was sick in France, we hadn't separated, hadn't gone to Switzerland, hadn't left him behind.

I was angry, especially now at my father. He and my mother, and Eva and Vittorio, were oblivious to me. They were absorbed in an endless chain of discussions. The armistice announcement had been vague, exasperating. Badoglio had spoken late in the evening, after the Allied announcement, telling the army its fight against the British and Americans was over. But war against the Germans hadn't been declared, and though the army wasn't to fight, it was still to resist if attacked.

"Attacked by whom?" my father asked. "Who is Italy's enemy? The Allies? The Germans? And what will become of the Jews?"

Vittorio was sure that Italy, which hadn't surrendered Jews in the past, wouldn't agree to doing so now. Neither he nor my father could know that soon, in little more than a week, there would be Nazis and Fascists at Lago Maggiore, tracking Jews as if hunting for animals and, sighting them, shooting them down. Still, on and on the discussions went.

And I was angry at Joel for not being strong—and plagued

by guilt for my anger at him. Only Daniel, of course, and Enzo, who was isolated by his ignorance of French, were exempt from my anger and guilt.

As we traveled the roads Vittorio chose, we never met the Germans. Nor were there ever any cars. They had either been cleverly hidden or already requisitioned, and though we knew that there was bombing elsewhere, and that in recent weeks or months there had been bombing here, the countryside through which we drove was peaceful, day after day. Only the shellholes told of the war, and yet, despite the hills and olive trees and vines, all that I could feel was my anxiety.

We must have stopped a hundred times to show our papers to soldiers—Italians—stationed at barricades, near cannons covered by leafy branches, or to get their advice on which of the roads might be traveled by Germans or bombed by the Allies, or to ask for news of the rest of the country. At dark, we'd look for a farmhouse to keep us till morning, and every time we stopped, and I heard this unknown language, I thought of Ondine and Aaron and worried for them and for me.

It was Vittorio, of course, who made our journey possible. He was still in uniform, but more important, he was upper-class. He spoke with assurance, with authority, and when he told the story that he and my father had concocted between them, it was always received as fact.

I don't remember how many days we rode in the wagon, and when later we talked of the trip we never could fully agree. Whether the number was four or five, they were days when the source of our news—when not obtained from other people on the road—was the radio, heard in a farmhouse kitchen, translated by Vittorio into French, and then, by my father, into Polish for Imma.

And of all of that news, there was nothing that encouraged us. German paratroopers found the place where Mussolini was imprisoned, and they set him free and returned him to power—whatever power, that is, they in fact allowed him.

Then, on the evening before we arrived in Florence, we were with people whose son had just gotten home from France. We were gathered, listening to Radio Rome, when the soldier, his jaw a little forward in a pose like Mussolini's, bent his arm at the elbow and thrust it toward the radio, slapping the biceps with his other hand, in that well-known gesture of defiance. Nor had I ever seen Vittorio look quite so grim.

The broadcast seemed endless. Then Vittorio said, "We're ordered back to duty."

My father asked, "What for?"

"To 'volunteer' to fight against the Allies. The Germans are here, Mussolini's back, and the armistice is finished."

It was Eva who asked him where he would have to report.

"The nearest German command, probably Florence." We waited to hear the rest. "No, of course not," he said, "you didn't think I'd go, did you? But other than that, I don't know."

My father seemed stunned. It was as if he, who'd been so slow to trust Vittorio, hadn't imagined being without him.

At last, he asked, "Should you and Enzo be in uniform?"

The farmer went out for civilian clothes. Soon he was back with some wearable things he'd bought with lire my father had gotten for francs in Entraque, as everything else had been bought since crossing the Alps. He also brought us some news.

On a nearby farm, there were two escaped prisoners of war, but they spoke only English and French, which neither he nor the other farmer understood. My father and Vittorio went to see them.

They were French Canadians. At the railroad station in Florence, they had escaped from a train that had been taking them to Germany. The city, they confirmed, was in German hands.

It had finally happened. For four years we had stayed a step ahead of them, and now, in mid-September 1943, when the war, we had thought, was close to an end, they would have us.

"But you see?" Vittorio said to my mother. "Part of the news should encourage you. Two hundred Allied men escaped from that train. Thousands—ten or twenty thousand—escaped from a camp at Laterina, by tearing down a barbed-wire fence. You see what that means? They're out in the country, finding shelter, somehow, with someone. And so will your sons."

He told us that we, however, couldn't stay on in the countryside trusting in luck—as my father wanted to do. We weren't young men. Besides, we had a good alternative. He'd find a place for us, if not together in his parents' home, then some in one place and some in another, with people he knew we could trust. My father, beaten down by his dependency, agreed.

Everyone was quiet, tense, trying to sleep, when Daniel, who normally slept beside my parents, stood up.

"I want to sleep with Ruth," he said.

"But you always sleep with us," my mother protested. "Why don't you want to tonight?"

He had already taken his pillow and moved from the mat. She leapt up and grabbed him. She needed him, almost as she had needed him when he was born, but he, decisively, pulled from her grasp, saying, "No, I'm sleeping with Ruth." With an utterly serious face, he settled himself at my side.

My mother said nothing but sat where she was, looking toward the two of us. At last, she lay back down.

It seemed as if hours had passed. I lay awake. I had slept in the wagon, and now I was waiting for dawn. The next day, or the day after that, or soon, I'd probably be on my own.

Daniel had curled himself up, his head under the cover, his sturdy little body pressed against me. His presence warmed me. His wanting to be with me brought me a measure of comfort and yet some discomfort as well. Eva had reproached me—I'd seldom played with him—and now I was filled with regret.

I sat up and uncovered his face. He was like none of us and like all of us. He was two and a half, and though he wasn't thin, like Joel he was small for his age. He was dark, with a face as beautiful as Nathan's, and with Nathan's good nature as well—but only up to a point. Then he became like Aaron—decisive, independent, strong.

As I watched him sleep, he stirred and changed position, so that his feet came off the mat and onto the floor. I reached across him to pull his feet back onto the mat and tuck the blanket around them, and for no reason I could see, I thought about the day Yvette had married Bernard. In the synagogue of the Châlet Ferrix, Daniel had sat on my mother's lap, serious, attentive to everyone under the canopy, the little thin Yvette, the lumbering Bernard, while I, like a child, had been bored.

I lay back down beside him and murmured his name, but he was sleeping soundly. Moved by a tenderness more powerful than I had ever felt for him, I curled my body around him and put my lips to his hair. "Daniel," I whispered, "I love you best."

VI

VITTORIO'S PARENTS, THE BELLINIS, HAD A VILLA ON the far side of the Arno. When you followed the road to the top of the hill, as we did on arriving in Florence, you stood in Piazzale Michelangelo, from where, it appeared, on a sunnier day you could see the entire city. On that day, through the mist, we could see the river, the many bridges, and on the other side of the river the *centro,* the old city, with its ocher Renaissance buildings and red-tiled roofs. Rising above them was something I wanted to touch, to hold between my palms and grasp, as if it were a simple object, like half of a large, red fruit, with a little pointed house above it, and on top of that a ball. It was the dome of the city's cathedral. Nearby, closer to the river, was the Palazzo Vecchio, its tower taller yet than the cathedral dome, and not very far away from them both and off to the right, another dome, simpler, smaller than the cathedral's, but in its own way intriguing, the onion-shaped turquoise dome of the synagogue.

I thought it was Vittorio's idea to take us there, and I thought it odd that he didn't go home at once, as Enzo had done with a quick *arrivederci* almost as soon as we'd entered the city. Vittorio, however, stood beside us, patiently, at the edge of the piazzale, naming the buildings across the river, telling us in French the meaning of Palazzo Vecchio and Duomo.

I didn't understand why we were there until my father, one hand on Joel's shoulder and the other on mine, said fervently, "Look. In its own way, it's more beautiful than Paris. We'll come to this spot again when it's over, all of us, you'll see."

"When will we separate?" I asked.

"What?"

"Who will go first?"

His mouth hardened. "Whoever has to."

It was cold and damp, and Joel was shivering, so without any more than a glance around the piazzale itself, we boarded the wagon, which the driver had already turned around, and drove back to the tall, yellow, shrub-enclosed Bellini villa, which a quarter hour before we had slowly driven past.

Now, after a reassuring smile at Eva, Vittorio leapt from the wagon and went by himself to the house, where an elderly servant, astonished, overjoyed, shouted, "Signora! Signora!" and let him come in. We all drew close to each other and waited in silence, and I—afraid we'd be turned away—kept my eyes on the door, unwilling to look at the villa and hope.

I was imagining Vittorio's reunion with his parents, seeing it as ours had been with Aaron. It seemed longer, however, than ours, and I was trying to believe we'd manage without the Bellinis when at last Vittorio came to the door with his parents beside him. His mother clung to his arm and, tears still shining on her face, welcomed us in.

I don't remember what impressed me more—the villa itself with its gray marble floors and dark-blue frescoed ceilings, or Vittorio's parents, aristocratic, his mother short but almost regal, elegantly dressed in navy blue, and wearing a green jade necklace and earrings on an ordinary day at home, as my mother used to do in Warsaw.

Vittorio introduced us, first Imma, then my parents, Joel, Daniel, me, and then finally Eva. His mother took Eva's outstretched hand, held it a moment in both of her own, and then, with a searching look and a smile of approval, said, *"Bellissima."*

We bathed, and though clothes had been hard to get because of the war, there were clean ones for all of us. Those for my parents, Eva, and Imma were clothes the Bellinis had worn, of fine quality, but they fitted my family poorly, looking like hand-me-downs from shorter and heavier siblings. I laughed aloud, not understanding, as Joel did, that for them, being reduced to this was nothing to laugh at.

But the Bellinis didn't have clothes for Daniel, Joel, and me, so Signora Bellini sat at the phone, unworried, smiling, patting her lustrous hair with perfectly manicured fingers, calling friends and relatives who might have children's clothes to spare, giving them clues to our sizes only by telling our ages. In less than an hour some clothes had arrived, and I dressed in the ones she had gotten for me, slowly, luxuriating in the very act of dressing in a real bedroom, which had beds, sheets, pillows, a wardrobe, and a full-length, hand-carved, wood-framed mirror—as if we were back at home in Warsaw, or in Paris, or St. Martin-Vésubie.

Joel, insecure because of his size and always worried about his appearance, came in from another room, grim, in clothes that on others his age would have fit, but that on him were much too large. "Are you going to laugh?" he asked.

I shook my head, too involved with myself to talk, and Joel left. I was wearing a checkered dress, dark green and much too short for me, but perfect around my tiny breasts, I thought of Yvette, whose breasts were hardly larger. How would she nurse a baby? I wondered. And where were they now?—she, her father, and the awkward Bernard. But I didn't have time to think of the Hartmans for long.

We were starting over, in a country, Signor Bellini said, that made France look simple by contrast. In Italy, there were the Allies, the king, and Badoglio in the south, and the Germans all over the center and north. Between them was the line of battle. And again there would be Mussolini, whom the Germans had freed from prison the previous week, and whose future role in Italy was still unknown.

As he told us who held power where, I scrutinized his face, looking for a feature that was different from Vittorio's, but the differences were those of age. The same straight hair and heavy eyebrows, the same full lips and cleft chin that I had thought attractive in Vittorio I saw in the elder Bellini.

I presumed, correctly, that he was older than my father, because Vittorio was six years older than my sister, but my father looked older by far. Next to the heavier, broad-shouldered man, my father looked drawn and thin. I glanced at my mother, who was tired and visibly nervous, and then at the languid, self-assured, and well-kept Signora Bellini, and I saw how my mother had changed in the past four years. I thought of how angry I'd been at my parents, and of what Imma had called me the day Bernard had married Yvette, and I felt myself truly, unforgivably heartless.

"Excuse me," my father said, "but—all this complexity—what does it mean for the Jews?"

"Nothing's happened to them," Bellini said. "We have many acquaintances among them—one is a friend—we'd have heard. Others, foreign ones, went to the archbishop's palace, asking advice, and his secretary, Monsignor Meneghello, advised them to stay in the city and wait for the Allies."

"Don't they go to the rabbi?"

"They do. I don't know what he tells the foreign ones, but he's warning the Florentine Jews to hide. Anywhere—in or out of the city."

"And which do they choose?"

"Some aren't hiding at all. He's young—a few years older than Vittorio. Before the racial laws, the man was a brilliant physician and scientist, highly esteemed, but young, so some of them question his judgment on this. He's been out on a bicycle, going to their homes, persuading them, or trying to. If he's right, he ought to have gone into hiding himself."

"What do *you* think?" my father asked. "Is he right?"

"We've heard terrible things. Perhaps it's propaganda—England has lied in the past—but if the Germans really are doing these things, and, I know it's hard to believe, but if they are . . ." He shook his head.

"And if they leave the city, where does this rabbi think they should go?"

"To the outlying villages, where no one knows them. Here—perhaps Vittorio has told you—they're registered as Jews, and their addresses are available. Badoglio could have had the lists destroyed—he had a month and a half—but, despicable coward, he didn't."

"They'll be done in by index cards," my father said. "As in France."

"It costs a good deal to leave," Bellini went on, "but the device is simple. They say they're from towns in the south that the Allies have captured, and they buy false documents to bear this out. And *because* the Allies hold the towns, no one can check and discover the papers are false."

My mother asked him how many people could do this before they would start getting caught.

"Any number at all," Bellini answered. "People *are* coming from the south—Italians, Catholics—escaping the war. There's continuous movement. Some are going to Florence and Rome in the hope that no one would *think* of bombing such places. And some are escaping from here and Rome to the villages, thinking they will."

My father asked him what it would cost to go to a village.

He said he didn't know. "To begin with, there are the counterfeit papers. If they catch the forger, you can guess the penalty—so the price has to cover the risk."

He paused, long enough to say that Daniel, who wanted to roam around by himself, was welcome to go wherever he liked. My mother asked me to take him, but I wanted to stay, so Joel, as I might have expected, offered to go in my place.

"But aside from the forged papers," Signor Bellini said, "which you'll need even here for buying your food, what Italian Jews can do is not what *you* can do. Off by yourselves, you won't have any idea whom you can trust."

My father asked his advice.

"Vittorio has told you. Stay here with us."

"And endanger *you* by our presence."

"For the time being, it isn't a problem. You're safer for us than the Jews from Florence would be. You, at least, can walk in the streets. No one will know you, and no one will follow you back."

"Don't worry," Signora Bellini said. "The Allies are coming. Archbishop dalla Costa's optimistic."

"Please understand," my father answered, "I'm grateful to you both, as I am to Vittorio, but it's my nature to worry. I'll worry much less if I know I've considered the dangers."

"Will you truly?" Signor Bellini said. "Then I'll tell you the rest. Our house might not be entirely safe. A cousin of ours is one of the men who voted against Mussolini. He was a Fascist, of course, on the Grand Council, but at the end, when it really mattered, he wasn't Mussolini's friend. Another cousin was an anti-Fascist leader from the moment Mussolini came to power. He was for years in exile in France, until Mussolini fell. Then he came home and now is in hiding. Still, I don't expect reprisals. Not against us. If I did, we'd have left. But if you want to know everything, it *is* a possibility, though remote.

"More important," he continued, "is the matter of Vittorio. He's supposed to report for duty, and, as you know, he won't. Will they come looking for him? Probably. If they do, will they search the house? Possibly. Will they find whoever else we might be hiding? And the men who come here to search—will they be Germans or Italians? Will they be interested in taking anyone except Vittorio? And if they are, how will I say you've come from the south—that you're Italians—if none of you speaks the language?"

He paused, as if waiting for the answers. "These are the dangers," he said. "We, I believe, are a greater threat to you right now than you are to us. And still, I think you'll be safest here."

As my father sat there, silent, deciding on what to do, I didn't feel worried. I couldn't imagine danger here, with these cultured people, in this lovely house. I looked at the life-size portraits hung on the walls, at the figures in the frescoed ceiling, at the delicate furniture carved by hand.

"You must assure me," Signor Bellini said, "that you know it's not my intention to frighten you off."

"I know," my father said. "I can't thank you enough. And *you* must assure *me* that you know I trust your judgment. Still, I want to meet this rabbi. If the synagogue is open, I'd like to go there now."

Signor Bellini agreed he should, and he stood up, ready to show the way and to act as interpreter.

"Please," my father said, "I've been dependent for far too long. The rabbi, I'm sure, will speak either German or French."

I asked my father if I could go too.

He turned to my mother, who was looking at me as if I were mad. "There are Germans!" she said.

"It's the building with the green dome," I said. "I'd so like to see the buildings with the domes."

"It wouldn't be dangerous," Signor Bellini assured her. "They haven't done anything yet."

My mother was afraid, but she was a guest, and not secure enough to stand her ground.

Sharing her fear, my father said, "We'd be showing the

neighbors we're here." Then, "All right—this one time. Then you stay in, no matter how long it takes."

"Go the long way around," Vittorio said. "Show her a bit of the old Florence. Cross the river on the Ponte Vecchio."

Joel and Daniel had just come back, and, without consulting Joel, I asked my father to take us both, but Joel declined, ashamed of the fit of his clothes.

Armed with directions, we went alone, my father and I, on what for me began as an exhilarating walk that made me think of the day we'd walked in Paris when Joel was down with bronchitis.

The street where the villa was, Viale Michelangelo, curved around to meet the Lungarno, the riverside road. At the Ponte Vecchio, we crossed the Arno, as in Paris we'd crossed the Seine, but soon I felt the two were in different worlds.

In Paris, in early 1940, people were handsomely dressed, while here, now, there were soldiers in makeshift civilian attire, trying to keep their desertion a secret, but blurting it out through their mismatched clothes. There, on the wide boulevards, I had walked with my head held high, unafraid, looking through open spaces into the distance. Here, in the narrow streets of an earlier time, with Germans nearby, I felt endangered, as once invading armies must have felt endangered by the houses pressing in on them from left and right, enemies lying in wait. My father's silence rang with a matching unease, and though Vittorio had thought I would enjoy this walk, I didn't.

After an hour or so we stood in front of the synagogue, marveling at this Jewish temple that looked to us like a Byzantine church. But neither the Moorish arches over both the portico and elongated windows nor the bulb-shaped domes above the turrets could prepare us for the rich, exuberant interior. There were intricate patterns in blue, red, and orange on the walls, vaults, and central dome. There were simpler patterns in the stained-glass windows. There was green, gold, and red in the inlaid marble floors. There were glistening mosaics, black marble columns flanking the ark, candelabras rising from the railing around the balcony, shining wood that was carved like lace, gleaming brass.

I thought of Joel and what we'd have said to each other, but I didn't miss him. The one I truly missed was Daniel. Just as my father had wanted me not to forget the Champs-Élysées, I wanted Daniel to see and not to forget this temple in Florence. I wanted to hold his hand, silently, and turn him around toward the ark, as my father had turned me around toward the Arc de Triomphe.

But my father was impatient. The rabbi, we were told, was in the offices in the adjacent building, so we went to look for him there and found him surrounded by people, talking with one of them quietly, listening, nodding. We stood to the side and waited our turn.

His name was Nathan Cassuto. He was thirty-three years old, but he had the presence of an older, confident, more experienced man. He was clean-shaven, of medium height and build, but athletic-looking, and with thick, dark, wavy hair and full, sensuous lips. He wore round, black-rimmed glasses.

The people who surrounded him had just arrived in Florence, and some were destitute, with no one to turn to. He spoke to them each at length, calmly, questioning. Some he directed to people in Florence—Gentiles—who'd rent them a room or an empty garage. A few young men, each without a family, he sent to the archbishop's palace, where Monsignor Meneghello knew a priest who'd shelter them.

One of the poorest-looking women had a distant relative in Italy, a wealthy, influential woman who might take her in, but she wasn't sure of the city—she thought it was called Perugia. The rabbi asked her the name and for a description, and said there was indeed such a Jewish woman in Perugia—highly respected by everyone, Catholics and Jews—but with the Germans holding the city, she might not be able to offer protection. Still, the woman wanted to try, so he gave her the money to pay for the fare, and for the return to Florence as well if she didn't find help.

At last he came to us. He listened to our story, told in a minute, a summary of our days in Paris, Lyons, the countryside, and then St. Martin-Vésubie. He asked if we needed money.

My father admitted our money was almost depleted, but he told him about the Bellinis—our connection with them through Eva, their offer to protect us, and the dangers—and asked his advice. And the advice was the same as from the Bellinis, but we should stay in touch with him, he said—it might change.

"There's something else," my father said. "I'm afraid to be where I don't understand the language I hear. Do you know of someone who—for a fee, of course—would teach us Italian?"

"Yes!" he said, surprised and enormously pleased. "I do. A young woman. Like you, she wouldn't take money. She's looking for work, and this would be perfect." He went to the doorway and called, "Matilde?"

She was Matilde Cassin. She was in her teens, or perhaps as much as twenty, and no taller than I. She was slim, with long, dark hair and a fine, delicate, even-featured face. Smiling, she greeted us both in Italian, and then, when my father excitedly answered in French, she repeated the greeting in French.

"I *know* of you!" my father said. "The Jewish girl who helped the foreign Jews in camps!"

"Italian camps," she said. "It was possible."

"Matilde," the rabbi said, "they'd like to have somebody teach them Italian. Will you run to Luciana Bianco and ask?"

"In a second," she said and went out. Soon she was back, offering me a package, and when I turned to my father to ask his permission, she said, "Please, monsieur—it's chestnut cake. We've had a wonderful harvest of chestnuts."

She left. There was nobody waiting to see the rabbi, and my father seemed very reluctant to leave. Abruptly, as if he had struggled and finally made a decision, my father asked if the rabbi was willing to talk a bit more.

I had to go out for several minutes, and we were there for ten or fifteen minutes after that, until some women arrived, looking for help, but in those few minutes my father behaved in a very unusual way.

He had always had friends, but he'd never achieved a genuine closeness with any of them, as if he'd been saving all his love for the family. Not even Hartman, who had shared so much with us, had been spared his reserve.

But now, when I reentered the room, my father and Rabbi Cassuto were seated facing each other, each with his elbows on his knees and his hands clasped, faces a foot apart, eyes locked on each other. My father's voice was impassioned, anguished, as if he were facing my mother or Imma.

"I was *somewhat* observant," he said. "But not because I believed—I doubt I *ever* believed, except as a boy. I was observant out of my oneness with Jews—that was all. But now, facing the possible loss of my wife or a child, I *have* to believe, as never before. Do you understand?"

"Yes, of course," Cassuto said.

"Is it the same with you?"

"About need, yes, but I've always believed."

"Don't you sense we're facing the end?"

"Personally? Individually? Yes, often I do. But this hasn't changed my belief."

With wonder—almost amazement—in his voice, my father said, "There seem to *be* people like you. People with a gift through which they sense a presence, God, as others have a gift for sensing music. Sensing the *existence* of God, unmistakable. Hearing in their mind, like music, what no one else can hear. *I* have neither gift, so I've told myself that even though I don't believe, I *should*, I *must* believe, because *somebody* does, someone more gifted than I."

Again he asked if the rabbi understood, and Cassuto nodded.

"I've made it a matter of will," my father said. "Since I'm pulled in two directions at once, I have to say yes to one and no to the other. It doesn't mean I've found the truth. It just helps me live."

My father glanced at me, hesitated, and went on.

"I had wanted to talk like this to my children—the older ones—but I didn't want to admit my doubts. I didn't want *them* to have doubts." Abruptly, perhaps distracted from his subject by the thought of children, he asked, "Do *you* have children?"

"Three. We're expecting our fourth. Any day now. Aren't we fortunate, you and I?"

My father nodded and suddenly smiled. How long it had been since I'd seem him smile. "Where *are* your children?" he asked.

"In hiding."

"Then why don't you go into hiding yourself?"

"And who will be here for people like you?"

"You've never considered it?"

"I have, but never for long."

The rabbi asked him to tell about us—the children—and my father relaxed, told of wanting to keep us united, of Nathan's break with Aaron, and it was then that some women came into the room, and my father stood up.

With no hesitation, he and the rabbi smiled and embraced—quickly, as if they would soon be together again. I thought it a marvel. Only once had I seen my father embrace a man who was not in the family, and that one was Vittorio.

We left for home, arm in arm and silent, but now the silence was peaceful.

"Papa?" I asked. "What did you mean? *What* don't you believe?"

"We'll talk about it when you're older, dear, all right? But for now, if something should happen to Mama and me—rely on Rabbi Cassuto. And, Ruthie, I said some things you shouldn't have heard. Please! Don't repeat them. Even to Joel. For now they're a secret, just between the three of us."

If Vittorio had become my brother, the rabbi had become my father's.

When we got home, my father told the Bellinis, "I never doubted that Eva should stay. I wanted you free of the rest of us, but if you really are willing, I would be grateful."

The Bellinis repeated he needn't worry for them, and the matter was settled.

Next he told them of having arranged for a teacher, and about cost, which he didn't yet know, and there was a flurry of talk among the adults, all agreeing not only that money for this would be money well spent, but that it was safe for the teacher to come to the house.

She arrived the following day, early, and I saw her just as she entered the house and told the servant her name. I'd expected, simply because she would teach us Italian, that she'd also *look* Italian, *my* idea of Italian, dark and, if we were lucky, as pretty as Matilde. But by typical standards she wasn't pretty, and yet, for the first time in months—not since I had drawn Ondine—here was a woman whose portrait I wanted to draw.

She was in her mid-twenties—older, that is, than either Matilde or Eva. Her face was small, and her nose was slender and large, shaped like the beak of an eagle, so different from the noses of Hollywood stars, who were my heroines even then. And yet, she had a glamour equal to theirs, derived in part from her carriage, her appearance of self-assurance, of almost too *much* self-assurance, as if she were happy to have this marvelous nose. Her chin was pointed, rather sharply, and receded a little, but, oddly, it seemed to be right—as if only this modest chin could be right for this proud nose.

Aside from her well-worn clothes—a white blouse, dark-green sweater, and a straight, short black skirt—everything else was flamboyant. Her hair was a shining auburn, thick and heavy, and reached to her shoulders in waves, and when she tossed her head, which she did in a bold, theatrical way, the waves would fall apart and then reform. Her skin was flawless, and her eyes were large, green, gleaming, and flitted from object to object and face to face.

She greeted my parents in Polish, formally, and they, astonished, having expected Italian or French, answered in Polish, formally too. Then, as if establishing the rules and setting up a barrier between herself and us, she resumed in an almost imperious tone.

Her name, she told us, was, for present purposes, Luciana Bianco. Knowing Polish, she could teach us all, including, she said with a toss of her hair, both the "old woman" and the little boy.

My father was slow to respond. Luciana conceded that—perhaps—he was right to expect her to tell him more. She would tell him as much as she thought he should know.

She was a Polish Jew who had come to study in Padua and had been there in 1939, when the war broke out in Poland. She had stayed in Padua and now, in 1943, had fled to Florence, where nobody knew her. She'd found a room, she knew the city, and she felt she was safe. Until she was offered a better job, she'd come to the villa to teach us, but only till then.

My father hired her, happy to pay her whatever she asked, and since she was there, he suggested, perhaps she would start our lessons at once.

She agreed, and they were difficult, unlike the ones with Piotr, which had been almost a lark, with my mother and Imma allowed to refuse. Here, now, refusal would never have entered their minds. Still, no amount of effort—anyone's—was ever enough for my father.

He was relentless, convinced that knowing the language was crucial to saving our lives. The rabbi was sure the Germans would search for the Jews, soon, before the Allies could save us; or Luciana might decide to leave us for a better job; or the Fascists might appear at any moment looking for Vittorio—whatever justified his desperation sprang to his lips if he heard a complaint. He insisted on lessons that lasted for hours, until Joel or my mother was close to tears, and Luciana, never tired, never exasperated, complied.

I didn't understand, though I think my mother did, that she had decided against "a better job"—that my father's intensity had struck a chord in her and that she'd committed herself to him and therefore to us.

She was formal with him, as she was with my mother and Imma, but with my sister, who was two or three years younger than she, she was too familiar, superior, as if Eva were a child, and Luciana, as teacher, had a right to intimidate, scold, badger her into submission.

It was only of Daniel that she didn't make demands. He stayed with us, playing nearby, hearing whatever was said and absorbing it, as children do. What she taught him directly she taught him casually, in lessons lasting for moments—and only when he would address her. Whatever he said or asked in French, she changed to Italian, and then answered, again in Italian.

Luciana, quand pourrai-je sortir?"

"Quando potrai uscire? Non lo so, Daniele, non lo so, amore. Devi aspettare un pò più. Il giorno verrà"

We weren't allowed to translate for him, and in a matter of days Italian fragments had entered his French.

Except in his case, though somewhat in Imma's too, she'd never let a mispronunciation pass. She'd hammer away until she was pleased enough for the moment, then she'd stop abruptly, and pleasantly—insincerely, my mother and Eva said—she'd turn to the matter of structure, showing us how similar Italian grammar was to that of French, or calling up the Latin Eva and my parents knew. Or she would turn to designing our next assignments—exercises we would work on when she left, always enough to take us through all of the day and into the evening, sometimes until it was time for bed.

Never had I been so ambivalent. My mother and Eva resented her bitterly. They said she was arrogant, insufferable, and my mother—the Warsaw matron again—called her "this shtetl girl," this nobody, who, just because she had studied in Italy, thought she was cultured. Imma was silent, but Joel, humiliated by the extra work Luciana gave him, was close to rebellion.

For my part, nothing she asked was ever too much. Though I wouldn't have dared to admit it, I liked how we worked, and for me to dislike her, as loyalty seemed to demand, I'd have had to concede that my father was wrong. He heard my mother and Eva, and disagreed, patiently, trying to placate, but his admiration for Luciana grew, visibly, with every passing hour, despite my mother's icy looks. What made it harder still was that—in my eyes—she had become beautiful, as had the far less glamorous Ondine, and, in a way I could not have defined, I felt that although she never openly praised me, she was partial to me, and for this I felt honored and proud. And at the same time, I was afraid that Joel, above all, was angry at me.

One evening, at the end of the first week, when Eva was off somewhere else with Vittorio, Joel threw down his pencil and said, "I give up."

My father answered, "Don't be silly. We don't give up. Stop and rest, and go back to it later." Joel was shaking his head. "You're not doing badly," my father said. "You don't speak well, but you do understand, and that's what counts. You'll see, you'll do just fine."

"No, I mean it," Joel said. "I won't go back to it at all. I can't learn from that girl—she's a witch."

"A witch?" my father said. He was puzzled, oddly it seemed, as if he'd heard nothing of what had been said in his presence for days, "Luciana?" and then, suddenly, enraged, "A witch?" He jumped up, grabbed Joel by the shirt, and pulled him to his feet, and now in a voice more menacing than I had ever heard from him, soft and tightly controlled, he said, slowly, "You will do whatever Luciana tells you to do, do you hear? If she says to study twenty hours a day, you'll study twenty hours. If you get lazy, I'll teach you your father can beat you. I'll beat you within an inch of your life, do you hear?" Suddenly, raising his voice to a shout, "Don't you understand, you stupid boy? I want you to live!"

Joel went white. Daniel started to cry, Imma's hands flew up to the sides of her head, and my mother sprang to her feet. She threw herself at my father, striking his shoulders and back with both of her fists, once, twice, and again. Astonished, my father let go of my brother, swung around, and received some blows to his chest before he could catch my mother's wrists.

"Again?" she shouted. "It wasn't enough you humiliated Nathan? Now it has to be Joel? For the sake of that horrid girl? What is she to you that you would treat your child like this? Why do you terrorize him? What is she to you?"

Trapped in my father's grasp and trying to wrench herself free, she started to cry. Roughly at first, he backed her into the chair from which she had sprung, almost toppling her, and then, gently, sat her down and released her hands, letting her cover her face. He waited until she was quiet, and when she didn't look up, he lifted her chin.

Softly, he said, "Luciana is my children's savior." He fastened his eyes on hers, and for endless seconds he was silent. "Don't you see, Magda?" he said at last. "It doesn't matter so much if *I* die, or if you or Mama dies. Maybe one of us *will* before this is over—the rabbi's heard what happened up north. He thinks they'll be shooting at Jews in the streets. But the children have to live. I was younger than Ruth when my father died, but I've had a good life—I wouldn't exchange it for anyone else's. I want Joel to grow up. I want him to fall in love and marry. I want him to have as good a life with the girl he finds as the life I've had with you."

Again my mother broke into tears. Imma took Daniel's hand, signaled to Joel and me to follow, and led us out of the room.

During that first week in Florence, while we were secure and studying, Mussolini was reestablishing a government. A new bureaucracy arose of Fascists dedicated to him even then. Beside them, the Germans continued to rule, and they repeated that Italian officers and men were to report to them for duty. Some would go to labor camps in Germany, and some would go back to fighting against the Allies.

Vittorio didn't report, and one evening, during our second week in the city, Enzo, on a rusty bicycle, its wheels wrapped in rags, came to the villa asking for shoes, which—like bicycle tires—couldn't be found in the stores. His army boots revealed him to be a deserter; civilian shoes could prevent his arrest on the street.

Again, as when she'd asked for children's clothes, Signora Bellini sat at the phone, while Daniel, two and a half years old, stood before Enzo, studying—and commenting on, in French—the long feet that wouldn't fit into the short Bellini shoes.

The rest of the talk wasn't as funny. Trains were leaving the city, taking Italian young men, many of whom were seized on the streets, to work in the German camps. In the north, where men and boys were hiding or joining the Partisan bands, the Fascists and Germans were taking reprisals—not against the men, whom they couldn't find, but against their families—and soon, Vittorio said, it might happen in Florence as well.

Still, he and Enzo were forming a Partisan group in the hills—they couldn't tell where—and Eva was going with them.

The following night, after a show of bravery from Imma, Vittorio's parents, and mine, they left.

The next day, Luciana didn't show up when she normally did. When at last she arrived, almost four hours late, she acted especially carefree and tried to begin our lesson at once with no explanation of why she'd been late.

My father refused to sit down. "Something's wrong," he said. "You'd better tell us what."

At first she denied that anything was, but then, for the first time since we'd met her, we could see there were tears in her eyes.

"I've been evicted," she said. "I thought that for me they would take the risk." Then, tossing her hair, she added, "But it doesn't matter. Rabbi Cassuto heard of a room, and Matilde took me there, and I agreed to take it, so let's get started."

"Where is this room?" my father asked.

"It doesn't matter."

"Eva and Vittorio are gone."

"Gone? Arrested?"

He shook his head. "Unless what you've found is better than living with us, I'll ask the Bellinis to keep you here."

"Have they gone to the Partisans?"

"Luciana," he said, "we don't have to tell each other everything. Do you or don't you want to stay with us?"

"I'm staying in a cellar, on a street near Piazza del Carmine, near the Ponte Vecchio. The space is small and dark, and Matilde said I didn't have to take it, but I did."

"I'll talk to the Bellinis," he said.

As he had expected they would, they said she could stay. Luciana went back to the room near Piazza del Carmine, retrieved her clothes, hurried back to the temple to tell the rabbi where she would be, and moved in with us.

During the same week, Florence was bombed for the first time, and though we didn't believe the Allies wanted to harm civilians, some civilians where harmed.

At the end of our third week in the city, the Germans requisitioned the Excelsior Hotel and a number of the private villas. They might have allowed the owners to stay in part of the house, but the Bellinis decided that if theirs was taken, they'd leave. They worried about their possessions, but they concluded that whether or not they stayed, the fate of their things was up to the Germans.

As for their personal safety, there were friends who would take them in. The problem, they said, was finding a place for us, not in a week or two, but at once, and to do so was harder than asking for clothes. Still, hard or not, they would try. They already had people in mind.

My father said that the job should be his—that he'd go to the temple the following morning. Neither could know what was happening elsewhere in Florence regarding the Jews, nor did we understand it fully until ten months later, after the city was freed by the Allies.

Rabbi Cassuto, and some Italian Jews who, like Matilde, had

been helping him, were swamped by the needs of the refugees. Desperate, the rabbi went to the archbishop, Elia dalla Costa, and dalla Costa summoned to his palace, one at a time, two ostensibly different men.

One was Don Leto Casini, a priest, forty-one years old, from a parish called Varlungo, on the outskirts of Florence. He was an attractive, soft-spoken, almost self-effacing man of medium height and build, and dressed in black. He had pleasant good looks and lively, intelligent—indeed, mischievous—eyes, but there was nothing about his manner or dress striking enough to attract any special attention.

The other was a student in his mid-twenties—Padre Cipriano Ricotti. He was tall and slim, decisive in his movements, and he wore the long white robes of the Dominican order. He was as hearty and open in speech as Don Casini was quiet, and when I met him, weeks later, I thought of Luciana. Though she, with her eaglelike nose and receding chin, might not have been as beautiful to others as to me, Padre Cipriano—handsome in spite of his crowded teeth—was. There was an air of theatricality about him, of extravagance. He might have been a magician, top hat, tails, and all, or a flamenco dancer, one who looked appropriately brooding while he danced and then, offstage, might explode in a joyous, triumphant, and mocking laugh.

That evening, at the archbishop's palace, the two priests, separately, hearing of our need, and knowing the risks they were taking, said they would help. Before they left, dalla Costa gave them each a letter to the convents in and around the city—men's as well as women's—asking the convents to open their doors to the Jews.

It was on the following morning that my father went to the temple again. Rabbi Cassuto was off at a meeting, and my father left without having seen him, and without finding out that there were two committees forming, each with six or seven members, some Catholics, some Jews. At the heart of one were Don Leto Casini, Rabbi Cassuto, and Matilde Cassin, and leading the other was Padre Cipriano.

Late that day, during a lesson with Luciana, Matilde appeared at the villa, bringing us news. An elderly woman from Poland had come to Florence, alone. She had a relative in Italy, a niece who had been studying in Padua.

Luciana, her voice shaking, stood up. "My aunt? Alive?"

They had taken her aunt to a convent and, thinking Luciana would want to be with her, had made arrangements for them both.

We had thought that when we left the villa, Luciana would go with us too. She stared at Matilde, her uneven features in striking contrast with Matilde's fine ones, and, hopelessly, she turned to my father.

"I have to," she said. "I'd rather stay here with you, but I must." Then, facing my mother, as if to justify this strange confession, she said, "I didn't like this woman—she tried to prevent me from going, badgered my parents to keep me at home. But she's my aunt, and she might even know where my family is."

"Can't you find out," I asked, "and then come back?"

She shook her head and went for her clothes, and my father, in his halting Italian, questioned Matilde.

Luciana returned with her clothes in minutes. "I'll be back," she said. "I'll be there as long as she needs me, of course, but I'll leave her for part of the day and come back."

I asked Matilde, "Where is this convent?"

"You heard your father, Ruth," Luciana said. "You don't have to know. But don't stop doing your lessons, or I'll be harder on you than on Joel."

"Luciana, don't come back," my father said. "We won't be here. The rabbi will know where we are. If he thinks you should know, he'll tell you. If not, we'll find each other later."

"How, Papa?" I asked, worried in a way I hadn't worried for my sister or Ondine, who had gone away protected by men.

With a toss of her hair and a barely audible *Arrivederci,* Luciana took Matilde's arm and left.

My father sat down. "I've done it again," he said. "The way I got complacent in Lyons, that's how I've been in Florence. Captivated by the comfort, by the idea of studying—under the nose of the Germans—as if the house and Luciana and knowing the language could save us."

He stood up slowly. Matilde had told him where he could find the rabbi, and he left.

As soon as he had, my mother said, "Imma and I have things to do. Take care of Daniel, but study as much as you can. You, too, Joel, do you hear? Finish the lesson."

"Are we leaving?" I asked. She nodded. "Together?" I asked.

"I don't know," she said. "Probably not."

VII

HERE AND THERE IN THE CITY, ARRESTS OF JEWS HAD begun.

My father and Rabbi Cassuto arranged that my mother, Imma, Daniel, and I, as paying guests, would enter a convent. We'd stay in our room, always, except for meals, which we'd take in the refectory with all the other guests. The Mother Superior knew who we were, but the story we'd tell to others was that my father was Italian, an executive in the Paris branch of an Italian bank, who was now returning to Italy, and my mother and Imma—*her* mother—were French. They were in mourning—my mother's younger brother had recently died. They were therefore depressed and silent most of the time.

"If they say much more than you can answer in Italian," my father instructed my mother, "say, *'Mi scusi. Non sto bene.'* " Please, I'm not well. "That's easy enough."

He turned to me. "If they ask you what's wrong with your mother, say, *'Mio zio è morto.'* " My uncle has died. "If they ask about your father, I'm in Rome, finding an apartment." He turned to Imma and took her hand. "Don't give us any trouble, Mama, please. They mustn't suspect we're Jews."

"Where will you and Joel be?" she asked.

"With good people. Don't worry, the worst is past."

He had met Don Casini and knew they'd be staying with him.

The next morning, we said our goodbyes, first to the Bellinis, and then, by ourselves, to each other.

Joel and I were on one of the sofas, and I asked if he knew where he and my father were going.

"I can't tell," he said. When I said it frightened me that everything was such a secret, he said, "If anyone gets caught, he'd better not know where the rest of us are."

I asked him if that's what my father had said.

"It's what I figured out. Eva knew where she and Vittorio were going, but she didn't tell us. And Papa knows, I'm sure, but he didn't tell Luciana. So no one can make anyone tell."

As I thought about someone making me tell, I remembered the day of the truck. My hands began to tremble, and I hid them behind my back.

"Ruthie, don't be afraid," he said. "*You* won't get caught. You're too smart. You're as smart as Aaron—better than me at everything. That's why Luciana likes you so much."

He had never said anything like that before, and hearing it frightened me. I was afraid his words were a testament.

"Stop it!" I said. "We'll go to Czestochowa, both of us."

"What?"

I thought he'd forgotten that night in Warsaw, and I didn't want to explain, so I shook my head. "Nothing, I don't know why I said it."

"I do," he said.

From the other side of the room my father was watching us closely, and when he saw me look at him, he approached us and asked if Joel would give him a turn.

Joel went off to Imma, and my father sat down. His clothes had been properly altered, his self-assurance seemed restored, and I thought he was as handsome then at forty-five as he had been in Warsaw ages before.

"What did Joel say that frightened you?"

"I don't remember."

With a sad little smile, he said, "You do. You don't have to lie. Not to me."

My hands were back in my lap. He raised them to his lips, kissed them, and set them down.

"I've hidden nothing from you," he said. "I haven't allowed you to be a child."

I thought he was apologizing, so I said, "You have, Papa, you have."

He shook his head. "No, and I can't allow it now, because soon you might be alone. Ruthie, listen. No one must know who you are. See everything, hear everything, remember everything, and trust your judgment. Luciana taught you more than you realize now. And when you make mistakes—of any kind—only then may you remember you're a child, with special rights to make them, more of those rights than I ever allowed you."

"Why will I be alone?" I asked. "I'm going with Mama."

"I hope you *won't* be alone, but I want you to think in advance, so that if you have to separate, you'll be prepared. Think of what might happen *before* it happens, always look around for ways to be safe—that's the trick to staying alive." He took my hands again and said, "Of this I'm not so sure, but maybe it's also the way to be brave."

"Will you know where we are?"

"Yes."

"Where will you and Joel be? Why won't you tell us?"

"We'll be with a Gentile who knows that we're Jews and accepts us as brothers. You don't have to worry for Joel and me. And always, if you need any help, look for Rabbi Cassuto."

That was all. Matilde was due to arrive in minutes. She was late, and we started to worry. When at last she appeared, apologetic and cheerful, she left us alone and waited outside. We, indoors, held each other long and hard. In my father's breast pocket was a small rectangular book whose outline I felt on my chest.

"My darling child," he said. "Let's go."

We let ourselves out of the house together, all of us, and looked around in the quiet street. No one was out, and we entered the taxi Matilde had come in—Matilde up front with the driver, and Imma, my mother, and I in the rear, Daniel on my mother's lap.

We rode away, passing the houses and gardens slowly, we in the rear looking back at the villa. My father and Joel were watching us, Joel up front, looking especially small, my father behind him, resolute, strong, his forearms crossed on Joel's chest. As we reached the point where the street curved sharply away, we stopped.

The driver asked us, "One last look?"

We hadn't stopped looking, but now, finally, my father and Joel waved. When the taxi started again, I turned, and for the first time saw that Imma and my mother both were dressed in black, as if we were really in mourning.

We drove along the Lungarno, and at the Ponte Vecchio we turned from the river and took the road to the Porta Romana. We passed the Palazzo Pitti, and after a while we arrived at the convent, a squat brown stone building. During the drive, I committed to memory the names of all of the streets.

Matilde deposited us in the sitting room, under the eyes of some women doing their needlework, and went to speak to the Mother Superior. Minutes later, she returned with a nun, who escorted us up to our room.

It was small and furnished with narrow cots, four of them, inches apart, and with a tiny freestanding wardrobe off in a corner. A crucifix hung on one of the walls, and on another a print of a seated Madonna and Child. Imma shuddered and turned to the door, as the nun, apparently puzzled, watched.

I waited until she had left. "Imma!" I said. "What you did! We're not supposed to show that we're Jews."

"Aha!" she said. "The eggs are teaching the hens."

Before very long, the room would become like a prison, but then, small though it was, it promised us safety. We unpacked and sat on the cots, facing each other, looking for something to do.

It was the first of many such stagnant days. We left our room to go for our meals, which we ate in silence, answering briefly when others addressed us, smiling wanly, and afterward leaving the women slowly, as if we were forced to by grief.

Among them were two who caught our attention, who didn't look alike, but who we presumed were closely related and probably sisters. They had come from the south, they said, escaping the war. One had four young children: a newborn girl, a boy of Daniel's age, an older boy, and a girl who looked rather young, but who had so serious a face that I believed that she, like Joel, was older than she looked. The other woman had a girl somewhat older than Daniel and a boy substantially younger.

I wanted to talk to the oldest girl, but we'd look toward each other and look away, denying ourselves even trivial talk. Daniel was not as restrained. He wanted to play with the boy his age, and he would try to pull away from us and go to him, but my mother, afraid that through the children we would be discovered, wouldn't allow it. As soon as she could, she'd hurry us up to the room, and there, early on, we argued it out.

Daniel sulked, cried, struck out with his hands. I, sensing my mother's ambivalence, nagged. My mother was counting on Imma's support, but she didn't appear to have it. Imma was sure the people were Jews.

"They speak Italian!" my mother said. "In Italy, Jews are all in the north, not in the south."

I leapt to Imma's defense. "They *say* they're from the south—Signor Bellini *told* us. Besides," I said with authority, "they sound exactly like Matilde, so they're from the north."

As if I had insulted her, my mother said, "Since when are you a judge of accents?"

"I know these things," I said, though of course I didn't.

I had gone too far. Imma turned on me. "Again! The eggs are teaching the hens!" Then, assuming even more authority than I had done, she again insisted the women were Jews.

My mother, coldly, asked her how she could tell.

Firmly, she said, "My *heart* tells me."

When something couldn't be explained by reason, its answer was in Imma's heart; when a room was deliciously warm, she was warm in her joints; when she worked especially hard, she worked with her sides or intestines—they were Yiddish idioms that had always made my mother smile, but not now.

Her ambivalence was gone, banished in a flat, irrevocable "No! They cannot play with the children."

"I know," Imma said—reasonably, as if she had fully agreed with my mother right from the start. "My heart tells me they're Jews, but we shouldn't take any chances."

My mother was exasperated with us all, and though she had won, she was not enjoying her victory. These two women whom she didn't dare to trust were just the kind of women she'd have sought as friends—not in Warsaw or Paris perhaps, but in Lyons or southern France or now in Florence, after she'd changed in ways that couldn't be measured. When on occasion Imma reverted to speaking in Yiddish, she'd refer to the women as *die shayne,* the pretty ones, or *die aydele, die tsvay aydele*—the two refined ones, the modest, soft-spoken, gracious ones—and my mother and I would know whom she meant. They were women like Matilde, my mother once said, not like Luciana.

Still, I felt sorry for my mother and decided I'd forget the other girl. Daniel remained a problem, so we worked at keeping him busy up in our room, telling him stories, inventing endlessly repeated games that kept him satisfied until the next encounter with the little boy.

The only respite from each other was the visits from Matilde. Twice she came by herself, and once with a charming young man named Marco Ischio, who helped her carry some food to the nuns. They also brought us some news of my father and Joel—not of where they were, but just that they were safe. There was even a hint from Marco that soon my father might visit.

There was only one bad moment, when Matilde said my mother ought to place "the children" in an orphanage or private home, but my mother became so upset that Matilde dropped the suggestion.

It was then mid-October. In the month we had been in Florence, a lot had happened in Rome. Nathan was with Flavio's family, but other deserters had gotten there first—cousins who had tried to reach the Allies and failed, or so they said. If they knew there were Partisan groups in the city and the hill towns near it, they didn't say so. Instead, Flavio's mother begged him to let the Allies manage without him, and Flavio gave in. He, in turn, encouraged my brother to stay, but though Nathan stayed for more than a week, he wasn't at ease with so many strangers, all of them happy together and none of them speaking a language he knew. If he couldn't join the Allies, he said, he wanted to look for Theo's sister, and Flavio told him how.

Long before, Italian Jews had joined together in formal communities. In Rome, there were Jewish neighborhoods, one of them the former ghetto, but there were Jews throughout the city as well. The *comunità* included all of them and, as in other cities, had an office where it kept a list of members. There Nathan obtained Nicole's address, and, at a tiny Trastevere apartment, found her, together with her husband and baby.

Nicole, in her middle twenties, was small, pale, plain—very

much like Esther, her mother. She and her husband had had an astonishing week.

First, Ondine and Aaron had reached them, looking for Nathan and telling what little they could about Theo. When they asked about Partisan bands, Nicole and her husband told them that some had been formed in the hills, in the towns that are called the Castelli Romani. They also knew someone in Rome who would know about Partisans there in the city. Ondine and Aaron took the person's address, told them where we'd reunite in Florence, and left.

Two days later, Theo arrived. Convinced—before the world had confronted the "final solution"—that his sister was the only living member of his family, he'd walked away from the Jewish Resistance in France in order to find her. He reached St. Martin-Vésubie on the evening of the day we had left.

Like us, he went to Entraque, swinging his rigid leg in an arc, impatient people behind him, and terrible gorges below. He intended to find Nicole and then, if he felt she were safe, leave her and join the Italian Resistance, as Aaron had predicted.

It was three days later that Nathan arrived.

He said he would go with Theo, but Theo wasn't convinced his sister was safe. He wanted the baby and her to be out of the city. Nicole, however, said that in Rome the Germans were models of proper behavior even toward Jews, and that the *comunità*'s leaders, or most of them, had stayed. Under the windows of the Pope, she said, Jews would be safe—the Vatican, an independent state, had no racial laws, had given jobs to Jews dismissed under Fascist laws, and had admitted to its law school Jews excluded from the law schools elsewhere. She wasn't afraid.

Later that week, the Germans demanded fifty kilos of gold from the Jewish community. If the *comunità* didn't comply, two hundred Roman Jews would be arrested and deported. The Vatican offered to help with gold from its treasury, and Nicole was again reassured. On the second day, without having had to accept the Vatican's offer, the Jews of Rome delivered the fifty kilos of gold. On the day when Nicole surrendered her wedding ring, both Theo and Nathan were with her.

During the next two weeks, the Germans plundered both the treasuries and the religious treasures of the synagogue, the rabbinical college, and the two Jewish libraries. Then, at dawn on October 16, in the rain, the black trucks of the SS entered the Jewish neighborhoods with lists from the records of the Rome police, and, in what was later called the Great Raid of Rome, arrested some thirteen hundred Jews.

We, in the convent in Florence, knew nothing of this. The day of the Great Raid, or a day earlier or later, we were huddled in our coats when a nun came up and told us that someone was waiting to pay us a call.

My mother leapt to her feet. *"Mon mari?"* Then, switching to Italian, *"Mio marito?"*

"No, signora, una signorina."

Downstairs, in the midst of a few attentive guests, and smiling broadly, tossing her hair, winning the women over with her glamour and vivacity, was Luciana.

When we had moved to where no one could hear us, she said, "The disappointment in your face! Whom did you expect?"

"Forgive me," my mother said. "I thought the signorina was Matilde."

"Thank you!"

"You needn't be sarcastic. Two weeks, and we haven't been out. We've been living for her visits."

We sat down, far apart from the other guests.

"I've been as silent as possible," my mother said. "By talking so much I'm making the others suspicious."

"I'm here," Luciana said. "They'll *expect* you to talk."

"How did you find us?"

"By luck."

"Why did you come?"

"I missed you!" Then, quietly, earnestly, *"You* don't like *me* much, I know, but *I* missed *you*—all of you. I went to give you your lesson, though your husband had told me not to, but the Bellinis said you had gone—you with Matilde, and he and Joel later, alone."

"The Bellinis wouldn't know where we are. *Matilde* must have told you."

"She didn't! Last week, when she left me to visit somebody else, I followed her, hoping."

"Then she told you the name we've adopted, or how would you know it?"

"I don't."

Alarmed, my mother asked, "What name did you ask for?"

"I didn't. I just walked in—as arrogant and spoiled as any cinema queen—and said I wanted to see my family—all four of them: my dear grandmother, my sour, ungrateful, suspicious aunt, and my little cousins. Nobody even *asked* me the name."

"You really described me that way?"

"I *should* have."

"I don't know why you're saying these things," my mother said. "I don't understand you."

"I know, and it doesn't matter. But understand Matilde. She's risking her life for us—don't be suspicious." She paused. "Why are we quarreling?"

"I don't know," my mother said. "I'm sorry."

"So am I. Don't be disappointed. She'll come again, or if she's short of time, Marco will come. Has she ever come here with Marco?" Before we could answer, she said, "What? You've been here that long, and even the children haven't been out?"

My mother, exasperated, said, "How can they go out?"

"They are the ones who *can.* Who would know they're Jews? They can go for a walk like normal children."

"Normal" echoed in me like a drum, and my mother, as if hearing it, clapped her hands to her ears and lowered her head.

Imma said, "*Gevalt!* You'd never have said such things if my son were around."

"I wouldn't have *had* to."

"Ruth," my mother said, "take Daniel and go upstairs."

"Please, Mama," I begged, "if Luciana says it's safe, let us go, please. I'll hold his hand."

My mother stiffened, glared at me for a moment, and turned away. After a while, and reasonably, she said, "Luciana, I'm sure you mean to help, but you don't have children, you don't understand. You're only making it harder for me."

"But easier for them."

"They're children!" Imma said. "They'll get over it. If they have their mother, children are strong. So what if they stay indoors for a while?"

But my mother was being shamed. It was clear in the way her shoulders suddenly drooped, in her heavier breathing, in the way she turned from Luciana's gaze.

"I know it frightens you," Luciana said, "but they don't have to go by themselves. I'll take them, and no one will stop us, you'll see. And even if somebody did, you really should know me by now—I can talk my way out of anything."

My mother, though still afraid, was reconsidering. She lowered her head and clasped her hands in front of her mouth. Luciana pushed on, turning from Polish to Yiddish, using a Yiddish expression I hadn't recently heard. *"Ich ken zay faredn die tsayn. Ich ken zay* allemen *faredn die tsayn."* I can talk their teeth away. I can talk *anybody's* teeth away.

Softly, my mother said, "You can take Ruth. Not Daniel."

He was leaning against my mother, looking up at Luciana with wide, solemn, mistrustful eyes. She lowered her head toward his and pursed her lips as if she intended to kiss him.

"Why so serious, Daniele?" she said in Italian. "You're Mama's little love."

We walked out into the street, and out of sheer joy in this sudden, wonderful freedom I spread my arms and twirled around as I often did when especially happy. Luciana gripped my arm and told me quietly, "Don't do anything silly, and stop looking so happy. Look as if you've lived here all your life."

I was about to tell her how truly happy I was, and that I had missed her, when she said, "If German soldiers come along, and they will in the *centro,* they won't be paying attention to you, so don't be afraid. You're an Aryan, you hear? You can look at them or not, whichever you choose, but if you do avoid their eyes, it mustn't be in a way that shows you're afraid."

"I don't *feel* afraid," I said, and I meant it.

"And whether we meet any Germans or not," she said, "don't gawk at anything."

I didn't recognize the word for "gawk," so she said it for me in French. "Someday," she asked, "might you want to be a teacher? Like me?"

"Not really," I said. I unbuttoned my collar and showed her the top of my dress. "Did you ever notice my leaf?"

"How can I help it? You always wear it."

"You never asked me why."

"There are more important things I haven't asked."

"It was a gift from Ondine. I want to be a writer, like my brother and her. But, Luciana, she's not as beautiful as you." She laughed, and, subdued, I asked her, "Where are we going?"

"What do you want to look at? Gardens or buildings?"

"Buildings. The ones in the *centro.* The ones Vittorio showed us from Piazzale Michelangelo, especially the Duomo."

"What do you know about the Duomo?"

"That it means 'cathedral.' It's the most beautiful—that and the synagogue. I really like the domes."

"We'll save the Duomo for last. We'll start at the Palazzo Vecchio—where they govern from—and as you look around, I'll give you the lesson you need. And later you'll teach it for me to your mother and grandma. What language are you speaking in the convent?"

"Italian when we speak to *them,* but they think we're French, so we speak to each other in French."

"Then your lesson today," she said, "is in French."

I hadn't known she had planned a lesson, much less that it would be in French, but I didn't intend to object to that or anything else.

"Who is Ondine?" she asked.

When I told her, she asked about Aaron. Then I mentioned Nathan, whose name she had heard, but when I said he was my brother, she said, "Another one? *Six* children? To a bourgeous woman from Warsaw?"

I asked her how many her mother had had.

"Too few. I envy you. *And* your mother. I pity mine and envy yours."

I didn't understand and wished I did, but all I said was, "They're in Poland?"

"In one form or another, yes, and the worst is that we didn't know we loved each other."

I had only an inkling of what she might mean, but it saddened me terribly, and, sensing it, she put her arm around me for a moment, giving me a hug.

As we passed the Palazzo Pitti, she told me a bit of its history, and then, when we were crossing the Ponte Vecchio and stopped to look at the bust of Cellini, a bit about him. On the other side of the bridge, we began to encounter the German soldiers, but as she'd said, none of them paid attention to us, and soon, distracted by the unfamiliar city, I forgot them.

When we reached Piazza della Signoria, which was crowded, we stopped, and I stood in the large square, astonished. I had expected the Palazzo Vecchio and its tower, but not an outdoor museum of sculpture.

"Come," she said, quietly. "You're gawking."

She led me toward a covered porch of sorts, like a corner room of a building, huge, open on two of its sides, with statues out front and along its interior walls. It had a broad stone bench at the open sides, attached to them, and at the center, half a dozen stairs led up from the square to the room.

"That is the Loggia," she said. "We're going to sit in the empty space on the steps. When you've rested enough, you can stand and face me and look at the statues inside, as if you're ready to go but waiting for me."

"Why do we have to be careful?" I asked. "Nobody's paying attention to us."

"You have to *look* as if they're not, but you have to *act* as if they are."

We sat on the steps, silently, with people all around us, and I looked at the sculptures out in the square. Then, when a sizable group of people had left their place on the bench, we quickly moved to the vacated space. Luciana sat down, and I, to see the statue above her, stood there and faced her.

"Remember Cellini?" she asked. "This is his *Perseus Holding the Head of Medusa.* Your lesson is Catholic prayers."

"What?"

"In French."

"Why?

"Lower your voice. Because if you were French, you'd have learned them in French."

"But why?"

"How long can you stay in the convent with nobody getting suspicious? Look at the statues and listen. You'll have to repeat what I say."

"I can't. My father wouldn't want me to."

"Oh, Ruth," she said sadly, "you're your father's daughter—you should understand him. He *would* want you to. Anything to help you live—that's what he'd want you to do."

I turned my back on her.

She touched my hand. "I've tried to teach you what you need. Not a word about a game of any kind, ever, because you won't be playing." I didn't answer. "I've taught the language of the hunted. Words for raids, arrests, killing, torture—war and madness words. So that you'd recognize them if you heard them. So that you'd know how to use them and when you must hide. But it's not enough."

She waited, and I remembered the evening with Joel, when my father had shouted, "I want you to live!" As my mother's resolve had weakened an hour before at the convent, mine was weakening now. I turned back and looked up at the *Perseus*, at the sword in his right hand and then at his left one, high above him, the head of Medusa hanging from it by its hair. Then, slowly, I lowered my eyes and nodded.

"We'll start with the easiest," she said, "the Ave Maria. Listen. *Hail Mary, full of grace, the Lord is with thee.* Repeat it."

I repeated it.

"Blessed art thou among women, and blessed is the fruit of thy womb, Jesus. Repeat it."

I repeated it.

"Now, both sentences together."

I said them, and then she told me the third, which alarmed me more, but which I repeated. *"Holy Mary, mother of God, pray for us sinners now and at the hour of our death. Amen."*

She had me repeat the whole prayer.

"My mother and Imma never will say it."

"They will. Your mother's a sophisticated woman. So will your grandma if she has to—if not for herself then for Daniel and you." She stood up. "People are coming. Let's move on to the *Fountain of Neptune*. They call it *Il Biancone*, the big white thing, but some of it's lovely."

We walked to it, casually. With her back to the railing she watched the square, as she'd done from the Loggia's bench, while I looked at the chariot's horses.

"Now," she said, "the second prayer, the Our Father. *Our Father, who art in heaven, hallowed be thy name."*

I repeated it.

"Thy kingdom come. Thy will be done in earth as it is in heaven."

I repeated it.

"Give us this day our daily bread. And forgive us our trespasses, as we forgive those who trespass against us. And lead us not into temptation, but deliver us from evil. Amen."

After a failure or two, I learned it.

"Good girl," she said. "Someday you'll come here to look at the rest, but I want to make sure you see the cathedral. And on the way, you'll practice the prayers."

"Then will I be finished?"

"There's one more, and it's the longest."

As we made our way through the narrow streets, I mumbled the prayers. Suddenly, across a narrow square from where we were, stood the cathedral, gigantic, overwhelming, rising from among the smaller buildings, the little area before it utterly unlike the space—the vastness—in front of Notre Dame.

"Don't gawk," she said quietly. "And use the time—we don't have any to waste. Just keep practicing."

She pulled me toward the Baptistry, and as we walked I looked back at the Duomo. I had thought cathedrals were made of stone, ordinary stone, but this one was of marble, pink and green, colors in which I'd never known marble existed. Luciana tugged at my arm, and I turned. A German soldier was there, his hand held up to prevent a collision. I thought my heart would explode. Again Luciana tugged at my arm, gently, taking us out of his path, but he had looked at her with so much interest that I felt my hands turn cold. I stuffed them into my pockets.

Quietly, she said, "It's all right, Ruth. The square is full of people, and all of them look like us. We'll stroll, first around the Baptistry—I want you to see the eastern doors—and then we'll circle the Duomo. But meanwhile listen. This is the Credo. *I believe in God the Father Almighty, Creator of heaven and earth.*"

I said I couldn't concentrate, but she insisted. *"I believe in God the Father Almighty.* Say it."

Frightened, but thinking she was not, I started to say it, but as we rounded the Baptistry, directly before us were other Germans, one of them distracted by the doors, the other one turned aside, facing us squarely. He looked at me and then at Luciana, who smoothly switched from French to Italian and changed the subject to hats. We went on, but she moved us several feet away from the railing. I begged her to let us go back to the convent.

"No," she said, quietly, glancing backward. "They have no interest in us, no reason to follow us, and they're not—if you don't believe me, look and see. I didn't intend this to happen, but since it has, we'll put it to use."

"Luciana," I begged, "I don't want to see the rest. I'm afraid."

"So am I, but you need this, and I'll walk you around this place all day if I have to. You'll learn the Credo now. Do you remember the line, or do I have to repeat it?"

I was silent.

"Ruth," she said, "the sooner you learn it, the sooner we leave. And you'll have discovered that even when you're most afraid, you can make yourself think."

"My father will be furious at you."

"He won't. Your mother will. By now, she and your grandma are hysterical—they'll never allow me to take you again—so why don't you try the prayer."

"I believe in God the Father Almighty, Creator of heaven and earth."

"There!" she said. "I *know* you. Even at the worst moment you heard me and remembered. Now, *And in Jesus Christ his only Son our Lord, who was conceived by the Holy Ghost. . . ."*

I repeated it from the beginning. Again we approached the soldiers, but now they both were turned with their backs to the doors, facing us, and when they saw us, one of them looked directly, frankly, at Luciana, with a hint of a smile.

She turned toward me, and again in Italian, she said, "But I don't like the way you look in it. It's a color for me but not for you—it makes you look like an olive with hair."

When we had passed them and taken another few steps, I managed to say, "All right, go on."

"But on the other hand," she said, turning away from the Baptistry, "we needn't be foolish. I've made my point, so now we can move a bit farther away."

We strolled toward the Duomo, and from across the narrow space that surrounds it, we circled it slowly, perhaps five or six or seven times, or perhaps even more, and finally, without hesitation, I recited, *"I believe in God the Father Almighty, Creator of heaven and earth. And in Jesus Christ, his only Son our Lord, who was conceived by the Holy Ghost, born of the Virgin Mary, suffered under Pontius Pilate, was crucified, died, and was buried. On the third day he arose again from the dead. He ascended into heaven, and sits on the right hand of God. And from there he shall come to judge the living and the dead. I believe in the Holy Ghost, the holy Catholic Church, the communion of saints, the forgiveness of sins, the resurrection of the body unto life everlasting. Amen."*

"Brava!" she said. *"Bravissima!"* Her eyes were filled with love and pride. "I'm sorry I had to do this, Ruth, truly I am, but someday, when we're free, we'll come here together and look at the Baptistry doors. Now we have to go home. We'll stop at a church on the way, and I'll show you how people behave in a church. And then I'll prove that I trust you."

We left by way of Via del Proconsolo, and when we got to the Badia Fiorentina, Luciana stopped and said, "Nobody's noticing—turn around. Now you can gawk."

We took a long last look at the cathedral, and then I continued saying the Credo over and over.

"I know it," I said. "Now can we talk?"

"About what?"

"How is your aunt?"

"She's fine."

"Do you like her better than you used to?"

"Yes, I do, very much."

"Why did you leave your family?"

"They wanted to arrange my marriage, a good one according to them, with a man in Warsaw in fact. But I didn't want a life like the one your mother was living. To be an idle, jeweled, dressed-up ornament—the visible proof of a man's success—for me, that wasn't a life."

"You didn't love him?"

"No. I don't think I loved anyone then. I don't know what I had in place of a heart."

"My grandmother called me heartless once. There was this Belgian girl—Yvette, she was Jewish—when we were in the south of France. Her mother was dead, and her brother too—shot at from airplanes. She was skinny, and her hair was like straw, and I said so, not to Yvette herself, but my grandmother called me heartless. Someday I'll tell her how sorry I am."

"The girl? Life has treated her worse. And you didn't say it to her, so she doesn't know."

"But I want to. I'll say I'm sorry for not being friendly. My father said we'd find them after the war."

"When did he say that?"

"When they left St. Martin-Vésubie for Nice."

"You won't be able to. The people in Nice were caught—they're probably dead."

"They aren't!" I said. "How do you know?"

"Oh, Ruth," she said, "everybody knows by now—everyone who wants to know. That's why I'm so hard on you. You mustn't let them catch you."

I didn't want to believe it, and I didn't want to argue.

"Is your name really Luciana?" I asked.

"No, of course not. But it's pretty, isn't it?"

At a church on the way we stopped, followed a little old woman inside, and mimicked her—dipping our fingers, crossing ourselves, genuflecting, choosing a pew.

"Do I have to say the prayers?" I whispered.

She shook her head.

Before going back to the convent, we went out of our way—I didn't know why—to stop at Piazza del Carmine.

"Do you remember the name Piazza del Carmine?"

"Yes," I said, "from before you came to stay with us. The cellar room—you said it was somewhere near here."

"Yes. When I left the Bellinis, you wanted to know where I'd be, and now I trust you to know. There: the Convento del Carmine. Only four people know: the rabbi, Matilde, Marco, and you."

"I won't tell anyone else."

"I know. Do you know why you wanted to see the Duomo and synagogue?"

"I told you."

"You told me you like the ones with the domes, but I know you better than that. You—like your father, I'm sure—you knew those buildings by instinct. Labor and love—that's what the two of you always respond to, labor and love. Look at the love and labor that went into making that temple and church. Remember—especially, today when so much is being destroyed by hate—remember what people were willing to build out of love. Transcending the self." And then, as if making sure I understood, she said in Polish, *"Nie zważając na swoją jaźń."*

When we got back, my mother was in the sitting room, near the door, apart from the other women, and when she saw us, she touched the wall for support.

Quietly, matter-of-factly, she asked Luciana, "Do you know how long you've been out?"

"Yes. I'm sorry, truly. I taught her some things you should know, and I hope you'll let her teach them to you."

Reasonably, but firmly, my mother said, "You aren't helping us. Please don't come here again—I can't allow it."

"I *am* helping you. You don't know what's going on. The SS arrive in trucks. They cordon off the streets and post their guards, and no one can hope to escape. They search the houses floor by floor, room by room. But you, you don't even know what to do if somebody challenges you—if you should have to pretend you're Catholics. Look around you. I know that none of these people are Poles, but is there really no one here who'd betray you? Is every Italian good?"

My mother was silent. She had voiced her suspicions to Imma and me of one of the guests—a woman with a shiny grapelike mole at the base of her nose, between her nose and cheek. She was a loud-mouthed, vulgar woman who several times had spoken of prostitutes, so that I, bitten by curiosity, had nagged my mother until she explained. Last evening the woman had asked me some personal questions my mother had never expected and hadn't prepared me to answer.

"But no one," my mother said, "no one has taken my child and kept her for hours. You told me a walk—I thought for an hour. And no one but you has questioned my wisdom. Does your arrogance make you wise? And no one has challenged my rights. Ruth is *my* child, and even if you think you're cleverer than I, you cannot talk *my* teeth away. Not anymore."

Resigned, Luciana turned toward me and solemnly said, "One more thing I forgot to say. Act brave even when you're not, and they'll think you are."

Before I understood her, she was gone. I didn't know whom she had meant by "they"—my mother and Imma or somebody else.

I followed my mother up to our room. Imma closed her eyes, sighing with relief, and Daniel asked me where we had been.

"No, Daniel, no, darling," my mother said. "I want to talk to Ruth myself."

But she sat there silent, and I, as if I could encourage her to let me off, said, "Mama, what does *nie zważając na swoją jaźń* mean?"

"What? What has that to do with anything? *She* must have said it—you should have asked *her.*"

"Can't you even tell me *that?*"

"Do you think I don't know? It means to think of something besides yourself. But *she* can't *do* that. And what about *you?* You should have told her to bring you back." She lowered her voice, sounding open-minded, reasonable. "Why didn't you?"

"She was teaching me something important."

"Oh, yes, important."

"Like how to behave in a church."

"You went into a church?"

"Yes."

"What else?"

"Catholic prayers."

My mother, silent, merely looked at me, but Imma, softly, her hands holding the sides of her head, said, *"Gevalt."*

"But I didn't say the prayers in the church. Mama, if she came here again, would you let me see her?"

"She won't come again." Then, mimicking Luciana's solemn tone, "'I forgot to tell you, Ruth, act brave and people will think. . . .' Can't you see? That was goodbye."

"But if she was sorry, and she did come back?"

"No."

"Just to sit in the sitting room together?"

"No."

"But I like to be with her, Mama, and she's alone."

"She's not. She has her aunt."

With no compunction now about lying, I said, "She doesn't like her. She wishes *we* were her family."

"I know she does, with an exception or two, and then you really *would* be her family."

"What do you mean? She won't do it again. Why won't you let her come?"

"What's wrong with you—don't you hear me? I don't know what she's teaching you."

"I just told you what she taught me, and she said I should teach it to Imma and you."

"You won't! She's turning you into something you're not, making you insolent, just like her, as if *you* know everything. I don't like it! You're only a child, and already you're acting like her. I warn you, you'd better not say any more."

I was glad I'd become like Luciana, but at the same time I was miserable, and I wanted to strike back.

"You shouldn't have sent her away," I said. "Her parents are in Poland too, just like yours."

VIII

I HAD HURT MY MOTHER, OF COURSE, BUT SHE DIDN'T SEEM angry at me, nor could I be angry at her for long. If there were other conflicts, or indeed if, even in the earlier years, there had been conflicts among my brothers and sister beyond what I've told, I've truly forgotten them. I don't, in fact, believe that there were.

From early on, we'd been somewhat apart from the Gentile world, even when it seemed we weren't, and we were conscious of barriers, overt or disguised. Whether we were typical of other Jews or not, whether our feelings for each other arose from my father's childhood memories or not—because it was he, rather than my mother, who had taught us the meaning of family—this is how we were, and especially so in the convent.

We lived as we had to. We accepted being confined, our cots only inches apart, with little conversation even with the two young women Imma thought were Jews, and not another child for Daniel. We stretched our legs when we went for our meals, we listened carefully to learn the language, and we waited for Matilde's visits.

She came to us often, bringing the nuns additional food—bought on the black market at horrendous cost—and to us she delivered friendship, ration cards used by the nuns to buy our food at legitimate prices, and assurances that Joel and my father both were safe. And once or twice, Marco Ischio came in her place.

We knew nothing about the committees working to save us—that one, which had Don Casini, Rabbi Cassuto, and Matilde, had two Jewish girls, teenage sisters, doing for others what Matilde did for us; that there was a foreign Jew, and that Marco, a Gentile, was his secretary; that Raffaele Cantoni, a Jew from Milan, had connections with Jews in America, and that he was bringing in from Switzerland money to pay for counterfeit documents, rent for hiding space, and of course for food; nor that Mario Finzi, a young Bolognese Jew, a brilliant musician and lawyer, was taking the train almost every day, carrying photos Don Casini gave him, together with money Cantoni had brought, returning to a counterfeiter in Bologna, and, on closely watched trains, bringing back the documents.

Nor did we know that linked to that committee, loosely, was Padre Cipriano's, which had a Catholic lawyer, a Jewish woman who had long before converted to Catholicism, and again Cantoni, and other Jews and Catholics.

We knew only what was happening to us, and a little about the course of the war. About Rome we knew nothing at all.

There, on the night before the Great Raid, Nicole was roused by an old acquaintance, a Catholic policeman, who had heard of the impending German raid and come to warn her. Before the trucks reached her building in Trastevere and the street was cordoned off, she fled with her husband, her child, Theo, and Nathan, to the home of a Catholic friend, an artist like her husband and herself, who had an apartment across the Tiber, on Via de' Conti, near the Colosseum and the Roman Forum.

Nicole's parents-in-law, however, in the old gheto, were caught in the raid. Certain he could get them released, her husband ran to the local police, who sent him to plead with the Germans. He was taken and never returned.

Nathan was sure we would hear of the raid and think he'd been caught. He knew by now of the Delasem, which had been formed some years before by Italy's Jews to help the foreign ones fleeing from Hitler to Italy. In September 1943, when the Germans crossed the border, the leaders of the Delasem went underground. They delivered their records and funds to some Catholic clergymen, who then took over their work. In Rome, the man who directed this help for refugee Jews was a Capuchin monk, Padre Maria Benedetto.

Nathan went to the office of the Delasem for help in sending a message to us. The black-bearded, rather taciturn Maria Benedetto turned out to be Benoît-Marie, the monk whom he and my father had known, who had worked with the banker Donati toward saving our lives in France.

On that day, after the Great Raid, when *L'Italia libera,* the Resistance newspaper, reported the Germans had gone on a manhunt through Rome, seizing people "for their furnaces," not a single other paper carried the story. No official made a public protest, and neither did the Pope.

In the next few weeks, semi-autonomous gangs emerged in the streets, empowered to hunt for the Jews who hadn't been caught. The bounty—when the value of the lira was a hundred times what it is today—was five thousand lire per male, two thousand per female, and one thousand per child.

We, in the convent in Florence, knew nothing of this.

Then, on a day at the end of October, I think, after Matilde had come and gone, we were back in our room when again we were told that there was a visitor. We took it for granted that it was Luciana. We all went down, I eager to see her, but worried about what my mother might say.

But it wasn't Luciana. From across the sitting room, a priest approached us, quickly, with a jaunty step and a broad, beautiful smile surrounding a mouthful of teeth crowded together. He wore long white robes, a habit I'd never seen. Everything about him dazzled me, as Luciana had done.

He started to speak in Italian, but my mother, missing a word, stopped him, saying the sentence Luciana had drilled into each of us: *"Mi scusi, non capisco. Parla francese Lei?"*

"Yes," he said, a long-drawn out "Sìììì," and switched to French. He was Padre Cipriano, he said, and he had brought us a message. "That is," he said, "I've been making inquiries, and I think it's for you. Do you have any sons in Rome?"

"Yes!" my mother answered. "Two of them."

"Nathan and Theo?"

"Nathan and Aaron. Theo is our cousin's son."

"It's from Nathan and Theo. They're well. Safe."

"Where are they? With whom? What is the message?"

"That they're safe and well—that's all I know. The message came through a friend."

My mother thanked him again and again. Imma, who had understood, was wiping her eyes, and Daniel, wide-eyed, leaning against my mother, tugged at her arm and asked, quietly but distinctly, why a man would be wearing that long, white dress.

Padre Cipriano laughed—a loud, delighted laugh. "They are the clothes *dei Domenicani,"* he answered, mixing Italian and French. *"Domenicani!"*

When he had left, we realized he hadn't said through whom he had gotten the message—whether he'd meant a friend of his or of ours. We went to our room, overexcited, all talking at once, wishing we could tell our news to others.

We thought that Flavio, through a priest in Rome, had gotten in touch with this young Dominican, asked him to find us, and told him where he should look. The Bellinis then would have sent him to Rabbi Cassuto, who'd have sent him to us. And Nathan's finding Theo, my mother went on, must have happened through Flavio too—as a Roman, he'd know how to find Nicole.

Hardly an hour had passed, and again we were told of a visitor. Now my mother became uneasy, and her face revealed it, but I, thinking Padre Cipriano might have thought of something more, asked the nun, *"Il padre?"*

"Dice che è l'impiegato del padre."

"Un momento, per favore," my mother said, and the nun left.

It was a man, my mother said—you could tell by the noun.

Imma started wringing her hands. Matilde had already come, she said, and then that good young priest—wonderful visitors twice in a day. Now she was sure our luck had changed, and she didn't want us to see who it was. She was sure that whoever it was, and whatever might be his evil intentions, he would leave if we didn't come down. "For a convent," she said, "he'll show some respect."

The problem was that we didn't know what *impiegato* meant and couldn't guess who a priest's *impiegato* might be. Luciana had said there were clusters of words, and if we could find the heart of one, we could figure out derivatives.

"Piega," I told my mother, "from *piegare.* But what does *piegare* mean?"

Suddenly, I didn't know whom the nun had meant by *padre.* "Mama!" I said, "Maybe there's another word for priest. Maybe she thought I meant my father, so maybe it's not the priest's *impiegato* but my father's."

My mother became impatient. "Enough *pilpul,"* she said referring to Talmudic disputation. "We're going down." She moved to the door and stopped. Turning to Imma, she said, "No, not all of us. Stay with Daniel. If it's safe, Ruth will come for you."

Pretending not to be worried, we went to the sitting room. At the far end, facing us, stone-faced, was my father. Despite his forbidding expression, I could have flown across the room, but my mother's hand was gripping my arm.

"Look at him. Not worried, but something. Distant. Like a stranger. Act formal."

We walked to him slowly, and he bowed to my mother and said, "Madame."

We sat near the door, out of earshot of anyone else, and my mother asked, "Who did you say you are?"

"A clerk employed by your husband. Tell me everything."

"Where are you staying?"

"Darling, please."

"But it's somewhere in the city?"

"Yes.

"Far from here?"

"Yes, or I'd have come here sooner."

"Marco said you would. You couldn't bring Joel?"

"I could have, yes, but he has a little cold. It's nothing, really, he's been very well."

"Darling," she said "don't get excited. Nathan and Theo are also well."

"Oh, thank God."

"A young priest was here. He only just left. A Padre Cipriano. He brought us the message from someone in Rome."

"How did he know where to find you?"

"I don't know. And all they said is that they're safe. Do you think it implies that Aaron is not?"

"It means they aren't together, but Aaron will find them, you'll see."

"Yes, I know, I know. How are you spending your days?"

He put his hand in his pocket and took out a package. "I make shoes."

"Shoes?"

"These are for Ruthie and Daniel. I also make boots. Make old ones usable."

"And Joel?"

"The same. He's learning his grandfather's trade."

"To whom do you sell them?"

"I don't sell them—I give them. To Partisans, escaped prisoners of war, British, American, whoever has boots that are falling apart."

"They come to you looking for boots?"

"No. They're in the hills, waiting for the Allies. To join them. How are Mama and Daniel?"

Afraid, my mother asked, "You *deliver* the boots? Joel too?"

"Magda, please. Joel doesn't. How are Mama and Daniel?"

"Joseph, you have to tell me the rest."

"Yes, I deliver them."

"How do you know where to go?"

"Through Vittorio, mainly."

"Vittorio? You see Eva too?"

"We arrange to meet. She brings them food."

"*Brings* them? She isn't *with* them?"

"Vittorio wouldn't let her stay. He doesn't know whether he'll stay around here or leave for the south, or so he says, though *I* think it's just that he can't allow a woman to fight."

"Then whom is she with?"

"People in a little hamlet. It's so peaceful you wouldn't believe there's a war, except that you see only women, children, and elderly men. They have a garden—vegetables—and rabbits and chickens. Darling, by now a clerk would have left. How are Daniel and Mama?"

"But going around to the Partisans—she's in danger."

"From the Partisans? And which of us is not in danger?" He looked around. "She doesn't go far, and if Germans should stop her, she can explain—the food is for a sick or pregnant woman, or an exchange for something else. And she can still explain in German why she doesn't speak Italian well. Magda," he asked, "who is that woman in blue?"

It was the woman who had asked us the personal questions. Her embroidery and hands were in her lap, and she was watching us frankly, her black mole no longer visible across the room.

My mother answered, "Just a woman. What is Eva's story?"

"Her mother was German, her father French. They raised her near Nice, and when the Italians were there, she married an officer. When he left, he brought her to stay with his parents in Florence, but *they* had left—she doesn't know where—and *he's* at the front, fighting the Russians, while *she's* in the country, waiting, where as long as she works she can eat."

My mother, proud, smiled. "How ironic. She said she'd never speak German again."

"Magda," he said, "I don't like the looks of that woman. Tell me, and let me go. How are Daniel and Mama?"

"They're fine, darling. God bless the Mother Superior. But please! Tell me the rest. If they catch you carrying boots, what will you say?"

"They won't catch me. I'm too old to have been a deserter, so why should they stop me? And I don't carry the boots. I wear them into the hills and trade them for those that are useless. If the old ones are small, I cut them open in front. If they're large, I stuff the toes with paper. If they have no soles, I wrap them onto my feet with rags. And I do it gratefully, not because I was asked, but because as Aaron said, it's worth it." He paused. "There's something else. If the children have to go off for a while, you mustn't object."

Pulling back, sitting rigid, my mother said, "Joseph, are you mad? Daniel has never been out of my sight for an hour."

"I know."

"He's a baby! What would he think?"

"I know. But if Matilde or the rabbi says it's necessary, do it."

"Matilde herself is a child!"

"And the priest with news of Nathan? Didn't you tell me he's young? Magda, listen, whatever Matilde or Cassuto says, do!"

"I don't promise anything."

"Magda, you do. So far as I'm concerned, you've promised. Now I have to go. Kiss Daniel and Mama."

"You can't—I promised Mama Ruth would come and get her."

"No. That woman's been watching me since I came in."

He stood abruptly and bowed, and in seconds was gone. He had said nothing directly to me, nor had he so much as touched us.

As we climbed the stairs to our room, my mother gave me the precious package of shoes. "Not a word to Imma, do you hear? Not a single word about my letting Daniel go, because he isn't going, and neither are you. Nathan should think for himself, but *I* should *not?* When a man can bear a child, I'll ask his advice on what I should do about mine."

It was clear. My mother dismissed the idea and rejoiced in a wonderful day. My father had come, Eva and Joel were well, and Nathan and Theo were safe. We knew nothing about the raid in Rome, nor about the bounties, nor about gangs in the streets hunting for Jews. Nor did we know that similar gangs were forming in Florence and elsewhere.

A month went by, and at breakfast one morning we heard of a new decree declaring the Jews—including Italian ones—enemies of the state. We assumed we would now be cut off from Matilde, who would go into hiding herself. I don't know where she was hiding at night, if indeed she already was, but during the day she continued to come, a lovely young girl on a bicycle, doing for us exactly what she had been doing before.

One morning, the Mother Superior sent for my mother, who as always when she'd have to speak Italian told me to come. For the first time, I didn't want to go, and I said so. There had been bombing during the night, and during a lull, when I'd fallen asleep, I'd had a disturbing dream, a part of which I remembered. There was a funeral, like those I'd heard about in Warsaw, with black horses and a black carriage. In the dream, someone spoke with contempt of whoever it was who had died, and I was depressed by the shameless remark.

"You *have* to come," my mother said. "What's come over you?"

Resentfully, I said, "Don't you know? I'm heartless!"

"What?"

I started to think it was I who had made the remark in the dream and, since Luciana was sure Yvette was dead, that the funeral had been Yvette's. "Nothing," I answered. "I'm coming."

The Mother Superior, rigid and unsmiling, was waiting for us in her somber office.

In fragments, slowly, she said, "I'm sorry. But I have to tell you. The convents aren't safe. Not for you. Forgive me. But, because of you, not even for us."

"What?" my mother asked me. "We have to leave?"

I nodded.

"There were raids," the nun went on. "Last night. By the SS. Three places. A recreation center. There were Jewish men in hiding. And at the Convent of the Sisters of Saint Joseph. And at the Convent of the Franciscan Sisters of Mary. There they arrested not only the Jews. They arrested the nuns. And they probably know there are Jews with us."

My mother was pale. "But where can we go?"

"I'm sorry. I really don't know."

"The signorina," my mother said. "Can we wait for her? She'll come. She'll know."

"Yes. But try to think while you wait."

"On Viale Michelangelo. We have friends. How do we get there?"

Slowly, the Mother Superior told us the route.

"Those convents," my mother said. "Were they far away?"

"The Sisters of Saint Joseph are on the other side of the river. The Franciscan Sisters are near. In Piazza del Carmine."

I felt as if I'd been struck.

"What's the matter?" my mother asked.

I wouldn't let myself believe they'd found Luciana. She had said Convento del Carmine, not Franciscan Sisters.

"But there are *two* convents there," I said. "Aren't there?"

"No, child," she said, "there is one Convento del Carmine.

The Franciscan Sisters. There are many Jewish women there. They haven't been taken away. Not yet. But they are under arrest. Both them and the nuns."

My mother was watching me, squinting, suspecting me of something. I wanted to shout, to accuse her, as if it were she who would harm Luciana, but in the presence of the nun I couldn't, nor even later on the way upstairs.

By the time we were back in our room, worry had displaced both my anger and my mother's curiosity. She explained to Imma and started to pack, convinced that Matilde—or if not Matilde, then Marco—would have heard about the raids by now and would arrive at any moment with a plan. The morning went by, however, and the whole long afternoon, and neither one appeared.

The next morning, at breakfast, we saw that the two young women Imma had been sure were Jews—and their six children—were not in the room. Now we knew that Imma had been right, but it was not until nine months later that we learned who the women were. One was Anna Cassuto, the wife of the rabbi. The other was his younger sister, Hulda Campagnano. They had fled to Gentile friends, and each, with her children, had found a room to hide in, in different parts of the city.

Daniel asked us where the little boy had gone.

"I suppose to his papa," my mother said.

Across the table from us and a bit to the left was the woman in blue, the one who'd been watching my father. "Jews," she said with distaste. "I'm sure they were Jews."

For several seconds I didn't look up. I drank my coffee and ate my bread, finding it hard to swallow. There was now some discussion of Jews, most of it, it seemed, sympathetic to us in general, and none a threat to us in particular, except perhaps what I heard from the woman in blue. We had to depend on what we could read in their faces, as much as on their words, many of which, since they spoke quickly, we didn't understand.

Afterward, sitting on our cots, we compared impressions. My

mother and Imma, who relied primarily on faces, were sure we had something to fear from the woman in blue—she would leave the convent and bring the SS. I began to believe they were right. Distracted by the Jewish children, I'd almost ignored the Gentile adults, whom, if I'd really remembered my father's words, I'd have watched.

In early afternoon we went to the Mother Superior, saying we'd leave before we were trapped. We would dress in all of our clothes, since we didn't have many, and leave without any bags, as if we were out for a stroll. We'd go back to where we had been, and from there to wherever the rabbi—or perhaps the Bellinis—could find us a place. The Mother Superior thanked us and wished us success, but if we had to, she said, we could come back for the night.

Now, bundled against the winter, the worst of the trip wasn't the cold or the fear of the Germans. The worst was the distance. Imma and Daniel were soon exhausted, and my mother carried Daniel, until Imma, calling up a strength she hadn't had in years, took him out of her arms and into her own. After a while she gave up. She clung to me, her hand heavy on my arm, and Daniel walked beside my mother, holding her hand and whimpering, while my mother said, more than once, "But that woman is farther and farther away."

I had stopped thinking of the woman. I kept my eyes on the names of the streets, recalling the day in Lyons when Eva and I had fled from the round-shouldered, green-faced neighbor and found we were lost. Aside from learning the streets, I wanted to get to the villa and pray.

I wanted to pray for Luciana, in Hebrew, but I didn't have any idea of what prayer I should say. The ones I knew were those for the Sabbath, and the *Sh'ma,* which declares that there is a single God, so those were the ones I thought I might say, and God would know what I meant.

And I wanted to pray for the nuns at the Carmine, but I wondered if Catholic prayers must be said in a church. I would ask Signora Bellini, without, of course, telling her why.

We walked on, along a route a little different from the nun's suggested one. My mother didn't believe there was anyone following, but Imma insisted we go by this improvised route. She couldn't say why, but her heart had told her we should, and now my mother wouldn't dispute my grandmother's heart.

As we came to each new intersection, Imma hesitated, looking up and down the streets for Germans, searching for safety and not being sure where it lay, and therefore turning or not turning, as instinct decreed. She probably didn't add to the distance, but she must have increased my mother's fear.

And yet in a way—for me—having nothing to say about the decisions was good. I spent the time on a different decision entirely: I'd persuade my mother—by raising the question in front of Signora Bellini—to let the signora take me to church. My mother, embarrassed, would hardly refuse. In the church, I could properly pray for the nuns, and since anyone knew I couldn't get into the synagogue, I'd pray for Luciana with Jewish prayers. Once I had made the decision, my anxiety eased.

Then, where the riverside road and Viale Michelangelo come together, my spirits soared. We couldn't see the Bellinis' house, but I could feel the comfort of an openhearted welcome, the warmth of a fire, and the freedom of lots of interior space enclosed by the safety of walls. I started to run.

"Wait!" my mother called. I ran back. She was breathing hard. "The rest," she said, "you'll do by yourself. Go to the house. Whoever answers the door, if it's a servant you'll say in Italian, 'Please, may I see Signora Bellini?' That's all. If then the Bellinis are there, tell them we're here, and may we come in. If they've gone away, and if it's the Germans, God forbid, or Italian policemen, tell them, *'Mi scusi,'* and come right back."

I walked by myself to the house, listened at the door for several seconds, but didn't hear a sound. I rang the bell and found myself facing a German soldier.

"Mi scusi," I said. "I need the Bellinis."

"Not here," he said, with a wave of his hand, and closed the door.

I went back. "Germans," I said.

We turned around. We knew we'd get into the convent again, but we didn't know what we could say to the guests if they asked us where we had gone.

"Why don't we say we wanted to see the cathedral?" I asked.

"Sightseeing?" Imma said. "On a cold day like this? They'd think we were crazy."

"To pray," I said.

Imma said, "Ach," dismissing it entirely, but my mother, after a while, said, "It's a good idea."

Almost two hours later we were back at the convent, and, as she had promised, the Mother Superior let us come in.

I didn't know the verb for "pray," so without having warned my mother I'd do this, I asked the Mother Superior, "Where do the sisters talk to God?"

"Vuoi dire pregare? Dove preghiamo?"

"Sì."

"Nella cappella!"

I wasn't sure what *cappella* meant. When we left her, my mother, who had understood my simple question, said, "What a foolish question you asked."

"Well, I didn't know," I said, "and I was curious."

"You could have asked *me*. They pray in a chapel, where else? It's that room over there."

When we came to the table for dinner, our faces still red from the cold, it was obvious we were exhausted. Imma could hardly sit up, and Daniel was fast asleep, but food was scarce and the rations small, and they needed the meal.

My mother woke Daniel, and as he looked about the table, half-asleep and blinking, the women smiled, including the woman in blue.

"Poveretto"—poor little thing—she said, with too much compassion for me to believe. There was a momentary quiver of her nose, a broad, flat nose flanked by the mole, a quiver as if she

were stifling a smile. "Why?" she asked my mother—innocently. "Why did you keep him outdoors for so long?"

Gesturing toward me, my mother said, "My daughter speaks better."

The woman turned to me. "That was a very long walk."

"Because we don't know the city. We got lost."

"You should have asked our advice. What were you looking for?"

"The Duomo. We wanted to pray in the Duomo."

"Truly? I've never seen you in the chapel."

"No?"

"No. So did you find the Duomo?"

"Yes."

She didn't pursue the subject at all.

The meal was meager and over with sooner than I would have liked. We stood up and left, but as we reached the stairs I walked away, telling my mother, "I'll soon be up."

"Ruth!" she called, but I continued walking toward the chapel, knowing that—no matter what she thought I'd do, or how she felt about it—then, with so many eyes on us, to stop me was out of the question.

The chapel was dark, except up front, where there were a pair of candles, one at each end of a simple, narrow piece of furniture, a short, upright frame of sorts with ledges one above the other—something I had never seen and later learned is called a prie-dieu. Beyond it were stairs, three or four, that led to the altar. There may have been light enough from the candles to reach to the walls, but I doubt it. I wasn't at all aware of the walls.

A little frightened, I crossed myself, genuflected, and finally recognized pews. Hesitant, I chose one, several rows from the rear of the room to the left of the aisle. I knelt, unable to see if I was alone.

I bowed my head, and softly, for Luciana, whose green eyes

and beaklike nose I saw in my mind, I prayed, *"Sh'ma Yisroel, Adonoi Elohenu, Adonoi Echod."* Hear, O Israel, the Lord our God, the Lord is One. In the absence of a prayer to save Luciana's life, I offered the prayers I knew: I thanked God for commanding us to kindle the Sabbath lights, for bringing forth bread from the earth and providing the fruit of the vine. And because my Hebrew prayers were short, I said the *Sh'ma* again.

Then, putting Luciana out of my mind, I tried to picture a nun from the Carmine, but all I could see in my mind was a habit, the nun inside it eluding me. "Hail Mary," I said, "full of grace."

I said them all, the Hail Mary, the Our Father, and the Credo, the three together longer by far than my Hebrew prayers. When I had finished, I stayed on my knees, feeling intensely happy, convinced that what I had done was right. Compared to the talk in the dining hall, careful, dissembling, fraught with danger, the silence around me was lovely, and the darkness, mitigated only by the pair of candles, was like the starless Alpine night lit by occasional matches, when Enzo had taken us over the pass.

Here I could think of Luciana, whom I finally knew I had come to love, deeply, as if she were my firstborn sister. She had seen in me much more than I believed was there—more than I *knew* was there—because she had loved me, and not me alone but my father too, whom I longed for, now more than ever.

Behind me there was a sound—sudden, soft—a rustling as if from some tender leaves being brought indoors by the wind, startling me, unnerving me, as would a sign from God, and making me turn. A nun emerged from the darkness into the aisle, right at my side, and then another one behind her, and then another, and with nothing but that rustling of their habits, and the whisper of soft-soled shoes on the marble floor, a hundred or more of them, sisters, in black habits in a black room, and with a movement perfect and unbroken as a quiet stream, made their way toward the front of the chapel, each one genuflecting, taking her place in a pew, one to the right, one to the left, with no hesitation at all. With the crack of an elderly knee, the nun who had led them knelt on the lower ledge of the wooden prie-dieu, her black clothes now illuminated by the candles, her head toward the altar, bowed.

"Kyrie eleison," she intoned, raising the hair on my arms.

"Christe eleison," rose from the nuns, a hundred women's voices all in a single sound—pure, unearthly, disciplined, certain, safe.

"Kyrie eleison," the single voice repeated.

"Christe, audi nos," the hundred voices answered.

"Christe, exaudi nos," the voice.

On and on, in the darkness, the single, vulnerable voice, and then the answering choir always in unison, enveloping, filling me. I thought my heart would break from the beauty of sound.

Then, abruptly, it ended. The nun who had knelt near the altar rose, genuflected, turned, and left by the center aisle, her face as she passed me devoid of visible feeling. As if at a signal discernible only to them, the nuns in the row that was nearest the altar rose, moved—flowed—one from the left and one from the right to meet in the aisle, genuflect, and, side by side, move to the rear of the chapel. Then the second row, and the third, their timing in coming together perfect, always, till the last of the sisters had gone. I stayed in my pew, too overcome to move, and a nun emerged from a room to the side of the altar, blew out the candles, picked up the wooden prie-dieu, and carried it back to the room. Soon she returned, came carefully down the steps and into the aisle. She faced the altar, genuflected, turned and moved toward the rear of the chapel, just as the others had gone.

I stayed, and when my heart was beating normally, I rose from my knees and entered the aisle. From the far end of the opposite row, a woman approached me. Frightened, I stopped. It was the woman in blue. She nodded, genuflected, and left. I followed her out, and when she turned her head a bit and said good night I answered.

"Why did you go there?" my mother asked.

I couldn't explain. I had almost forgotten why I had gone. I knew I was feeling a terrible sadness and didn't know why. I looked for an answer, and finally, knowing it wasn't the truth, but needing an answer to satisfy Imma and her, I said, "The woman in blue. She was there. Now she'll believe we're Catholics."

My mother said, "Oh." She sat on the bed, took my hand, and pulled me down, gently, beside her. Putting her arm around me, she said, "We'll sleep in our clothes and leave here at night if we have to." I nodded. "Aren't you exhausted?" she asked. "Don't you want to go to sleep?"

I was truly exhausted, but, though I was still a child, I lay immobile and couldn't sleep. Something was wrong in what I had done, I was sure, and a thousand questions assailed me. Why had I been so moved by the communal prayers? I felt myself drawing away from my family, wanting Luciana, sure that she, rather than Imma or my mother, and rather than Eva, my only true sister, would know the answer.

Why had I sensed such beauty down there in the chapel, in that choir of innocent voices?—a beauty like that of the piano Eva and I had heard in St. Martin, addressing the high, unanswering Alps. It was there, in St. Martin, that Eva had warned Vittorio that there were things that never changed, that she would be a Jew, always, no matter where it might lead. Nor had I forgotten that Aaron, Ondine at his side, had said the same—so long ago—to her father. And yet I had prayed in a church, fervently.

And for what? Would God protect the nuns at the Carmine? Because of *my* prayers? Would he protect Luciana? Whom could I ask? Not my mother. Surely she knew I had prayed, but she thought I had said the Catholic prayers as a ruse, only out of necessity, and I couldn't tell her the truth. How then could I ask what I needed to know? And yet, she was my mother. What had I done?

The night wore on. Daniel and Imma fell asleep, and then my mother, and later, much later, so did I.

IX

THE FOLLOWING MORNING, I PUT MY THOUGHTS OF the chapel aside. An hour before breakfast, while the other guests were in their rooms, we were called to the sitting room, where my father and Joel were waiting, trying with modest success to smile. They had been up since long before dawn, and Joel, thinner than ever, was coughing again, a rasping, body-rattling cough, worse than at any time I could remember, but in sheer relief at being together with nobody watching, and holding each other, no one referred to the cough.

As if we hadn't parted and were just continuing a briefly interrupted talk, my father said, "Disasters. One right after the other."

"The convents?" my mother asked.

"Including Luciana's."

Shocked, my mother turned to me. "Oh, Ruthie. I'm sorry. I'm so, so sorry."

"There's even more, much more," my father said, "but now go back. Put on whatever fits under your coats, and don't carry anything—I have bread. We're leaving the city."

"You too?" my mother asked. "Is that why Joel is with you? To whom can we go?"

"The people Eva's with, or if not, then to somebody else."

"But if nobody takes us, we'll have gone there for nothing—how can you ask it of Mama? Or Joel—he's already worn out."

He said we would rest on the way, and as we went to our room my mother said, "It's impractical. If we wait a few hours, Matilde or Marco will come."

But then, as we dressed in all of our clothes, she came up with a plan and told me what I must ask the Mother Superior.

"You will try again?" the nun asked, slowly, clearly.

"Yes," my mother said, "But, please," and pointed to me.

"A *padre* came to see us," I said. "Do you remember?"

"Un frate, penso, si. Un Domenicano. In white robes."

"Yes. Padre Cipriano. Do you know where he is?"

"At the Convento di San Marco. On Via Cavour, at Piazza San Marco. On the other side of the river. It's far. It will be hard for your grandma."

"I know where the Duomo is," I said. "Is it near there?"

"In that direction farther away. As far from the Duomo as the Duomo is from the river."

"Then it isn't too far," I said. "We can go."

"Be careful. When you reach the Duomo, ask for directions. Always ask women—men might be in disguise. And let me hear you recite the route—I want to make sure you know how."

Her concern was so clear that my mother, suddenly tearful, embraced her.

"Dio vi benedica," the nun said.

We joined my father and Joel, and as we left the building my mother said, "Joseph, remember who brought us the message from Rome?"

"You told me a priest."

With a child's sense of proportion and timing, I stopped them. "Papa?" I said. "The word for 'priest' is *frate,* I think. The Mother Superior used it."

My father answered as he and my mother had done when danger was farther away. "No, dear, 'priest' is *prete. Frate* is 'brother,' but I don't know the difference."

"That's all you have to think about?" my mother asked.

"Magda," he said, "allow us an innocent pleasure."

If my mother was shamed, she didn't admit it. She walked ahead, quickly, remembering the route I'd recited, not even asking my father where he had meant us to go. When we had caught up with her, she said, "Instead of crossing a city to someone we don't even know, we'll find this Dominican priest."

In a moment, my father agreed that for now, it was a good idea. If we could stay a night or two, he'd go to the country all by himself and try to arrange something else. As we walked toward the Ponte Vecchio, he questioned Daniel, relishing his childish voice and answers, and afterward me, ignoring my mother's request to hear what other disasters there'd been.

Then, at the bridge, we stopped, and as we ate the bread he had brought in his pockets, he said, "The first disaster was on Friday night. Don Casini went away—we don't know where—and he hasn't come back."

It was the first time we had heard the name Casini. It confused us—it was so much like Cassin, Matilde's name—and my mother stopped him.

"He's a priest," he said, "with whom Joel and I have been staying. His niece is there too, and she's heard—I don't know from whom—that he's under arrest."

"For what?" my mother asked. "Why did they take *him* and not you too?"

"They didn't catch him at home—he was with Rabbi Cassuto.

They both were arrested. And about Mario Finzi I don't have any idea."

"Mario Finzi?" she asked. "Who is Mario Finzi?"

He looked at her in surprise. "No one," he said. "Forget I said it." And this, of course, ensured that I would remember.

"But this priest and the rabbi," she said, "why were they together? I don't understand."

"They were *working* together—through the rabbi we were with the priest! But now the Germans will search at the parish, so we left, but by then we'd heard of the raids on the convents."

My father, however, knew only part of the disaster of that end-of-November weekend. Time was to tell us the rest.

On Friday evening, at seven, Don Casini, Rabbi Cassuto, and most of the committee had met at the Palazzo Pucci, near the Duomo. They had been meeting every day, always at a different place, to report and to take their assignments. Missing from the meeting was the Milanese accountant, Raffaele Cantoni, who—as often—was elsewhere, gathering the money Don Casini needed for expenses.

Most of the others had assembled. Matilde arrived a few minutes late, and the concierge, a woman, refused to allow her into the building, denying heatedly that anyone was in the room to which she said she meant to go. Minutes later, Matilde, waiting across the street, perplexed by how the concierge had acted, saw the committee come out, flanked by a group of SS.

The men were taken to Le Murate, the city's prison for men, and separated, each of them put in a cell that was far from the others. The two teenage girls, sisters named Lascar, were taken to Santa Verdiana, the prison for women. It was later that same night that the recreation center, the Convent of the Sisters of Saint Joseph, and the Convent of the Carmine were raided too.

The next day, Cantoni, hearing about the arrests, managed to find the rabbi's wife, and together they looked for anyone on the committee who—by chance—might not have been caught. They found Marco Ischio, the charming young man who had helped Matilde in everything—buying food, making deliveries, and visiting the convents, including ours.

He too, he said, had been arrested, but he was an Aryan, he'd proved it, and—acting bewildered—had told the Germans that all he'd done was blunder into a room that was not the one he had wanted. Just as they had arrived! They believed him.

He didn't know who could have been the informer, he said, but in the prison there was surely someone who, for a bribe, would agree to arrange the committee's release. He, Marco, knew some well-placed people, and he would do what he could. He'd meet them the following day in Piazza della Signoria.

At the prearranged time, the rabbi's wife, together with Cantoni, and with the husband of the rabbi's younger sister—the other young woman we'd met in the convent—reached Piazza della Signoria, hoping Marco indeed had arranged the bribe. Moments later, in the shadow of the Palazzo Vecchio, he was beside them—with the SS.

Anna Cassuto was taken to Santa Verdiana, where the teenage sisters were. Cantoni and the rabbi's brother-in-law were put with other Jews aboard a train, a third-class passenger train that was to meet a cattle car waiting in Verona. From there they were to go to Auschwitz.

On the train to Verona, Cantoni wrote a message to Matilde, who, as he'd learned from Marco, hadn't been caught. He threw the message onto the platform, where a witness retrieved it, as so many others were then retrieved, and—knowing the risk to himself—mailed it. The message was brief. Marco is a spy.

We, however, on the way to Padre Cipriano's convent, which, ironically, had the same name as the spy, knew nothing of this. Joel was coughing frightfully, and Imma, whom I had never heard curse, wished every German dead.

But what did *we* know of despair? On that very day, the SS, having promised safety to the Lascar sisters, took them home—by car, as if they were friends—to their elated parents, and then rearrested the girls and the parents as well, and shipped all four of them to Auschwitz.

We merely walked. At Piazza del Duomo, I went to an elderly woman and asked for directions.

"San Marco's a convent for men," she said, but she pointed the way, listing the names of the streets.

We walked on, and when we reached San Marco my father and Joel went in, taking Daniel, while the rest of us waited. In less than a minute, Joel called us, and we were in a long, gray, high-ceilinged hall with walls of stone. There were benches on each side, but before we had time to sit down, a forbidding-looking man in ordinary clothes came out of a small receptionist's booth. He led us away to a room with badly faded frescoed walls.

"Wait," he said, and the word echoed as if in a cave.

Years went by before I discovered that there, in that room, Padre Cipriano used to sit, and, with the seal of a Sicilian city captured by the Allies, he'd prepare the false identity papers with which he could ask for the ration cards needed for buying our food.

As he entered the room now, he looked at us all, and with a toothy smile for Daniel, who was falling asleep, he said, "Ah, you see, I'm wearing my dress." Then he turned serious. He knew both Matilde and Don Casini, and he knew about the raids.

"First," he said to my father, "we'll talk about you and your son. You can stay at San Marco, but you must promise me you won't go out. Some of your people are undisciplined. They want to see their wives, they go out, their accents are heard, and some have been caught. They endanger us all."

My father apologized, said he'd been hoping to leave, to look for a place for all of us out in the hills.

My mother interrupted. "Joseph, don't argue. There might be nothing better. We might even be caught on the way."

He said he was sure we wouldn't be caught.

"Listen to Joel's cough," she said. "He'll be burning up with fever—he shouldn't be walking so far in the cold."

My father was shaking his head. He wanted the freedom he'd had in delivering the boots.

"Listen," my mother said. "If you promise you'll do as he says, take care of Joel, never leave him, I'll do as you said with Daniel and Ruth. Otherwise, Joseph, no."

At last, defeated, he said, "All right."

Daniel, asleep, heard nothing of this.

"Now," Padre Cipriano said, "I know of a woman who'll take the women and girl, but little children cry, and neighbors hear. But I assure you—I know your concern—when this madness is over and you have him back, he will not have been baptized."

Evenly, my mother said that if it came to that, she would agree. But if the woman could see this child, have him for a single night, she'd see there was nothing to fear—he was more than two and a half, he never cried, he never got sick, he was not afraid of anyone, so couldn't they try?

He hesitated briefly. It was an attic room, he said, far from most of the neighbors, and though he had his doubts, maybe my mother was right. Yes, we could try.

We rested a bit, said goodbye to my father and Joel, and left for Via Torta, a narrow street that leads to the Church of Santa Croce. At a tall, yellow stone building, and after what seemed to be stairs to the sky, we stopped.

Before us stood Signora Pietranera, small, thin, almost bald, and with fine lines in her tiny face. She was Imma's age or older, and after glancing at us all, she singled Imma out and showed her to a chair. Daniel, making himself at home, went to Imma and sat on her lap.

Quietly—Daniel didn't hear—Padre Cipriano said he hoped signora might have reconsidered, might accept a child.

Erect, her heavily veined hands gripping her upper arms, she looked at Daniel. The boy, she said, was attractive. He didn't look French. He could pass for Italian. But the answer was no.

Daniel was talking to Imma, and my mother, with Padre Cipriano as interpreter, tried to persuade her, but the woman stopped them quickly with her slow, clear, simple language.

"You," she said, "are afraid of danger *to* the boy and want him to stay. I, whose house you want to keep him in, am afraid of danger *from* the boy, and want him to go."

My mother understood.

Still, Signora Pietranera added, it was late, and if we wished, we could stay for the night. Moreover, she knew of a childless couple, in their early or middle forties—good, reliable people, he a professor—who wouldn't take people like us, but perhaps would be willing to welcome the boy. If in the morning my mother was willing, she'd go to the woman and bring her to meet us. Later, when the professor got home, they could come for the boy before the beginning of curfew. If my mother didn't like the woman, or if the woman wasn't interested in Daniel, we'd all have to leave.

My mother was satisfied. She was convinced that Daniel, who was discussing the stove with Imma, would capture the heart of the good signora, as the little blond girl in Lyons had captured ours, and also in a single night. She was sure we'd be able to keep him. His mission done, Padre Cipriano left.

Signora Pietranera brought us food, and after we'd eaten she said, "*He* is a priest. It's his *duty* to love. *I* am an ordinary woman. I must know when to stop."

Still, we slept, all in one bed, tired from the march, unwilling to think of the future or even to look at the room. In the morning the signora came back, bringing us coffee and bread, but her mind was made up. My mother thanked her and said we would leave.

We went back to San Marco. Padre Cipriano had been called away, we were told by the man in the booth, but he'd be back in a matter of days. And no, nobody else could help us.

My mother picked up Daniel, though he wanted to walk by

himself, and carried him all the way back. We climbed the stairs, and when Signora Pietranera opened the door, my mother merely nodded.

Imma sat down on the chair in the attic, her head bowed.

"Play a little game with Daniel, will you, Mama?" my mother said. "Tell him what happened when Joseph started to read."

She drew me away to the far edge of the bed, where Daniel, distracted, couldn't hear. She'd let those people see him, she said, and if they wanted him, and *if* she trusted them to have him, Imma would take him aside while she and I—and they—continued our talk. She'd ask them to take his sister as well, because—though of course she wouldn't say this to them—otherwise, who could be sure they would give him back.

But we needn't have wondered whether we'd trust them. The woman arrived in midafternoon, a pleasant-looking, educated woman, simply dressed. In the evening she came with her husband, he somewhat older but boyish in manner, and both of them eager, fully prepared to cherish this child. Their name was Leoni, Alberto and Lina.

They carried a bag with bread for us all, and for Daniel a boat and a truck. Signora Leoni invited Daniel to sit on her lap, and he accepted. She stroked his hair, gently, and she and her husband spoke in the simple Italian they thought he would know or could guess. Bread. Cheese. Boat. Truck. *Cavallo.*

"Cavallo?" he asked.

"Cheval," I said. Horse.

Soon, they said, he would see the horse. It was out in the street. They had come in a carriage. They had borrowed a carriage to give him a ride. Behind a horse. A pretty black one. Yes, all the way home to their house in a carriage pulled by a horse.

Daniel was enchanted.

Though he protested, Imma took him aside, and my mother and I asked the Leonis the question—would they take another child. I was almost twelve years old, I said, and strong. Never sick. I could help the signora at home, lighten her work, and if I was with him Daniel wouldn't be frightened.

All we succeeded in doing was making it hard. They could explain a little child's arrival, but an older girl would ruin their plans. There were neighbors, they said. With a call to the local police, there were things to be gained by betraying us—*and* them.

Nor would they tell us where they lived. They were afraid of a "chain of arrests." Besides, since we couldn't leave the attic, what point would there be to our knowing? Signora Pietranera had a niece who'd visit them and bring reports. We'd see, the child would adapt, but reminders of us would upset him. The way to avoid any anguish for him was to wait till the Allies could get to the city.

The Leonis were both so nice, and the old signora so forbidding, that my mother agreed to whatever they said. Signora Pietranera had insisted, and in this we were sure she was right, that Daniel not be told he was leaving until he was well on the way. We couldn't assume the risk of having him cry in the house, or even in the street in front of it, where anyone might see, suspect what we were, and alert the police.

We would therefore all go down—my mother, Daniel, and I. We might be seen, of course—and the sudden appearance of strangers would need some explaining—but this was a smaller risk than a tearful goodbye. We'd get into the carriage, we three and the Leonis, and ride away. At the corner, when the driver turned to the left, we would explain to Daniel: from there he'd go with the lovely signor and signora, to their lovely apartment, so much better than our attic, and where *lovely* toys, dozens, were waiting for him. Later, when Papa and Joel could come for Imma, Mama, and me, Signora Leoni would bring him to us, and we would go back, together, to Vittorio's house, where everyone would be assembled—Vittorio, Eva, Nathan, and even Aaron and Ondine.

We rode away in the carriage, a black, rickety carriage drawn by a small black horse, Daniel on Signora Leoni's lap, silent with excitement. When we turned the corner, my mother began to explain, reasonably, calmly. Daniel was quiet. The carriage stopped, and my mother stood up, not hesitating for a moment. She kissed Daniel quickly, as if he were perfectly safe and leaving for less than an hour, but Daniel moved to follow her out. Signora Leoni grasped him, held him firmly against her chest, and as my mother's feet reached the ground, Daniel shouted in French, "Wait, Mama, wait! Why are you leaving me? Mama! Why?"

My mother stood on the pavement beside me, erect, throwing him kisses, demanding I do the same. The carriage started, and as we watched it roll away from us, so slowly that if we had decided to we could still have overtaken it, Daniel, hidden from view, shrieked, "Mama," and again, "Mama, Mama, Mama."

For as long as we saw the carriage, we heard the frantic screams. I think we heard them longer than the screams were really audible. Then my mother fell in a heap to the ground, and I didn't know how I'd be able to get her back to the house.

When we had left, Imma had seemed to be fine, but when we got back she was curled on the bed, her long gray hair entwined in her fingers as if to be ripped from her scalp.

"Imma," I pleaded, "I need you."

She lifted her head. Seeing my mother crumpled beside her with hands pressed to her mouth, she rallied. She sat up, bent down to my mother, and held her. "I know, darling, I know," she said. "Just don't fall apart, just don't cry. It would be terrible if, after all this, we were caught because *we* had cried."

But my mother indeed started to cry. "I did it all wrong. I should have prepared him—how could I have been so stupid? What will he think? How can he *live* believing I gave him away?"

After a while, she sat up. Imma and I sat beside her, each with an arm about her, each of us holding a hand.

That evening, when Signora Pietranera brought us food, she

said, "There's now an Italian SS. Anyone envious or resentful—any neighbor, any shopkeeper, any acquaintance—could betray me. No one is safe."

Silent, unforgiving, I lowered my eyes.

"Besides," she added, "it's better for your boy. Now he can live like a child."

We were not convinced.

Then, two days later, others were sharing our room. A young Jewish woman, born in Florence, had found her way to the attic. She too had a child, a baby of less than a year, and she begged the signora to let her keep him. She'd gotten some drugs, and she'd keep him drugged as long as she had to. There'd never be noise. The old signora stood firm, and the young one as well. She'd been staying a few nights here and a few nights there, her baby constantly drugged, until the courage of the people keeping them had failed. She now accepted the night of refuge, and the morning afterward, she and the silent baby were gone.

"The signora's right," my mother said. "Daniel's better off."

I, however, couldn't forgive. "I don't like her," I said.

"You don't have to," she answered.

"And *she* doesn't like *us*. She thinks that Catholics are better than Jews."

"She doesn't. And even if she did, I don't care what she thinks. I only care what she does."

Within days, I envied Daniel. At the convent, our room, small though it was, had been large compared to the space in the attic, and perhaps more important, it had been clean. My mother, repelled by the dirt, struggled at scrubbing the floor and walls, but, not having soap, she soon got discouraged and stopped.

Imma, strong when we'd needed her, again was weak. She sat immobile, all day, or lay in bed, waiting for the war to come to Florence, for more bombs to fall on the city and for men to fight in the streets.

But in early evening she would come alive. Padre Cipriano had come back, and every night at nine he'd pay us a visit. Once when my mother was ill, he brought us some medicine; often he brought us some food, and always a word from my father. "And Joel?" Imma asked. Joel was coughing, he said, but he'd been coughing before he had come to San Marco, so nothing had changed for the worse. God was our father, God would protect him.

Imma believed him—this handsome young man, who, to her, was hardly more than a boy. In this utterly unreal, unprecedented world, anything was possible—a Catholic priest could be sent as an angel of God. He had never suggested we ought to convert. He had found us this place, bad as it was, and it wasn't bad at all when he was there. "He lights up the room," she would say. And every evening he would come to us, bounding up the stairs, smiling. He came to encourage us, to tell us the worst had passed, that Signora Pietranera's judgment could be trusted, Daniel would be safe with the Leonis, and Imma believed him in everything, always. She wished devoutly—to his enormous amusement—that he would rethink his life, find a girl as beautiful and good as he, get married, and have a family.

To me her love for the priest—inconceivable before—was a sign that, though perhaps I shouldn't have said the Catholic prayers, I hadn't committed a crime.

I started to long for the convent. I tried, more than once, not to think of the chapel, but it fought to enter my thoughts, bringing the limited light of the candles, the sense of boundless space, the single female voice invoking *"Kyrie eleison,"* the unified voices answering, the sentences lengthening, one by one, gathering words that had to be heard, not understood—and all of it mysterious, hypnotic.

And with no guilt whatever, I thought of the room where we'd taken our meals. I heard the language my mind had raced to untangle. I looked at the faces stamped in my memory, each with details I couldn't remember. I dreamed of drawing, which I hadn't done since leaving France. Someday, when I could, I would draw the face of the woman in blue, her broad flat nose and shiny mole, like a small black marble stuck in a corner, sent to the spot by a boy's small hand.

And I thought about Luciana. Always.

One night, Padre Cipriano didn't come. Nine o'clock had passed, and then ten. Imma lay down and wept. More than four years earlier, when Germany had marched on Poland, Imma had wept for her children there. I had seen her cry again when Aaron reached Entraque, but not since then. Now she wept, bitterly, her head under the pillow to muffle the sound.

We tried to comfort her, and when her crying finally stopped, she said, "They've caught him. They're killing the angel of God."

We reminded her he'd gone away before and then come back, but she was sure he was in Florence, caught—she knew it in her heart. She pulled the covers up to her eyes and refused to answer anything else. My mother decided to let her be, but I was afraid she would die if we did. I talked to her softly, childishly, as if she were Daniel, and when I couldn't elicit an answer I pulled the covers away from her eyes. They were lifeless, unseeing, withdrawn from the world. She had aged a thousand hours in one.

"Imma," I begged.

I circled her with my arms, I sat up and stroked the back of her head, I talked, but I couldn't get a response. Time passed, half an hour perhaps, and from somewhere in the house I heard Signora Pietranera's voice—pleased but angry as well, almost a shout, as if at a young, irresponsible child. "You've finally come! I was so worried—where have you been?"

My mother, in a sudden ecstasy of expectation, pulled me away from Imma, threw her arms around me, and held me close in a quick, crushing embrace.

And then he entered the room, not as he always did, with a jaunty step, but with a long slow one, and then another one, on tiptoe, with his slender head tipped forward, a mischievous conspirator, his mouth in a large O-shaped smile as if he were saying, "Surprise!"

Imma didn't hear him come in.

Reaching her, he said, "Signora Levy." She didn't move. All at once he understood. Gently, he said, "Madame Levy. Oh, *ma pauvre amie.*"

She stirred, turned, and looked at him oddly with dull, expressionless eyes, and then with suspicion. Suddenly she recognized him. With tears welling up, she looked toward my mother and me. She struggled to sit up, grasping his arm, accepting his help.

"You've come," she said. "They haven't taken you. You weren't caught." And again she was ready to live.

He didn't tell her, nor did he tell any of us then, the truth of why he'd been late. He said he'd needed to visit some others before us, and though it wasn't a lie, it was an evasion.

He had, in fact, been caught, but not as Imma had pictured the capture. Someone in Florence had taken the train to Milan. On the way, he'd confided to somebody else, a companion, that a Padre Cipriano, in Florence, was protecting the Jews. Someone else overheard and informed the Milan police. They, in turn, informed the Florence police, where an anti-Fascist official, Vincenzo Attanasio, a Sicilian who had helped Padre Cipriano and Matilde many times in many ways, warned him that he would be followed.

On the night he was late, he had started in time to reach us at nine. When he was a block or two away, two policemen, as tall as he and twice as wide, came up from behind, grabbed him, and swung him around, and one of them, grasping his robes at his throat, pinned him against a house.

They told him they finally had him—they knew exactly what he'd been doing. How long had he thought he could work for the Jews—Italy's enemies—before he'd be caught? He said he had no idea what they meant.

Endless minutes went by, and, for motives I can only guess at, they released him, but with a simple warning—that if he didn't stop, they would destroy San Marco. They left him there at the building and marched away, noisily now, into the night.

"Funny, no?" he asked me in later years. "Like a comedy. Something to laugh at. But then, when it happened, I sat down in the street like a child. Kill *me?* Fine—I'm working for God. But destroy San Marco? Another matter entirely. I got up, walked away, kept looking behind me, took a different street, walked in all directions, visited someone who wasn't a Jew, then another one, just to make sure they had left, and worried about the *convento.* Then I went back to you."

But that was not what he said to us when Imma was dabbing her cheeks.

"And what if they *had* caught me?" he asked with a smile. "It wouldn't have been the end of the world. I'm only one man."

"No," she said. "You are our angel. You are our world."

I loved seeing him. I too waited for his visits, if not with the love that Imma had, with something resembling it. But I was a child, and what I felt even more was the need to escape, to get out of the attic, to depend on more than him, to do something other than wait, to see other people, the people I loved, people I didn't know, anyone, anything part of a larger world.

I begged my mother to let me go out.

"Out?" she repeated. "Soon you'll be twelve, and I have to tell you everything as if you were a child. People would see you. Even if no one informed, the signora would think they might. She'd tell us to leave!"

I couldn't persuade her—we hadn't been there for long. All the bonds that had been formed, between Padre Cipriano and the rest of us, between Imma and Signora Pietranera—this one an odd but powerful bond—all this had happened in weeks, and in the same way, every hour that we were confined was a day. One night, I awoke in my mother's arms, feeling her rocking me, hearing her hush me.

"Ruthie, wake up. It's only a dream."

It was the same dream, the funeral in Warsaw, with black horses and a black hearse, but the hearse was a simple carriage, the horses small and thin, and they weren't adorned. They were more like the one that had drawn the carriage Daniel was in. The coffin was small, but large enough for a body like mine. As I came more fully awake, I saw that the body was Joel's. I buried my head in my mother's breast, grateful to be in her arms, but refusing to tell her the dream.

I knew I had to go looking for Joel, and I didn't have long to wait for my chance. During the nightmare, I had wakened not only my mother but Imma as well. Afterward there was a bombing, not in the city but north of us, near enough to be heard if not to present an actual threat. We were awake for much of the night. The next day, tired, and looking for any escape, my mother and Imma went back to sleep, close together for warmth. I, tired or not, opened the door and left. On the way down, I met a woman, said a polite *buongiorno,* and went on my way.

I went to San Marco to ask about Joel, hoping I'd see my father and him. Hoping to visit was foolish, and I knew it as soon as I looked at the man in the booth. Though I hesitated at the mention of a visit, he didn't hesitate to tell me no.

But asking him more about Joel was easy. I had learned the language Luciana had given me—nouns like "refugee" and "prisoner," adjectives like "wounded," verbs for "capture," "kill," "shoot," "massacre," "ambush"—verbs I hadn't yet had occasion to hear. The simple, everyday *morto* was easy.

"Dead?" the man asked. "Your brother's a boy. Why would he be dead?"

I didn't know the word for "cough," so I showed him.

"Oh, that," he said with annoyance. "That's not dead! That's only *tossire!*"

I left, satisfied, indeed rather pleased that Joel was coughing. He was accustomed to coughing, and to being confined because of it, so being confined for coughing wouldn't be half as oppressive as being confined for being a Jew. Nor could he be bored with my father, who was surely giving him more to do than he would have liked.

From satisfied I graduated to triumphant. The nightmare had

changed my life. I had been close to my father and Joel, and I hadn't been caught, so I wouldn't allow my mother and Imma to keep me up in the attic forever.

I walked to the Duomo and around it, and around it again, under the eyes of the Germans, who ignored me, across to the Baptistry and around it, back and forth between them, and just as I started to leave the piazza a group of what I believed to be tourists, led by a guide, passed me.

I was thinking I might join them, when one, a slender, wall-eyed woman, faced me. I had seen her before—there was no mistaking her face. She had waited behind us in Nice, at the reception center, where she had talked with Bernard and Yvette. My heart leaped. These people were refugees—going toward safety—and the Germans didn't know. I flung out my arms and whirled around in a circle, triumphant again, and left. I ran to Piazza della Signoria and around it, too excited to stroll, looking at the clock on the Palazzo Vecchio, at the *Perseus,* the *Biancone,* the replica of *David,* the pigeons soiling them all.

Here and there on the buildings warnings were posted, threatening death to traitors—anyone who helped deserters, anti-Fascists, Jews. Still, people were out in the streets, everywhere. I had known they'd be there, and yet it amazed me that others were living like normal humans—normal for wartime, that is—hungry, needing some soap for a bath, some shoes that would fully enclose their feet, thread for mending the holes in their clothes—but out in the open, without any reason to hide.

I listened to what they were saying, understanding most of it, knowing I would recognize a danger to my safety, aware that Luciana had done this for me. Walking among them gave me the feeling of being like them, and I wanted the feeling to last.

I thought of Ondine and Aaron, and of Nathan, wondering if they, by now, had learned Italian too. And then I thought of Theo, who had probably learned some Italian before, through his sister in Rome.

Nicole, safe with a Catholic friend, was distraught when her husband didn't come back, and the friend began to regret she had taken them in. Someone would hear the commotion, become suspicious, and she herself, uninterested in politics, would have to pay. She asked them to leave—there were limits to friendship.

Nicole became quiet, promised that no one would hear her again, and the woman appeared to relent. It was then that Theo and Nathan went out to Via Sicilia, to the new office of the Delasem, and, through Padre Maria Benedetto, sent us the message.

Then, during the next week, only the friend went out and gathered what news she could. The previous month, the Germans had captured the *carabinieri* barracks, and they and the Fascist militia had taken over patrolling the city. Now they were everywhere, and Italian men—those of an age to serve in the army, or in forced labor, and afraid they'd be caught in the manhunts—had gone into hiding, she didn't know where. Later it came to be known. They, and Jews, and officers, and members of the recent Fascist government who now were enemies of Mussolini, were hiding in cellars, caves, the catacombs, and even the domes of churches.

One day, the friend announced she was tired of harboring Jews. She hadn't been able to paint with a houseful of people—all of them idle, solemn, grieving.

The next morning, Nathan went off to Via Sicilia. Near dusk, when he got back, excited and happy, he was dressed in the Capuchin habit. He took Nicole, Theo, and the baby to a building on Via Madonna dei Monti, where a middle-aged woman was waiting.

"Her name is Signora Locieco," he said. "You're her nephew and niece. But despite what we're paying, we can't be sure of how long she'll be willing to keep you. Try not to get on her nerves."

He, however, would stay with the Capuchins. "I can help

Maria Benedetto, and I don't need Italian. In Rome there have always been foreigners—students, priests—studying, living with Latin, which I do know."

"Be careful," Theo said, "you're too excited—you'll get caught."

"I won't. And if I do, I do."

Theo said he would join him as soon as Nicole was ready to be by herself. "But if something should happen to either of us, the other should know what message to give. If it's you, what should I say to your parents?"

Nathan refused to answer, but later, at Signora Locieco's apartment, when he had given them Vittorio's address and was about to leave, he said, "Theo, about the message . . ." But he was having a difficult time beginning it. "I don't expect us to die, either of us, but if I do, there's something I'd like them to know. It's about Aaron and me. You know the way we were raised—*I* was the one to look after *him.* But I always wanted to *be* like him, even though it wasn't *in* me. Flavio said we wouldn't be able to get past the Germans to meet the Allies, so I didn't try, but Aaron got through—I just *know* it—either to them or the Partisans. But now I don't mind. *This* is what I was meant for—to help Maria Benedetto—and it's just as good as what Aaron will do. That's what I want my father to know."

"It's strange," Theo said. "*My* message is also about him—him and me."

"I thought it would be for Eva."

"No, for your father, about Aaron—*I* was supposed to take care of him too, remember?" He too was finding it hard to begin. "In the Resistance," he said, "at first, after we left Lyons, I was afraid. Not of dying, but of being remembered because of my leg. Of torture. Of betraying my friends. Then the wife of one of the men gave birth, and this fellow gave me a gift—something that, now, he wouldn't use. It was a cyanide pill. I stopped being afraid, but I never told Aaron why. But before I left for the Jewish Resistance, I wrote him a note, padded it, made it look like a letter, but it was the pill, and the note explained it was meant for him or Ondine, whoever he wanted to have it. At the time it seemed right—I had left him, broken my word to your father. But now I don't know. If he uses it, I want your parents and Imma to know that, right or wrong, I was trying to help him."

"Okay," Nathan said.

"And about Eva—so much time is gone. Do I stand a chance?"

"I don't know, Theo. She met someone else. The address I gave you is his."

"Then what's the point? If there's ever a future, I'll speak for myself."

All this, like so much of what was happening in Florence, I learned only later. But then, out in the streets, luxuriating in the sense of being normal, I thought of nothing but whether they spoke Italian.

It was only when I started back that I began to worry about myself. My mother had been adamant. I had been lucky, she said, on the day I had gone on the walk with Luciana. If now I went out by myself, and if a soldier or policeman stopped me, he'd know what I was.

When I climbed the stairs, Signora Pietranera was up in the attic. I assumed the neighbor had told her she'd seen me, but I didn't have time to find out, because my mother, without asking for an explanation, seized me and between clenched teeth said, and then repeated, "After I gave Daniel away?"

Then, with Signora Pietranera watching, she gave me the honor of being the first of the Levy children ever beaten by either one of our parents. On and on—the blows and, separating them, the question. I didn't utter a cry, and when my mother was finished, she was exhausted and unrepentant. I was younger, self-absorbed, and unrepentant too.

X

I WASN'T ANGRY AT MY MOTHER, AND I KNEW SHE'D GET over her rage at me. Signora Pietranera, however, said I must go—at once—so my mother's goodbye was simple and quick, without so much as a parting embrace. Had we had a few minutes alone, I think we'd have put the conflict behind us, but we weren't allowed to delay. Imma, not having punished me, could be a little more affectionate, and she was, but in deference to my mother, she only kissed me lightly and said, "Be good."

Signora Pietranera waited and watched, but I didn't resent her, or, if I did, I don't remember it now. This ordinary, barely educated woman, who had said her love had limits, had been going from grocer to grocer, baker to baker, buying one thing here and one thing there, partly because of the shortage of food but mostly in order to hide the amount.

Before we were out of the building, we met a neighbor, who peered at us both—for a good deal longer than she'd spent in greeting us—and, suddenly looking wise and complacent, went on her way.

Out in the cold I walked beside the signora slowly, holding myself to her pace, grateful not to be punished further with words. I needn't have worried. She was saving her words for my mother and Imma. She respected my mother for parting with Daniel, and to Imma, in fact, she was soon profoundly devoted. Two old women, they found each other through a dozen simple words—"widow," "son," "pain," "God," and a handful more. The signora wouldn't allow me to translate, to help them add to the little they knew of each other, as if language might intrude on something far more basic. Now, as distant from me as ever, she didn't offer a clue as to where we were going, and yet, because of Imma's and my mother's faith in her, I wasn't afraid.

The walk was a long one, over streets I didn't know, whose names I memorized—my lesson from Lyons—and then over streets I knew, over the Ponte Vecchio to a tall, brown, ugly building in the dismal working-class neighborhood close to the Carmine. Only then did the signora speak to me.

"You have to stay here, you hear? You mustn't come back to my house till Florence is free." And in a muttered aside to the walls, "If the bombs haven't killed us by then."

Again we were climbing an endless succession of stairs. The woman who opened the door at the top was thirty or less—short, not heavy, but broad-hipped and large-bosomed—and with a dark, round face that was pretty enough.

Without a *buongiorno* or smile, and with neither addressing the other by name, they entered a kitchen smelling of garlic, and I, uninvited, followed them in.

With a glance at me, the woman asked Signora Pietranera, "What do you want?"

"You're not afraid of anything," she said, "so hide her. She's a Jew. French."

"Are you mad? There's a Fascist official downstairs."

"Why should he know she's here?"

"Why don't you keep her yourself?"

"You're the one who's brave." Then, relenting, "I already have two of them, her mother and grandmother both. But *this* one . . ." She told her what I had done. "She's spoiled, she has to have something to do. Somebody new to talk to."

"In French? Me?"

"In Italian. What she wants to understand, she does. Maybe with you she'll learn to behave."

"And if not? What do I do? Tie her down?"

"If you have to, yes. If we're all alive when the Germans are gone, no one will care."

Annamaria—I learned her name only later—studied the older signora. "Where did you get them?"

"A priest."

"Priests! You and your priests."

"And you and your communists!"

"Better than priests."

"According to you!" Then, quietly, "From San Marco."

Annamaria, poised for another rejoinder, stopped before it emerged. Thinking, deciding, she said, "All right."

I wondered why "San Marco" had made a priest acceptable, if indeed it had. I also wondered if my hour or two of freedom had been worth all this. I really believed she'd tie me down if I didn't behave. Nor did I understand the strained relationship between the women, and I knew I couldn't ask.

It was Annamaria who asked the questions, but not in the older signora's presence and not at once. For a quarter hour or so, while she worked at the stove with her back toward me, I didn't move. At last, she pointed to a chair and sat across from me, her elbows on the table, her chin in the palms of her hands. She was staring at me with squinting eyes, as if gauging how thick a rope she would need. For this, I thought, for this I've given up Imma and my mother. I lowered my eyes. Act brave, Luciana had said.

I lifted my head and tossed my hair—as if I were indeed Luciana, green eyes, beaklike nose, and unlimited nerve. Annamaria was staring, even now, so I stared back. Seconds passed, but I would not look down.

"How much Italian do you know?" she asked.

"Everything."

She rolled her eyes in a way that said I was hopeless. "How old are you?"

"Fourteen."

"You are not. You have no breasts."

I didn't recognize the word.

She grabbed her own, fiercely, proudly, and thrust them before me. "These! And you think you know everything."

Hesitating for a second, I said, "My mother doesn't have any either."

"I don't believe you."

I shrugged.

"Tell me about your family."

"What should I tell?"

"Are there priests in your family?"

"Nessun prete e nessun frate," I said, showing off, making it clear I knew both of the words. "We're Jews."

"Stop!" she said. "Act superior to *me,* and you'll be sorry, you'll see. I meant *Jewish* priests."

She had shown me some limits. Yielding a little, I said, "No, signorina. No rabbis."

She paused, putting down her anger, and I remembered she'd taken me in at risk to herself. I decided not to fight her so hard.

At last she asked, "Any communists?"

"I don't know. In France I had a cousin who was . . . in French we say *socialiste."*

"Socialista," she said with condescension, "is not the same as

comunista, but for now it will do. But I meant closer relatives, here—are there relatives in Italy?"

I paused. Signora Pietranera knew a lot and might, if asked, reveal it.

"I think so," I said.

"You think so. Where do you think they are?"

"I really don't know. We separated, and we didn't tell each other. Except that my mother and grandmother, both, are with Signora Pietranera."

"That I *already* know. What other relatives?"

"A sister and some brothers. And my father."

"Where are your brothers?"

"I don't know."

"And where is your father?"

"I really don't know."

She was shaking her head in amazement. "Are you really fourteen?"

"Yes."

"Then you're not only spoiled, you're stupid. You *don't* know everything. Your Italian is atrocious."

There was no mistaking the words. *Stupida* and *atroce* in Italian, *stupide* and *atroce* in French. I would have been far less hurt to hear I was ugly.

At last, fighting back tears, I said, "I learned Italian since September."

"September?"

"When we came to Florence. I had a teacher—she didn't tell us her name. Every day, all day I studied. For almost a month. Now I learn when I listen. Everything stays in my head."

"Well," she said. "September. Then it's not so bad." She paused. "Your father—what did he do for a living in France?"

I didn't see the point in saying Poland. "He once had a jewelry store."

"Of course. Was there anyone in your whole family who ever worked with his hands?"

"When he was young, my father used to fix watches."

"Very heavy labor." She paused for a long time. Then, "Why should I help you?"

"I would help *you."*

"I can find others to help. People who are poor—*those* are the ones who get caught. Who can't pay a guide to take them to Switzerland. Don't have the money to go into hiding. Work for their bread and have to be out in the world. Seen!"

Ashamed that we hadn't been poor, I couldn't answer.

"Where is your father now?"

"In the hills."

"With whom?"

"I don't know."

"So how do you know where he is?"

"He came to Florence."

"What for?"

"To see us."

"And when he isn't visiting, how does he amuse himself?"

"Amuse" came as a shock, and I didn't answer.

Probably thinking I didn't know what *si diverte* meant, she asked, "When he's out in the hills, what does he do?"

Uncertain, wondering if I was giving too much information, but proud, I said, "He makes boots. And shoes."

"No wonder yours are so good. And the others? He sells them for a million lire a pair?"

"No!" She straightened up. "No," I repeated, softly. "He doesn't take money. He made a pair for my little brother and me. The others he gives away to Partisans or allied prisoners of war who got away."

Half a minute or more went by as she searched my eyes. "Are you making this up?"

"No."

Sitting forward, she said, "Why didn't you tell me?"

"I did."

Again she shook her head in amazement. "My God, but you

are stupid. You should have told me that *before* I asked you. Haven't you figured anything out? Haven't I given you hints? Think hard. If you were intelligent, is there anything else you'd have told me?"

It was Signora Pietranera who had brought me here, but I *was* here, and this one was trying to break me. I knew I mustn't allow it.

"I'm not stupid," I said. "If I think of anything else you should know, I'll tell you."

She paused for a long time. "If I'm allowed to keep you, will you go out the minute I leave you alone?"

"No."

"Never?"

"Never."

"Why not?"

"I want my mother to know where to find me."

She thought for a while, and in the silence my strength returned.

As if having decided she ought to relent, she said, "As soon as you speak, anyone can tell you're not Italian. So when you went out, weren't you even afraid?"

"No. I look like a child—you said so yourself. No one would stop me. In the convent I *always* went out."

"Convent?"

"Before the Germans raided the Carmine. I used to take my little brother. Today, at the Duomo, a million soldiers were out, and none of then knew I was there."

"I don't know," she said, shaking her head. "I'll have to ask." She hadn't told Signora Pietranera she would have to ask. "Maybe I'll even let you go out. But only if you won't until I say you can."

"I'll wait until you tell me."

She stood up, went to a bureau, and opened a drawer. "Here," she said, holding out a book. "She said you need something to do, so do something useful. Read."

"It was *Das Kapital* in Italian. I knew I had passed a test, and that my father and Luciana would be proud.

I worked at reading the book, picking out the words I knew, and since there weren't many of those I was grateful that Annamaria ignored me.

Late in the day, a wiry young man arrived, who I assumed was her husband. His eyes were heavily lidded, sensuous, and they stirred me in an unfamiliar way. His name was Enrico. There was a long black smudge on the middle half of his nose, and I wondered what work he did and when I'd be able to ask.

From across the room he asked, "Who's this?"

"What's your name?" Annamaria asked me—now, for the first time.

I told her.

"My *suocera* brought her," she said.

Had I known a *suocera* was a mother-in-law, I might have understood the tension I had seen between the old signora and this young one who was living not with the signora's son, her husband, but with another man.

Enrico's eyes swept from my hair to my shoes and back to my hair. "Why?" he asked.

"She has to be hidden. She's a Jew, French, but knows Italian. Her father seems to be helping the Partisans, or that's what she says. Can we keep her?"

"Complications."

"She brought me her ration card. And money enough for some food. And she'll sleep in the kitchen, of course."

"But can we trust your *suocera?*"

"Enrico, please! She'd never betray us. She doesn't blame me enough to want me arrested. Besides, she got the kid from a priest at San Marco. To her it's an order from God."

"So let her keep her herself."

"She has two already."

"And our little Fascist two floors down?"

"Enrico, he still doesn't know about *us.*"

"All right," he said. "Why not?" As quickly as that.

He moved forward, and I hardly believed what I saw. What I'd thought was a smudge on his nose was hair. Laughter was building inside me; I had to suppress it. *Another* astonishing nose. I thought of Luciana's, of course, but this one was handsome by anyone's standards—neither short nor long, like a Greek statue's, but the middle half had hair like an eyebrow, perfectly even in width, with each dark hair growing downward. I knew I was staring too long and forced myself to avert my eyes.

They shared their broth, bread, and peas with me, eating slowly, silently. Whenever I felt I could, I glanced at Enrico, seeing how the hair grew evenly, neatly. They finished the food with a sigh, an audible wish that there had been more.

Annamaria seemed hesitant. "Enrico, listen, you know why she's here? She wouldn't stay up in the room with the others."

"What others?"

"The ones my *suocera* has. Her mother and grandmother."

Appalled, he said, "She left her *mamma* and *nonna?*"

"So did I! Why don't you listen? When they were sleeping, she slipped away and went for a walk."

"Why didn't you say so? I don't want her. If she ever got caught, *they* would trace her to us."

"No, listen, they wouldn't. She looks like any other kid. She might have been yours—look at how slim and strong she's built. And she always goes out and never gets caught."

"No! One of these days her luck will run out."

"Enrico, would you stop and think? Think!"

Suddenly he understood. "No, no, no. She's only a kid."

"She's not a kid. She's fourteen."

He looked directly at my breasts. "She's not. Look at her. She's a stick."

"So are you! On what should she be fat?" Her tone became cajoling. "She's the perfect age. She only *looks* young, and it's good. No one would ever suspect. I'll tell the neighbors she's your niece—timid—doesn't like to talk to strangers. That Fascist'll never guess."

I was suddenly frightened, remembering the woman in the convent and her talk of prostitutes. I stood up and backed away. "No," I said. "I'll go back to the priest at San Marco. He'll send me to somebody else."

"Why?" Enrico asked. "What do you think she wants you to do?"

I turned away, crossing my arms on my chest to cover my breasts, holding my shoulders, my eyes closed.

I heard him jump to his feet, move in front of me, and I thought he would seize me. When he didn't, I opened my eyes.

Annamaria was standing too, holding the edge of the table.

"My God. Do you think I meant *that?*" she asked. "A *prostituta?*" I didn't answer. "Why? Why would you think so?"

Both she and Enrico loosed a flood of apologies.

"All I meant," she said, "was that once in a while you'd deliver a message. A piece of paper. To friends, people like those your father's helping."

Still frightened, but beginning to feel some guilt for what I had thought, I lowered my eyes.

"You don't even have to," she said. "Enrico, can she stay?"

"Of course," he said. "Of course!"

It didn't take long for us all to calm down, and again I was sitting with them at the table.

Annamaria, still apologetic, said, "Would you *want* to take a message now and then?"

"Yes," I said. "Where?"

"Different places, but always in the city. It's good your father brought you the shoes."

"I can go tomorrow."

"No, tomorrow I'll do it myself. I'd have to teach you the streets of the city."

"I already know a lot of them."

"Do you?" Enrico asked. "What streets would you take to get from here to the Duomo?"

"Via del Orto, to Via del Leone, to Borgo San Frediano, to Via dei Serragli, to Lungarno Guicciardini, to Piazza Frescobaldi . . ."

"Mamma mia," he said. And I hadn't even reached the Ponte Vecchio. He turned to Annamaria.

Astonished, she said, "She actually knows. But she told me. She keeps it all in her head."

They started to laugh, recovering from their amazement, split second by split second, visibly. My heart was bursting with joy.

"What else can you do?" Enrico asked.

I couldn't remember the word for "draw," and I didn't have any idea that drawing could help them. I only wanted to show them I wasn't a fool.

I asked for a pencil and paper.

Enrico brought them, but instead of writing, which I think he expected, I started drawing a face entirely from memory, not looking up.

"What I'm doing," I said, "what is the word?"

"Disegnare," he said.

He watched, seeing a well-shaped head, heavily lidded eyes, a fine nose, and then I had a decision to make. I longed to be brave, to show the nose as it was, but I was afraid. It didn't occur to me that if he'd disliked the hair he'd have shaved it off, just as he'd shaved the hair on his face. I wavered, but then, carefully, I penciled it in, one short hair at a time.

With surprise, he murmured, "Annamaria, it's me. And it's good. Look."

"Yes. Enrico, she could do more than carry messages."

"She could do drawings and maps," he said. "A kid. Who would suspect they'd come from a kid?"

He leapt up, laughing aloud, and seizing Annamaria, kissed her again and again on the lips, on the nose, on the forehead, kisses of appreciation, of thanks, as if with her own two hands his clever girl had manufactured me.

Finally settling down, watching me do the sketch, he said, quietly, "I don't know if she can do a lot right now, but later, when there's war in Florence. . . ." He paused. "She will. But even if not," he added, taking her hand, "it's nice, *carissima,* isn't it? I'm happy tonight. Are you?"

His *carissima,* smiling, nodded assent.

I was carefully shading his cheeks, when, abruptly, he turned from Annamaria to me and ordered, "Go to sleep."

It was a quick command that wasn't easy to follow despite the mat he laid on the floor.

I don't remember feeling the cold. I lay on the mat in the kitchen, in my clothes, covered with my coat, listening to their sounds, hearing sounds like those for the first time, and convinced that a part of their ardor was due to me—to this new co-conspirator, different from the others, bringing a spark of mischief, of fun, to their perilous lives, a girl they believed was really fourteen, who, listening to them now, could feel the start of desire, as if she truly were.

By the next evening, Annamaria had found me a blanket and cot, and also by then, there was a change in the plans they'd been making for me. At work, with a printer like himself, Enrico had gotten a better idea. "Timid" was not a reliable cover. They were afraid if someone induced me to talk I might say a few innocent words and reveal what I was.

Instead, Enrico had brought me a card. It carried a handwritten message in German of sorts, as good as the Germans probably thought Italians could learn. On the reverse was an almost identical message in proper Italian:

> Please! My daughter is a good girl. She is a deaf-mute. Have pity on a mother. Do not harm my child. May God protect you.

The card was to stay in my pocket. If anyone stopped me, no matter who, I was to hold up my hand to tell him to wait, pull out the card, and, after he'd read it, smile and go on as if I'd been doing this all of my life.

"Don't smile like an idiot," Annamaria said, "but like an intelligent girl. Always remember you're deaf. If anyone *asks* if you are, don't fall into a trap by nodding your head. Just look patient and then go on."

"She knows!" Enrico said. "She knows! She's fourteen—my mother had a kid by then."

Still, to make sure I wouldn't do anything stupid, we practiced. Enrico was a German soldier, Annamaria an ancient neighbor first and then a friendly child, and then Enrico presented the worst scenario either of them could imagine, and therefore the one he had saved for last.

He played an Italian, one of the "they" whom he was afraid I might lead directly to him. "They" were neither Germans nor ordinary Fascist bureaucrats, but Italian thugs and criminals, more than a hundred of them, organized into a band in early September, armed, and assigned to hunt for Jews and Partisans. They usually searched them out in their homes and almost always during the night.

Their leader, Carità—his actual surname, meaning "charity"—was a notorious sadist, and from his headquarters, now known as the Villa Triste, screams and moans of men and women under torture could be heard at any time. Or so Enrico said, and, in saying it, he brought to my mind something I'd stricken from memory—the French Milice, whose reputation was the same. He added that cities like Rome and Milan had similar gangs.

Since the gangs consisted not of French or Germans, but rather of Italians, I only half believed they were really as bad as he said, and the half I believed I dismissed from my mind. There couldn't be so much danger, I thought, in Florence or Rome. Not from Italians. We had a glorious rehearsal, with Enrico playing not only Carità but also various victims. It was a rehearsal filled with laughter inappropriate to screams of pain, and I don't know which of us enjoyed it most.

When several days had passed, and I had settled in, I thought I knew my place in their lives.

They had taken me in as an act of defiance—not only against the Germans but also against the Fascists—and there wasn't a sign of any affection whatever for me. The badgering Annamaria had done at the start had suited her purposes then, and later, trusting me, she never repeated it. Still, their early excitement faded away, and they took for granted my talents, such as they were.

I was simply their colleague, young, not of the communist faith, and therefore inferior, or at least unproven. If Carità or the Germans caught me, I'd be weak, and they didn't intend to tell me more than they had to. They didn't even inform me that some of the Florentines working at freeing the city—men who were not of the clergy at all—were living at San Marco.

All they would do was write a few words in code and slip the message into a pocket Annamaria had made in a sleeve of my coat, inches under my armpit. They'd say the address, give me directions, and then I would leave. Soon there were larger items added, and by their shape alone I knew what they were—identity cards, false ones, of course.

On other matters, they seemed to perceive me, if not as an equal, as someone willing to learn.

One evening, Annamaria asked me—mysteriously—what I knew about San Marco.

"It's a Dominican monastery."

"What else?"

"It's where this priest is—Signora Pietranera's friend."

She shook her head in wonder. "Why did you go to him?"

"To whom should we have gone?"

"Don't you know your troubles *started* with the Church? That they preached the hatred of Jews from the start? That exactly this order—the Dominicans—led the Inquisition?"

I didn't know what "Inquisition" meant but thought I should, if it involved the Jews. "It wasn't this priest," I said.

"But why to a priest at all?"

Enrico was looking at her with amazement. "Why? Because a *convent* took them in! The Carmine took fifty!"

"Besides," I said, "There's another priest too. He was helping my father, but he was arrested."

"For helping your father?"

"For helping the rabbi. They both were arrested—he and Rabbi Cassuto."

Enrico was shaking his head. "Listen, girl. Don't expect too much from the Church. Maybe one man, two men, three, but none with power. None of them can do enough, and neither can these nuns. But the rabbis have failed you more. Do you know what that rabbi should have been telling the Jews?"

I shook my head.

In one of the longest speeches I would ever hear him make, he said, "I'll tell you. Months ago he should have told them, 'Go and convert!' Because it's the Pope you need, not a simple priest, and if the Pope were helping anyone, that's whom he'd be helping—the ones who converted. The rabbis should have been telling your people, 'Pray our prayers, but in private, and in public pray what the Catholics pray. In public say whatever the Catholics *want* you to say. They'll never know what you have in your heart, so why not?' If that's what they'd done, more of your people would still be alive. But no, you trusted the Pope to protect you, and look at what happened in Rome."

"What happened in Rome?" I asked.

Impatiently, loudly: "They've *arrested* the Jews—*that's* what—in a raid, a big raid."

I didn't believe him. Then, gradually, as my heart started to pound, I did. "When?"

"Weeks ago! The middle of October."

"How do you know?"

"Partisans *know*."

"They're in prison?"

"Jews? Prison would be lucky. They locked them in trains and sent them east."

"But not *all* the Jews."

"All they could find—rich, poor, old, young, French like you, Italians who fought in the wars, all of them. Not a word from the Pope."

As if I could undo it, I repeated, "All of them?"

"A few they let go—maybe they caught too many to take."

I stood up and went toward my coat.

"What's the matter?" he asked.

"My brothers are in Rome. I'm going to San Marco."

Enrico got up and stood in my path. "Brothers?"

"One's a Partisan, and the other one sent us a message. The priest will find out."

Defiantly, as if I had offended him, he said, "But why would he tell you? The time to ask is after we've driven them out—Germans and *fascisti,* all. What you need for tonight and tomorrow is will. You have to hate them on principle—do you know that word?—*principle,* for what they do to anyone. Anyone! Don't even *think* about your own."

I sat down, intimidated. I told myself Nathan was with the Allies, or with Flavio's family, or with Nicole, safe. Aaron and Ondine would be with Partisans, out of the city entirely, or with Partisans in Rome, people as clever as they. Then I remembered. The message! *That's* why Nathan and Theo had sent it—to tell us they hadn't been caught in the raid. Tears of gratitude came to my eyes.

"Go to sleep," Enrico ordered. "And if you pray, pray that we're not on their list for tonight."

But I wasn't ready for sleep. "Enrico," I said, "you said we should say what Catholics want us to say. But what if *you* get caught by Carità, and they torture you, and they want you to tell them the names of your friends. Then, to make them stop, will you tell them whatever they want you to tell?"

"You have a good memory," he said, "and you can draw, but you still can't think. Are the two situations really the same? Are the evils—do you know about evils—are the evils really the same? Answer me."

"Why aren't they the same?"

He shook his head. "Figure it out. And while you're doing it, go to bed. Annamaria and I have better things to do than talk about religion."

I would have wanted more from them, and I'd have wanted to love them both in return, but I knew I had gotten all I could get. I already had what I'd longed for during the days in the attic. I could go out and be almost as free as if I were normal—as I then defined that ambiguous word. I could even have taken a tram if Annamaria were not so afraid.

"Walk," she insisted. "Your father made shoes. On a tram, in one place, someone will talk and make you forget."

"I'll show them my card."

"And flinch from a sound and prove you can hear."

Enrico sided with her, so I walked, concentrating on the names of streets, of which there were hundreds I felt I should learn, adding them one to the other, building a huge indelible map in my mind. Often I'd be near my mother and Imma, near the Church of Santa Croce, but it was only on the Ponte Vecchio that I'd stop, rest, and think of the people I loved. I had been there first with my father, on the day we had gone to the temple, and then with Luciana, seeing the bust of Cellini, and then again with my family, eating the bread my father had brought. Everything there on the bridge had been good.

On one of the days I carried the papers, I was detained. The woman to whom I'd been sent was away, but her mother was there and welcomed me in. She was old and bent, and I thought she had gotten that way from carrying things too heavy for her.

"You want my daughter, don't you?" she said. I showed her my card, and she read it and murmured, "Aah. *Poveretta.*" Poor little thing. *"Sordomuta."* Deaf-mute.

I could surely have left the papers with her—she wouldn't have known the code—but she was older than Imma, and I was afraid if I gave her the message and documents she would forget I had left them. I decided to wait.

She was washing women's underwear—a tubful—pieces enough, I thought, for an army of women, and each of the pieces she scrubbed by hand, without any soap. She had large, ugly, almost purple hands. Every once in a while she'd look up. *"Poverette,"* she'd say. Now she was using the plural: poor little things. I thought she meant deaf-mutes.

There were too many things in the tub for them all to be hers, and I thought she was earning her living this way. I was repelled. I'd forgotten that there was a time when someone had handled our laundry for *us.* I pictured myself in her place, rubbing all the dirty stuff of other women's bodies. I looked away, toward the farthest wall, where a cross was affixed.

After a while, she lifted her hands from the tub and carefully rinsed them. Then, from a wooden box, she took a piece of bread, cut it in half, and offered it, urging, "Take it, child, take it."

I shook my head, more, I believe, because of revulsion than principle.

"Poveretta," she repeated, putting the pieces of bread in the box.

It was late when her daughter got home, and I gave her the papers and left, but before I was halfway back it was dark, and the curfew had started. In the distance I heard the shots of revolvers, probably those of the newly established Italian SS. I had heard there were twenty thousand of them in Florence and elsewhere—some of them eighteen and younger, recruited from the boys' reformatory, and now, suddenly, holding legitimate power. They had sworn their allegiance to Hitler and then been rewarded with guns and grenades.

I hurried toward home, and to shorten the time I chose a route I normally tried to avoid, along the Lungarno, in front of the Excelsior, where the German headquarters were. Soldiers were out in front of the building—two whose faces I couldn't yet see in the darkness—and one of them came to me slowly, with no appearance of threat. He spoke in a blend of Italian and

German, kindly, and the gist of what he was telling me was that I shouldn't be out in the streets so late.

I lifted my hand to tell him to stop and gave him my card. Another, taller soldier approached us, looked at the card, and went with it into the building, where there was light. Soon he was back. He looked at me coldly, carefully, and waved me on.

I was elated, and when I got in, Annamaria said they'd been sure I'd been caught. I explained the delay, proud of how well I had done—my whole errand, but especially my meeting with the Germans. Then, quickly, I sketched the Germans' faces, pleased even more by Enrico's open approval.

"Good," he said, "but from now on, stay away from the Excelsior."

As we ate, I said, "Are they really so poor that the lady has to wash clothes?"

"Sure they're poor," he said, "but that's not why she does it. Figure it out. I'll give you a hint. Your father makes shoes and gives them away."

I felt a stab of recognition. "But *she* gets paid for it."

He shook his head. "Keep thinking."

"Whose clothes does she wash?"

"You got it! *Prisoners'* clothes—you knew it, didn't you?"

"But she was washing *ladies'* things."

"Ladies can't be prisoners? That's what her daughter was—the daughter you met. The Fascists thought she was helping some Englishmen, prisoners of war—men who escaped from a train."

"Enrico," Annamaria said. "Enough."

He paused, but as I knew, though they both could be loud and volatile, final decisions were always his.

"They put her in Santa Verdiana, but she's smart—swore she had met the Englishmen minutes before, there in the station. All she'd done was answer a question—as pure as the Mother of God. The Englishmen swore it was true, so, after a couple of weeks, the Fascists thought they'd made a mistake, and they let her go free. *Now* do you understand?"

I still didn't see whose clothes the old signora had been washing, and Enrico, seeing me so perplexed, shook his head as if he'd been wrong and I really was stupid.

"Now," he said, "they let her come into the prison to visit the women she met. Politicals. And Jews that are caught in the raids. More and more there are Jews. Ladies. All of them ladies in Santa Verdiana, some with their children."

"They let her take the *prisoners'* clothes to wash?"

"Why not? Why should the Fascists care if she does the ladies a favor? She even brings letters and food. If they ever get sent to the east, it's the end. And the old signora washes the clothes, but not for money." He put his hand on his chest. "For *amore,* girl, you understand? *Amore.*" And then, as if we were still discussing the Church, "And she isn't a priest."

I wanted to say she was not a *comunista* either—a crucifix hung on her wall—but, before I could, the full weight of what he'd said fell in on me.

The laundry the old signora was doing was *ours.* I didn't know then that among those prisoners was someone I had known—Anna Cassuto. But I did understand that by saying *poverette,* plural, the old signora hadn't been speaking of deaf-mutes at all, but rather of the women prisoners. Tears welled up in my eyes, and I didn't explain that the tears weren't for us.

Annamaria put her hand on mine, the first time she had ever touched me. "What's the matter?" she asked, with concern that, for a moment, I believed was genuine.

All I could do was shake my head and wipe my eyes.

"What's the matter?" she repeated.

"Nothing," Enrico said, impatient again. "Women cry. She's becoming a woman—haven't you noticed? Her breasts have grown."

If he really believed it, his vision was better than mine.

I remembered the day of the truck, and again I was thinking of hands. We had spoken of Santa Verdiana, not of the Villa Triste, but I started to think of Carità, whose picture I'd never seen, but who, for me, took on the image of our neighbor in Lyons—huge, green, hanging over Eva and me.

Carità, I believed, would be led by his evil instinct to follow someone like us. He'd go to the house where the good-hearted, bent signora had offered me bread, and there he'd uncover the proof that her daughter had tricked the police. His eyes would be drawn to the mother's hands, large, purple, scrubbing the clothes, and thinking he'd wrench from her mouth the Partisans' secrets, he'd take her away—not to Santa Verdiana, but to his own prison, where he'd break her hands.

I was sure that a woman like her would never give in, but I had to find out if Enrico had told me the truth, or if, to impress me with the dangers to which Partisans were subject, he had made Carità and his prison seem worse than they were.

One morning, at the end of December, my errand took me into a basement. Near the coal bin, against a concrete wall, was a structure resembling a bookcase, with shallow shelves a person could sleep on. Each of the shelves had a padding of sorts and a blanket. Sitting on some of the shelves were Partisans, some of them women, all of them young, and all of them silent.

One of them jumped from his shelf and accepted the papers. He was taller than Joel, but he couldn't have been much older—sixteen at the most. I thought of the risks he took, and of the hardship of living in that dismal, dank enclosure, and I felt that my cot in a kitchen was more than I had deserved.

I had reached the day of becoming an equal, earning my cot, by knowing what these others knew, at least by knowing what the Villa Triste was. It was far away, and I hadn't told Annamaria I'd go there. Minutes before, I'd been grateful to her for my cot, but now I was thinking that she and Enrico had secrets from me, so I was entitled to secrets from them.

But the trip was longer than I had expected. I rushed along on Via Ricasoli, and then on Lamarmora, for miles, worried, but going on. I reached Piazza della Libertà, an unusual square with a vaulted arcade, and then a broad, tree-lined avenue like those in Paris, and finally found Via Bolognese. I didn't look at the numbers on buildings or see the facade of the prison itself. I didn't have to. I knew I had found it long before I had reached it. Uniformed men were lounging outside, one of them leaning, others talking and smoking.

I walked quickly, purposefully, looking directly ahead as if I were lost in thought. When I was close, I heard not only their voices but more—the start of a sound, muffled at first, like the voice of a man beginning to sing. It was coming from somewhere inside of the prison. I reached the men, and the sound rose high in the air and exploded around me, slowly, in a strange, slow, fiery explosion, and I knew it to be what I'd thought—the voice of a man.

It wasn't a normal voice but a howl, like the howl of an animal, near and distant both, a cry of pain that might have emerged from a wolf, or from a man of any age—my father, the rabbi, Enrico, the boy who had jumped from his shelf. I stopped where I stood, paralyzed. I knew I had to go on, but before I had passed the uniformed men, who continued to talk, again came the hideous howl, piercing, unending, wild.

I clapped my hands to my ears and turned, abruptly, and ran, and instantly knew Enrico and Annamaria were right. I had panicked and shown I could hear, and if anyone followed, the card in my pocket was useless.

I didn't look back. Now, finally, whatever I had thrust from my mind in the past few weeks was inescapable and real. Capture. Torture. Death in the east. And all—or so Enrico had said, and now I remembered it clearly—all because none of the rabbis had told us we ought to convert.

There was no one behind me, and still I fled, reaching Piazza della Libertà, turning at a corner, turning again, ignoring the names of the streets, intent on getting away from pursuers—only that, I thought, nothing more—as Eva and I had fled from our neighbor in France.

Though I didn't know it, I was also running *to*—to human

touch, to the arms of anyone who truly loved me. I ran for as long as I could, and when I was close to exhaustion I stopped. I knew I was far from the prison and looked around for the name of the street. I had reached Via Cavour, through both experience and chance, and I wasn't far from San Marco. Only then did I know I had run to my father. And at the same time, I knew that the man in the booth would send me away.

Nor could I go to my mother. I'd been warned I mustn't go back to the house, but I hadn't been banned from the street. I went there slowly, regaining my breath. The city had never been bombed severely, and now, from a tiny piazza, I saw that the building was fully intact. I sent my mother a silent message, and after a minute or two of watching I left.

I went to a baker's, to a grocer's, to other stores, hoping to see Signora Pietranera, and at each I watched for her from a distance. If she wasn't in Santa Verdiana, or in the Villa Triste, I would conclude that my mother and Imma were still in her attic, and all of them safe, but I wasn't able to find her and couldn't be sure that they were.

There were only Enrico and Annamaria to go to. I started for home, thinking I shouldn't have put myself anywhere near the people that they were afraid of. When I got to the bridge, I stopped at the bust of Cellini to rest. I sat on the ground, facing the lower wall, my back to the vertical iron bars of the fence that surrounds the statue, hugging my knees and listening hard for the river below me. I couldn't have been there for long when I heard some voices behind me speaking in Yiddish.

A flood of warmth engulfed me. I saw St. Martin-Vésubie, and Eva and I were strolling, seeing the Alps, hearing the children speaking in Yiddish. I rolled the name of the language around in my head, finding it suddenly dear. At last—though it surely was nothing but seconds—I was back in the present. I wanted to jump to my feet and announce who I was, but Annamaria had warned me not to reveal I could hear, to anyone, anywhere, ever.

There were two men, and they were waiting for someone who should have been there. They wondered aloud if he had again been arrested. What else would explain why he hadn't returned? And then, an eternity later, with relief as profound as if this person were their missing child, they saw him coming.

At least a minute elapsed, and then in unison, almost in a shout, they said, "*Buongiorno, Don Casini, buongiorno.*"

I leapt to my feet and turned. Walking along, he'd seen me and wasn't surprised. The others withdrew from me—shrank from me. For a moment their terror bewildered me. I pulled the card from my pocket. One of them looked at it, shook his head, and handed the card to the priest, who read the message aloud in Italian, repeating *sordomuta, sordomuta,* and, seeing the word meant nothing to them, tapped his mouth and ears and shook his head.

In Yiddish, one of them said with relief, "Oh, thank God," and then, with shame, "God forgive me. Poor child."

"Poor parents," the other one added.

The whole transaction between them was brief. Don Casini asked them how much they needed and gave them the money. They thanked him, effusively, and he hurried them off and faced me.

"I'm not a deaf-mute," I said.

"Then who are you?"

"Ruth Levy."

His eyes lit up. "You must be the little daughter. And the card—it's to keep you from having to speak in Italian? Where is your father?"

"At the Convento di San Marco, with my brother Joel. Weren't you and the rabbi in prison?"

"I was released. *Providenza.*"

"When?"

"Only days ago. Christmas Eve."

"And Rabbi Cassuto?"

He shook his head. "Unfortunately."

"Sent to the east?"

"No, no, no. I'm sure he's still in the city."

"Do you visit him?"

"Visit?"

"I met a Partisan. She goes to Santa Verdiana to visit."

"In Le Murate I wasn't allowed any visitors, so it's surely the same for him. And if not, if the visitor were me, it would prove we'd been working together, and that would be bad for us both. But where are you living?"

"With Partisans."

"Why don't they keep you at home?"

"I carry things."

"Things?"

"Yes, things." Then, "Messages. Documents."

"I don't remember—how old are you?"

"Twelve."

"Does your father know what you're doing?"

"No, but he'd be glad."

"I doubt it. Do you need any money?"

"No, I didn't come looking for you. I heard when they said your name."

"Providenza. But the people who are keeping you are rich? If not, I'll give you some money for food."

I thought it over and shook my head.

"That's why I come here," he said, "but you mustn't repeat it."

"I can't tell them I met you. I'm not supposed to talk."

"I'll be here tomorrow, at the same time or earlier, for about an hour. Is there anything else you might need?"

Without having known I would say it—or even that I thought it—I said, "I need to talk to the rabbi."

"On a matter of faith?" he asked. "You can't discuss it with *me?"* I shook my head. "You want to talk to a Jew?" I nodded. "Do you know where the Church of Santa Croce is?"

I told him I did.

"Then tomorrow, earlier in the day, perhaps at ten, try to go there. Stay at the top of the stairs. I'll send you a brilliant young man. Would that help, do you think?"

I told him it would, and I left. When I reached the far end of the Ponte Vecchio, I looked back, and he was still there, at the bars of the fence, looking up at the bust of Cellini and waiting for Jews.

XI

IRRITABLY, ANNAMARIA ASKED ME, "WHY WERE YOU gone so long?"

"I was planning to make a map. I went north—to see the names of the streets."

"That's ridiculous. There are *plenty* of maps—that isn't the kind we'd want. And the longer you're out the greater the risk. From now on, you'd better get back as soon as you've done what I sent you to do."

I wanted to say she'd been rude—she oughtn't to talk that way to a person like me, fourteen, her colleague—but I held my tongue, pleased that I hadn't revealed where I'd been.

My pleasure in that, however, vanished. Taking its place were the feelings I'd had at the prison. I sat with Enrico and her, hardly hearing them, hearing the howl. I wanted to tell them about it, and about the strangeness of the aftermath—that by going to the prison I had reached the bridge at exactly the time Don Casini and the Jews were there.

"On the Ponte Vecchio," I said, "I saw some Jews—I didn't speak to them—but I felt as if something had led me to them. Providence."

Incredulous, Enrico echoed, *"Providenza?"*

"Well, yes," I said, becoming defensive. "A miracle."

"There are no miracles! Only simple coincidence. *You* go to the bridge, why not others—what's the miracle?"

I gave up. "In Rome," I said, "is there still a gang like Carità's?"

"Yes, but if you're worried about your Partisan brother, stop. We're managing nicely, aren't we? So will he."

By the next morning, when I left on my errands, I had changed in a way I could not have defined. I was noticing things I hadn't been seeing before. In the past, almost all I had let myself see was the names of the streets. Now I was seeing the city, but in a new and desperate way, as if it were soon to be taken from me and I had to record it: the mist that rose from the river, the tans and yellows of the stuccoed buildings, Renaissance *palazzi* made of beautifully proportioned blocks of stone, the white of plaster and pink and blue of interior walls where bombs had fallen, heaps of rubble, missing cobblestones, bloodstains—wartime Florence.

And now I was fully conscious of people, any one of whom, no matter who, or how involved or not involved with politics, might suddenly, without a warning, become a victim. I stared unashamedly at everyone who passed me.

The bombing had taken some homes, and from everywhere—both Florence and the countryside—people were moving about. In the absence of vehicles, they were moving whatever remained of their things in whatever could move them—carts, wheelbarrows, baby buggies, almost anything at all on wheels.

A boy a bit younger than Daniel was sitting in one of the

buggies, a large elaborate lampshade wedged behind him, to his left a box of saucepans, linens piled from his lap to his chin. To his right was an empty birdcage, its door ajar, hanging at an angle from the one remaining hinge. He was peering into the cage, as if with enough concentration he could summon a bird.

When I reached Piazza Santa Croce, the sky was clouded over, a cold wind was blowing, and rain appeared only minutes away. I looked toward the top of the church's facade, at the large blue six-pointed star, and I wondered, as I'd done when first I'd seen it, why a Star of David would be on a church.

I crossed the piazza and climbed the stairs. There was a large central door and, at each side, a smaller one in front of which, in the ground, was another Star of David. I planted myself on one of the stars and waited, watching people pass, ignoring the church, as if it held no mysteries, as if I were fully accustomed to being there, meeting a friend. Soon a slender young man of medium height was beside me.

"Excuse me," he said—softly and with a smile. "Ruth?"

"Yes."

"I'm Mario."

He gestured toward the square, and as we started down he offered his arm as if to a woman instead of a child. I took it and, as I did, I thought of my sister. I was suddenly filled with excitement, as if I were she and, for the first time, taking Vittorio's arm, my body close to a man's.

I remembered my father had mentioned a Mario linked to the rabbi, and felt as if fate had given me someone to trust. He might have been one of my bothers—he even spoke French. He was shorter than Aaron but as dark and slim, with eyes as gentle as Nathan's. And yet, what I felt was utterly new.

"Are you Mario Finzi?" I asked. He looked surprised. "I knew it! My father told us your name, but he said to forget it. He thought you'd been caught with the rabbi."

"No. I was elsewhere, doing the job that was mine."

"What do you do? I won't tell anyone."

"No, Ruth, let's talk about other things. But I'm not a rabbi, you know."

"I don't care. Don Casini would have talked, and he's nice, but this—it isn't something I'd have asked a priest."

"What is it?"

I was intensely happy, and what had been troubling me only an hour before was suddenly distant. "I'm not so sure," I said. "Maybe I worry too much."

He stopped and looked at me oddly, a puzzled look that made me believe I'd wasted his time. I saw I had to consider what, in a minute of happiness, I had dismissed.

"Are they really killing the Jews they send to the east?"

"Yes."

"What I wanted to talk about is . . . I'm worried about my brothers, and what I wanted to talk about is . . . conversion."

He didn't answer.

"The people I'm living with," I said, "the man—he said we should have converted. That if the rabbis had said we should, and we had, more of our people would still be alive. And I didn't know the answer. What should I have told him?"

"That he's mistaken. He's thinking of Italy under Italians, Fascists, yes, but of the past, when Jews who converted were given exemptions. Now it's the Germans making the rules, and to them even converts are Jews. Have these people been trying to make you convert?"

"No. They say they're 'nonbelievers.' And they've been very fair to me."

"You don't have to convert out of gratitude, not to anyone, even for saving your life."

"It's not because of gratitude, but . . . Mario, have the Jews who were in Rome been sent to the east?"

"Where did you hear that?"

"From the people I live with."

"I hadn't heard that. I don't know. I know your brother is there, and I wish I could say he was safe, but I can't."

I drew closer. "I haven't told this to anyone: I prayed in a church. Catholic prayers."

"Did you?"

"In the chapel of a convent once at night. And it was so beautiful there, so peaceful. The sound—the prayers—lovelier than music. And it felt so safe."

"It made you want to convert?"

"For a while I think it did. But we Levys don't convert. When we were in Paris, my brother Aaron said he never would, and later, in St. Martin-Vésubie, my sister said it too, even though her boyfriend's a Catholic. Because why should we *have* to convert? And then, yesterday, I went to the Villa Triste, not to go in, but just to see what it looked like. And from inside, there was this . . . I heard this . . ."

I didn't want to describe it or even remember.

"Someone was . . . crying?" he asked.

I looked up at him. His eyes were filled with sorrow.

"Oh, Mario, it was horrible. And then I kept hearing it, and I couldn't sleep. I was worried about everyone—an old signora I met, and the Partisans, and Don Casini on the bridge, and my mother and father. And I thought: Carità is a Catholic, and so are the *fascisti* that my Partisans are so afraid of, so I'd *never* want to be a Catholic."

"But so is Don Casini a Catholic," he said, "and your Partisans—they probably haven't renounced the faith of their parents. That's not the way to decide on whether you ought to convert. And you don't decide because of a sound—even a sound more beautiful than music."

"But if it looked like converting would help—if my Partisan, even if he's wrong—if he said he was afraid to keep a Jew, but that he would if I'd convert. Then?"

"Oh, Ruth," he said. "Would that really happen? Do you plan to tell him you met me?"

"I'm not allowed to be talking to you."

"Then you can't admit you know—suddenly—that he's wrong. But you know him, and I don't, so tell me. What is he like?"

"When you get used to him, he's nice."

"Then I can't imagine his making such a request."

"But if he did?"

"All right, we'll consider it. Expediency—what may we do to protect our lives? In our religion, not only *may* we save our lives, but we're commanded to, and, in that, only three things are forbidden: murder, adultery, and idolatry. The question is: is conversion to Christianity idolatry? I doubt it. Surely not a conversion like this, not intended to last."

"Is that what Rabbi Cassuto would say?"

"I don't know. There *have* been Jewish martyrs, of course, people who felt that that was their fate, their privilege—to sanctify the name of God by dying. Even dying a terrible death."

"I'd never be that brave," I said.

"It's hard just to be an adult. There are terrible things to decide. Rabbi Cassuto might tell you conversion's allowed, and then refuse to do it himself. I just don't know."

"I think my father would say I could."

"If it came to that, I'm sure he would."

"Mario? I don't think I'll have to, but I feel better about everything already. It's like my finding Don Casini was a miracle. My Partisan said there aren't any, but there are."

He smiled. "Meeting Don Casini was coincidence. He's on the bridge every day, so it isn't so strange that you'd see him. The miracle is that—every day—he chooses to come."

He looked up at the sky, which was darker even than minutes before.

"I really should go," he said, "and so should you. It's going to pour."

"Please don't," I begged. "Not yet, Mario. There are other things too." Again we were walking. "About the Villa Triste. All you have to do is pass it, and you hear the screams. Why don't the people—the ones who are free—revolt? Why don't they do like the French when they took the Bastille?"

As if I had asked an intelligent question, he said, "Times are different. Unarmed people can't—every man in Florence might be shot. But a time will come, you'll see. The things you carry—Don Casini told me—I don't think your father would like it, you're so young, but those papers, they're like the boots he made."

"Were you ever arrested?"

"Yes."

"But not with Don Casini and the rabbi."

"No. Before the Germans came in. Before Mussolini fell. Badoglio freed me."

I was about to tell him about the old signora scrubbing the clothes, but an icy rain began to fall, and he said, "You have to go home. It wouldn't do for you to get sick."

"Can you meet me tomorrow?"

"No, but Don Casini will be on the bridge—you really don't need me. And if you like, send me a message through him."

"And you'll send one back to me?"

"Yes, of course. And be careful." He put his hands on my shoulders, kissed me lightly on the forehead, and left.

For a minute I stood where I was, watching him go, feeling I'd suffered a terrible loss. A minute later I was seized by joy. Don Casini would have said, *Providenza!* God had sent me Mario. He was handsome and young, he was my father's friend, and Don Casini's, and he had come to the piazza especially to meet me, and he had told me to send him a message, and then, *then,* he had kissed me.

I wanted to tell it to someone, but I knew I mustn't reveal it to Annamaria. For her I needed a plausible reason for being so late, but all I could think of was him, Mario, and any young woman who would understand what I was feeling—Eva, Luciana, and even Yvette. She had probably loved Bernard, despite what her father had thought, so even Yvette would know how I felt.

The rain had turned to a downpour, and the wind blew harder, but, wet though I was, I didn't feel terribly cold. I ran along near the river, and every once in a while I spread my arms and twirled around in a circle, my face to the heavens, crazily happy. People were huddled in doorways out of the rain, but I didn't have any desire to join them. All I wanted to do was shout my glorious news—that, and to run through the city, letting my feet announce my joy.

On the Lungarno Diaz, between the Ponte alle Grazie and the Ponte Vecchio, there was a large arched doorway crowded with people I didn't bother to look at. Before me, a taxi arrived at the river side of the road, and out of another doorway, a black umbrella opened slowly, and a couple emerged—a woman whose face I couldn't yet see, a small woman in a long black coat, bundled up, together with a man much taller than she. He was leaping toward the cab with long, ludicrous steps starting at his shoulders, steps I recognized.

"Yvette!" I called. "Yvette! Bernard!"

They didn't turn. They entered the cab, and I reached them just as the door fell shut. I spread my arms in a fierce embrace of the car and pressed my face to the window.

Strangers looked out at me, puzzled, silent, grave.

I backed away from them into the road. Chastened, I started toward the Ponte Vecchio, slowly, suddenly feeling the cold, while the taxi lurched from the curb in a quick explosion of sound.

As if truly deaf, I wasn't aware of the boots approaching behind me, until a heavy hand grasped my shoulder, making me gasp. A German soldier spun me around. He towered in front of me, over me, furious, as if I had forced him out of a shelter into the rain. I knew him at once. He was one of the two I'd met in the past, farther along the Lungarno, at the Excelsior Hotel when Providence had really been with me. The other soldier approached us too, but slowly, and stood at his side.

The one who was gripping my shoulder had taken my card to the light of the building, and here he was now, almost doubled over, his head an inch from my eyes, his cap directing the rain to my mouth.

"Yvette?" he bellowed. "Bernard?"

I didn't answer. I knew he must have been standing in one of the doorways—the one I had just gone past—and now that he knew my card was a lie I didn't know how to appease him.

He gripped my arm, pulled me backward across the road, and, releasing my arm, pressed my shoulder against a gate. In Italian he shouted, "Deaf-mute?"

The other one followed him, saying his name, "Joachim." They started to talk to each other, in German, ignoring the rain, ignoring the people passing us, Joachim holding me firmly and shouting, the other one answering softly, trying to reason, even to placate.

I couldn't be sure of what they were saying, except for a single, repeated, and unmistakable word. *Jude.* The second German nodded. I could see he conceded that I was a *Jude,* but I also could see he was willing to let me go on.

Joachim turned on me, angrier than ever, and releasing my shoulder, gesticulating toward my throat, shouted an order in German. I stared, terrified, motionless, trying to puzzle out the German words from what I knew of Yiddish. With both of his hands he opened my coat—not by unbuttoning it, but by ripping it open, starting with the button at my neck. Again he spun me around, almost toppling me, and grasping the collar, he tore the coat from off of my arms. He held it away from his body with loathing, as if it were covered with vermin, and searched in my pockets. He found my card, read it again, and it seemed to make him angrier still. He didn't discover the pocket that Annamaria had made, which was empty, but as if he believed my coat were a grievous insult directed at him, he crumpled it up as well as he could, darted across the narrow road, and threw the coat high in the air, into the river.

With hands on his hips, he watched for a while, ignoring the rain, and then, satisfied, he ambled back, as if strolling along in the sun. With a sudden change of face, a quick return from pleasure to rage that now I believe was deliberate rather than real, he shouted in German, a command I couldn't decipher and don't remember. Then, in Italian, and softly, his whisper an obvious threat, he said, "The last time, do you hear? The last time." With that he gave me a shove, turned to where he had come from, and, with his companion following, without a backward glance from either of them, left me standing alone.

"My God," Annamaria said. "My God. What happened? Where is your coat?"

I couldn't answer. I fell into her arms, and she sat me down on a chair and rushed for some towels, muttering, "Frozen, frozen." She tore my clothes from my shaking body, rubbed me dry, pulled her sweater off, and wrapped it around me, saying, "Sit here, I'll get you some more." She bundled me up in layers and layers of cloth, and still my shaking continued.

"Did somebody catch you?" she asked. I nodded. "The Germans?" Again I nodded. "Did they follow you here?" I shook my head, vehemently. "How do you know? Did you come right home?" I shook my head. "Did you go here and there, here and there, just to be sure?" I nodded. "Good," she said. "Then we're safe."

She brought me a glass and a bottle of liquor and held them in front of my face.

"Drink. It'll warm you up."

I'd gladly have drunk it, if only to show her how grateful I was, but my clacking teeth refused to open. She went for a spoon and came back.

"Up." Holding me hard at the waist, she helped me walk to my cot. She laid me down, sat beside me holding the bottle, and lifting my head with her arm she spooned some liquor into my mouth, through my teeth, spilling a lot of it onto my chin and the blanket, but persisting, never becoming impatient, telling me, "Swallow," with each spoonful, "Swallow."

As the minutes went by, and the liquor burned in my throat, my mouth relaxed, my teeth stopped clattering, and my violent shaking turned to a gentle shivering, less, I think, from cold and fear than from knowing that now I'd be sick, not in the care of my mother and father and Imma, but here, among people to whom I was sure I meant nothing.

"Drink," she said when I wanted to stop. "Better drunk than frozen."

Again and again and again, she spooned the liquor into my mouth. Afterward I slept—I don't know for how long, but when I awoke, at least a night had passed, and Enrico had gone to his job. Someone had changed my clothes again, and next to my skin was one of Enrico's sweaters, and on top of it another one, Annamaria's. On my feet were Enrico's socks.

My head throbbed, my voice was gone, and razor blades seemed to have lodged in my throat, but I wanted my leaf. With my finger, I drew an outline of it on my sleeve. Annamaria was puzzled, so I drew it again.

"Your jewelry?" she asked. "You want it? You wear it for luck?"

The answer should have been no, but I couldn't explain why I wore it, so I simply nodded.

She went to my clothes, which she had washed, and took the leaf from my blouse. "I put it back where you wear it," she said. "Who knows? Maybe you're right. You really have luck."

With the passage of weeks, I discovered what Joel had known for years—the pain of continuous coughing—but through it all, Annamaria never appeared to be worried.

"It's good they didn't take your shoes," she said. "This is only a sickness. It'll pass."

It did, of course, after a month or more went by. The nightmares, however, refused to abate, and I didn't know which was worse—the pain I had felt in my body when I was awake or the nightmares that still returned when I was asleep. Day or night, I lived with the hour on the street when, elated over Mario, I had caught Joachim's eye and felt his hand.

I had probably told them a lot in the hours before my voice disappeared, because, later, they didn't ask questions or even refer to my coat. And yet, whatever I said to Annamaria seemed to be something she hadn't yet heard. They were the things I wouldn't have thought I'd reveal to Enrico or her.

One day, as she stood at the ironing board, I said, "I have something to tell you." She stopped and came to my cot, slowly, apprehensively. "I've fallen in love."

With a quick expulsion of breath, a mixture of exasperation and relief, she asked, "For the first time?"

"Yes."

She laughed, but then, as if in apology, she said, "Good. But not with Enrico, I hope."

"Enrico is yours."

"With one of the Partisans?"

"Not exactly. Remember the day I saw some Jews? On the Ponte Vecchio, remember? They were with a priest. I heard them say his name, and it was the priest my father had lived with, the priest I'd said was arrested. So when they went away, I talked to him. I told him I needed to talk to someone who knew a lot about Jews, and he said he would send me this boy—this man—a Jew. And I met him and fell in love."

"Did you tell him where you live?"

"No. Do you think I would? Have I told you the name of the priest? Have I ever told you the name of the one from San Marco?"

"So what about this boy?"

"I was supposed to send him a message by way of the priest. Now he'll think I've forgotten him." I was hoping she'd offer to go and deliver my message, as I had been doing for her.

"How many times did you meet?"

"Only that once, because that was the day I got caught."

"But why *exactly* did the Germans stop you?"

I considered letting her know I'd been careless, but my courage failed me. "I don't know. Anyway, this boy, this young man, he said Enrico was wrong. That even if the Jews of Rome had all converted, it wouldn't have helped them."

"Yes, I know it."

"Why didn't you tell Enrico?"

"He's a man!" she said with a shrug. "They like to think they're smarter than us, so whenever I can I let him believe it. Who cares?" Then she added, "Listen. This boy. When all this is over, you'll find him, you'll see. The priest will know where to look."

"I know. I've thought about it. I mean, if he lives we'll find him. But so many people have entered my life. In Warsaw, all my mother's friends . . ."

"Warsaw?"

"Yes. It was too much to tell Signora Pietranera. Would you have cared that we started from Poland? But in Warsaw, all my mother's friends—from when she was a girl—they were still her friends when we left. But me, so many different people, in France, in Italy, and I don't believe I'll see them again. And I'm not even sure I'll remember them. One of my brothers told me I wouldn't."

"That's how it is during war," she said. "These friends of Enrico's and mine, once the shooting starts, maybe someone'll die. But I'll remember them—that I know. And you—the way you remember things—so will you. And with you and this boy, maybe things will be good. Why should you think of the worst?"

If Imma had been there, I'd have asked her to look in her heart and tell me if this was the worst.

One night, when I wakened from one of my nightmares, Enrico and Annamaria were standing over my cot, Enrico's hand still on my arm.

"Enrico," I said, "may I stay here anyway?"

"Anyway?"

"Even though I'm a Jew."

He looked as if he were solving a mystery. "You know, you have less in your head than you have in your breasts."

He didn't think his remark was funny. I had wakened him, and he wasn't amused. I, however, laughed—for the first time since I'd been caught. The laughter was brief and followed by tears, but though the episode ended with tears, Enrico's answer ended my nightmares.

More than my nightmares, however, had ended. In early February I was well again and asked if Annamaria could find me a coat.

"You don't need one," she said. "You're not going out."

"You could cut my hair. I could dress like a boy."

"And if they stopped you again? You're staying inside till the end of the war, and you'd better not try any tricks."

I was relieved, though I didn't admit it. I really didn't want to go out. Too much was happening "out," more than had happened before I'd been sick. Germans and Fascists were being attacked, and innocent people were shot in reprisal. Though most reprisal victims were men, political prisoners, I thought that because of Joachim the German the same could happen to me. I had offered to go only because I believed I should, and Annamaria's answer freed me of that. With nothing but a simple threat, Joachim had broken my will, and I truly believe that Annamaria knew it and spared me the shame of admitting it.

To her, what she called my reimprisonment became a kind of joke. She said I had joined the *sepolti vivi.* It was a term that, in the past, had referred to particular groups of nuns, women permanently cloistered, never in touch with the outside world, dependent all of their lives on a nun who was. It translated into "the buried alive," and now it referred not only to them but to others less lucky than they and I.

The new *sepolti vivi* were the Jews or anti-Fascists hidden away in narrow spaces created to hide them. A wall would be built in a room, a few feet in front of an existing wall, sealing off the person who would live between them. He wouldn't be there for any predictable time, but for as long as he had to be, and if the war went on at the pace it was going at then, maybe for years. In the ceiling of this doorless space, there was an opening cut to the roof—a trapdoor—and, through it, someone would lower the hidden one's food and lift out his waste.

I, who should have been grateful, had many ungrateful hours. I didn't understand, or had only forgotten, who I really was. The Italian Jews, in the decades before the thirties, had gotten accustomed to being accepted as equals, and some of them might have been taking for granted the help they were getting from Christian Italians. As a Jew from the east, I should have known better. I was aware that—compared to the *sepolti vivi*—I was free, but I thought of myself as deprived. There was so much I wanted, so many people I longed for.

Soon, Enrico and Annamaria sensed my need, and since now I was less of a danger to them than before, they were willing to tell me some more of what they were doing.

They handed me boxes of pamphlets urging the people to rise in revolt. As soon as the Allies were near, they said, they'd distribute them. Meanwhile, I assembled and packaged them, like a child who was helping her mother to bake. Next, they showed me some boxes of guns, and I knew at last that when I had delivered identity cards and messages, they had been carrying guns—often to the rendezvous the messages had specified.

They told me whatever they heard of the news of the city and areas close to it: Archbishop dalla Costa had gone to the German commander to say that the nuns—in taking the Jewish women into the Carmine—had acted on orders from him, and the Germans, with their respect for orders, released the nuns. *And,* with their respect for rank, released dalla Costa. At the Grand Hotel, which the Germans had occupied, a Partisan shot a Fascist militiaman, *and* escaped without getting caught. In Siena, however, boys who hadn't reported for duty when called were captured and publicly shot. On the roads leading into the city, cars were presumed to be carrying Germans, and therefore were bombed by Allied planes. On and on and on, and I waited eagerly for all this news.

They told me more. They told me the names of Fascist groups

who were searching for people like us in Florence or elsewhere—names I hadn't yet heard—the Koch band, the Muti band, the Decima Mas, the Guardia Nazionale Repubblicana, and every group, no matter where in Italy it was, bound me closer to them—to Enrico and Annamaria—in a way that carrying messages hadn't been able to do. I felt that by sharing this knowledge we also were sharing the threat.

In return, I spoke of my family far more freely than ever before. I told them about Vittorio, that his parents were wealthy, that he'd been an army officer but was now a Partisan, that I had brothers, even in Florence, whom I hadn't told them about. And yet—though of course I trusted them—I didn't disclose any names or where anyone was.

But one evening, Enrico, more agitated than I'd ever seen him, waved me away when I opened the door.

"What do *you* know?" he said with contempt. "You and your jeweler father, what do you know? Your sister's Partisan boyfriend, what do you know?"

Her hand at her throat, Annamaria quietly asked him, "Who, Enrico? Who was caught?"

She had guessed. The Italian SS had captured one of the Partisans, a law professor, a man they had worked with closely and greatly admired. For a moment Enrico was mute, unable to utter the name, and Annamaria said it for him in a horrified whisper. "Lorenzo?"

Enrico turned, approached me, and stopped a foot in front of me. His eyes were brimming with tears. "Your sister's boyfriend. He's an anti-Fascist? What was he doing before Mussolini disgraced the army? Answer me!"

"I don't know," I said, confused, frightened, thinking it was Vittorio who'd caught a Partisan, that all along he'd been deceiving us.

"The *true* anti-Fascists—not just workers, but professors like Lorenzo, who treated us as equals—they *always* fought the Fascists, not since *months* ago. No matter *what* the risk. You know why? On principle! Remember that word? Because this is Florence, where there are men of principle, and where was *he,* this boyfriend of your sister's, where?"

I stood like a stone.

His voice getting quieter, he asked, "Remember I talked about principle? Do you? Answer me."

"Yes."

He nodded. "Now they're anti-Fascists. As long as Mussolini won, they loved him. Justice? Did they care about justice? *Now* they care. Because he promised them an empire and he couldn't hold it. *Now* they're anti-Fascists. And look who got caught."

He couldn't go on. He sat in a chair with his head bowed, his elbows on his thighs and his hands covering his face, and Annamaria knelt on the floor beside him, her arms around his legs, her head at his knees.

I sat on my cot, trembling from my momentary fears about Vittorio, with my eyes averted, guilty—for everything, my bourgeois past, my ignorance, and for caring deeply, still, for Vittorio, soon to be my brother, who hadn't been an anti-Fascist soon enough.

After a while, Enrico got up and washed. "Come to the table," he said.

Annamaria had set a place for me, but I couldn't lift my spoon. I stared at the broth.

Quietly, Enrico said. "Pick up your head. It's not your fault."

XII

IT WAS NOW LATE IN MARCH 1944, FIVE YEARS SINCE MY FAMily had left our home in Warsaw, six months since we had entered Italy, and still we were waiting for the Allied troops, who were sustaining terrible losses and hadn't even gotten to Rome.

Preparing, however, for when they would reach us in Florence, the Germans had long before mined the gasworks, the central telephone station, the electric power plants, the bridges—all, that is, except the Ponte Vecchio, which they were planning to spare out of sentiment, probably Hitler's. Rather than mine the bridge itself, they had planted the mines in the buildings abutting it. Later, they thought, when the mines went off and the buildings fell, their rubble alone would block the bridge and keep the Allies from crossing.

Still, if Allied troops were distant, their planes were near. They had bombed and machine-gunned the roads to the city for months, and Enrico, leaving on Partisan business out in the hills, would go before it was light, enjoying the safety of darkness, while Annamaria the atheist prayed he'd get back.

But in another way, the city seemed quieter. Arrests of Jews appeared to have stopped. Those the Germans and Fascists could find had been taken away, including the ones in hospital beds and those in the home for the aged. Were it not for Vincenzo Attanasio, the police official who had given Padre Cipriano and Matilde lists of Florentine Jews who were due for arrest, fewer by far would have known they must hide.

In our own building, there was one disturbance, and that one involving a Catholic. At four in the morning early the previous month, a neighbor downstairs had been taken away, accused of political crimes. He was an elderly grocer, crotchety, but as apolitical as any man could be. His ailing wife had gone to the prison, sworn he was innocent, wept at his suffering, pleaded, but now, almost two months later, he had disappeared, and no one, not even our Fascist neighbor, would tell her where.

"Of course!" Enrico said. "To drive us crazy wondering who will be next. There are still anti-Fascists around, free! Even today! And this dumbbell is taken away."

These were the things I knew.

I did not know Padre Cipriano had been caught. A young woman on his committee, the one who'd converted to Catholicism, had been captured for Partisan acts unconnected to him. In her purse was a diary, and in it his name. One night, a Fascist official arrived at San Marco demanding to see him.

"Here!" he said, thrusting the diary forward. "Do you know what would happen to you if I'd shown this?" What he wanted of him was a halt to his crimes.

"No. That, no," he answered. "If you saved my life, I thank you, but the life is mine to be lived as I choose."

Nor did I know that in December, ten days after the SS had raided the Carmine, Luciana and the other Jewish women had been sent to Auschwitz.

Nor that at the end of January the rabbi and his wife had been sent to Auschwitz too.

Nor that in February Don Casini had again been arrested.

Nor that in March, in Bologna, Mario Finzi, who had been having counterfeit documents made, had been arrested too.

Enrico had told me Florence was quiet, so I waited, as my mother and Imma did, as my father and Joel did, as I was sure that Daniel waited too. I wondered if he could remember we'd slept in a farmhouse, his body curled with mine on the mat. But I didn't worry. I was convinced that we in Florence, and Vittorio and Eva in the hills nearby, and Mario, all were safe.

But confined with little to do, I thought about Rome—about Theo and Aaron, who had parted in France, about Ondine, whose leaf was still on my blouse, and above all, about Nathan.

In the months I had lived with Enrico and Annamaria, there were hardships in Rome, worse, I believe, than in Florence. Many Romans and a quarter million refugees, mainly from the countryside, were homeless, hungry, desperate. The water system had been damaged, and now that the roads going into the city were blocked, food as well was increasingly scarce.

At night, under the cover of darkness, waves of German ammunition trucks, tanks, and motorized artillery rattled the walls in the heart of this "open city," and the Pope did not protest. When the Allies, to disrupt the operations, dropped their bombs, he did. During the day, troops of the Fascist or German SS would arrive, seal off a street, move on to another one, and at each, arrest the men between the ages of sixteen and fifty-five, and ship them to the labor camps in Germany, refusing them even a word of goodbye to their families.

Romans, alone or in Resistance groups of every shade of anti-Fascist opinion, rebelled. As early as October, somebody armed with a bomb, riding a bicycle, attacked, so bicycle use was banned.

There was sniping at German and Fascist officials, so, to control it, they halted the life of the city at dusk, banning buses and trams. From then until dawn, in place of the normal sounds of the city were sounds of guns and grenades.

Nicole and Theo were going outdoors, blending into the masses of people. It didn't seem likely that anyone bent on capturing men for labor in Germany, or for the army, would bother with Theo.

Nathan too, in his Capuchin habit, was going about. For five months, he did what Matilde was doing in Florence for us. He went on his errands on foot, even when the trams or *filobus* were running, knowing that every so often the Germans would stop one, arrest the passengers, and take them away. And every few days, before the curfew at seven, he'd visit Nicole and Theo.

One day in March he asked Nicole, "Do you happen to know Celeste di Porto?"

"We met at a party," she said. "Do you know her?"

"No."

"She's eighteen. As gorgeous as you must have heard. Ask Theo—we recently saw her."

"Did *she* see *you?*"

"Yes, I waved, but she didn't remember me. You should see her, Nathan. Voluptuous, with eyes like fire. Her nickname is Stella." Star.

"She has another one, haven't you heard? La Pantera Nera." The Black Panther. "She's a spy."

Nicole, with a sound resembling a laugh: "Spy? For whom?"

"The Germans."

"Don't be silly."

"She searches the streets. Thirty feet behind her there are Germans. In civilian clothes. Whenever she sees a man she knows is a Jew, she stops him, talks to him, and then goes on, and the Germans come up and take him away."

"That's absurd! It isn't possible—the girl's a Jew!"

"I know! That's why she's effective—she knows who else is a Jew. From now on, you'd better stay in."

Nicole was silent. Then she said, "I think I'm safe. We met for a second, and then there was a wall of men around her. And at a party the subject of race doesn't come up."

"But your husband was born here—she'd know him. Did she follow you?"

"I don't think so. Theo, do you?"

"Who'd have thought to look back?"

Nathan asked them where, precisely, they'd met her.

"Down at the end of the street, near the vegetable store. That's all we go out for—water, food, and to give the signora a rest from the baby."

"Stay in," he said. "I'll bring you whatever you need."

But before he left, Signora Locieco came in, agitated, frightened. In a tone that said it was useless to argue, she gave them an hour to get out—strangers were out on the street, not refugees but well-dressed men, with jobs, it was obvious. Maybe police—just hanging around, watching. What was the use of the money they paid her? Her husband and sons would need it when Germany let them come home, but if *she* got killed, she asked, what was the use of it?

She agreed to extend the hour to an hour and a half, to the start of the curfew. Nathan ran off and was back in less. Out in the street, he hadn't seen anyone hanging around. He'd gone to Via Sicilia, to the Capuchins, and found them a room in another apartment.

Theo carried a bundle of clothes, and Nicole carried the child. As they walked toward the corner, four men in civilian clothes emerged from a building, seized Theo and Nathan, and pinned them down on the ground. Nicole shrieked and begged, and from the opposite side of the street, Celeste di Porto arrived.

"You thought I'd forgotten you," she said. "But you and your husband are artists, and I never forget a creative Jew."

Nicole's pleas were useless. She had disappointed them—they'd expected to capture her husband too. He'd *already* been captured? di Porto asked. Oh well. As for this Capuchin, in the prison they'd see if he was a Jew or a Catholic. Anyway, why should Nicole be worried? Didn't the name of the prison, Regina Coeli, Queen of the Heavens, assure her? No? Then she, Celeste, would visit them often, no one should worry. Besides, they really were lucky. They wouldn't be sent to the east. At least for the moment, they could be sure they'd be staying in Rome. As for Nicole and her child, nobody wanted them yet.

The date was March 10, 1944. As Allied bombs were falling on Rome, Nicole, holding her baby, ran to the Capuchin monks, who took her away to the promised room to wait for the Allies. They'd been stopped at the Anzio beachhead, as they had been stopped at Cassino. In the hill towns near Rome, the Castelli Romani, to which Aaron and Ondine had gone, the Germans were killing Partisans, and the Allies were dropping bombs.

Nicole was still in the apartment two weeks later, on March 23, the twenty-fifth anniversary of the founding of the Fascist Movement. It was a bright, sunny afternoon. Not far away, in a formation a hundred yards long, escorted by an armored truck, 156 German troops, recently brought to enforce the occupation, marched from the north to Piazza di Spagna, singing, their thundering boots shaking the walls. Their gray uniforms and helmets had the SS emblem, a double bolt of lightning. Each had an ammunition belt, a rifle, and a pistol. They passed the Spanish Steps and, turning left, entered Via Rasella, a narrow sloping street close to the southern end of Via Veneto.

It was three forty-five, and it was the route they had taken every day. In a city sanitation cart, near a semiabandoned building whose number, by an odd coincidence, was 156, there was a bomb. When the column entered the street, a waiting Partisan lit the fuse and hurried away. At the moment the column filled the street, the bomb went off. The Partisan escaped.

Thirty-two of the Germans were dead. In the following hours another one died. There was a flurry of meetings, and there were calls both within and out of Italy, to authorities of many ranks, including General Kesselring and Hitler, and by eight in the evening the final order came: within twenty-four hours, ten Italians were to die for every German.

By word of mouth, news of the Partisan action spread through Rome, but there was no announcement in the papers or on the radio of either the attack or the German order of reprisal. Rome and the Partisans waited, but there was no warning of the consequences if the Partisans responsible did not surrender.

The next day, 335 men and boys were selected from the Roman prisons, which, like the Villa Triste in Florence, had torture chambers. One was the Queen of the Heavens, the Regina Coeli.

Among the men and boys selected, seventy-five were Jews, sixty-seven imprisoned for "race" alone—twenty-six betrayed by Celeste di Porto. The final eight Jews, and the 260 Catholics—a few already near death from having been tortured—were accused of political crimes. Most had never been tried. The youngest was fourteen, and the oldest seventy-five. They were in the learned professions, in the armed forces, in the creative arts, in business, in industry, and in government. There were peddlers, servants, waiters, students, and one was a priest. They were a portrait of Rome.

With their hands tied behind their backs, and linked to each other in groups of three, they were loaded on trucks and, under armed escort, taken away through the Porta San Sebastiano, at the start of the Appian Way. Less than a mile from there is a fork in the road where Peter is said to have asked a vision of Jesus, *"Domine, quo vadis?"* The trucks went off to the right, along Via Ardeatina. Soon, on the right-hand side of the road, between the Christian catacombs of Saint Calixtus and Saint Domitilla, they stopped at a clearing, where the men were made to climb down. They faced an opening into a hill, leading into a network of tunnels.

Still shackled, they were marched through the tunnels to some preselected sites. There, while others waited their turn in the clearing, they were forced to their knees, and German soldiers, taking each of the men and boys in turn, placed a gun near the nape of each one's neck and, as instructed, with an eye to economy, tried to kill with a single shot through the cerebellum upward, out through the top of the skull. Too often the single shot, poorly aimed, was far from enough.

Corpses lay where they fell, becoming a heap, and each new captive was forced to climb to the top of the heap, until the first was a pyramid five feet high, and a new one was started. They climbed, their executioners behind them, and knelt on the corpses of others, adding their bodies, tier on irregular tier.

The executions had begun at half past three. They were finished at eight, punctually, as ordered. Explosives were placed, and the caves were sealed.

There were five more corpses than the ten-for-one. When, long afterward, the Germans, meticulous—correct—were asked to explain, they admitted that taking the extra men had been a mistake, and that they had killed them because they were there.

Within hours the city had heard, but not till the following day did the papers carry the news of either the Via Rasella attack or the German reprisal. Nicole, and all of Rome, waited to hear or see the names of the men, but no list was published. It was not until June, when the Allies had liberated Rome, that the caves were opened and the men and boys, slowly, and with the difficulties no one need explain, were identified.

The Pope, who had been begged by one of his priests to speak to the Germans, to plead that they not go through with their plan, of which he knew, had declined. Instead, as the massacre was being carried out, the Vatican newspaper carried an urgent appeal to the people of Rome, telling them that ill-considered acts would only injure innocent people. It also told the clergy its mission: "persuasion, pacification, and giving comfort."

But when the caves were opened in June and the bodies removed and examined, a note was found in the pocket of one of the dead. He was Domenico Ricci, thirty-one years old, a clerk, the father of five children. He was a Catholic. He had written, "My dear God, we pray that You may protect the Jews from the barbarous persecutions. One Paternoster, 10 Ave Marias, one Gloria Patri."

The next day, the papers in Florence as elsewhere carried a brief report. On the 23rd, it said, criminal elements, communists and followers of Badoglio, perhaps with help from the British and Americans, had ambushed a column of German police. "The German Command," it said, "has therefore ordered that for every murdered German, ten *comunisti-badogliani* criminals be shot. This order has been carried out."

Annamaria and I sat at the table, silent, worried, each with different people in mind, and Enrico, gravely, mimicking the voice of the Pope, stood before us, intoning, "People of Rome: accept oppression. Do not bring calamity upon us by rebellion."

"Please," Annamaria said.

He sat down and faced me. "I told you a lie. It wouldn't have helped to convert. The Pope won't protect *anyone* if it'll make the Germans angry."

"Please!" Annamaria shouted. "We know!"

Shouting back: "She doesn't! I told her a lie!"

Less from generosity than childish arrogance, I said, "It wasn't a lie. You believed it, so it was just a mistake."

"And you," he said. "When we listen to Radio London I look at your face, but I can't see into your head. When you hear what London says about extermination camps, do you believe it?"

"I don't think so," I said.

He didn't argue. Quietly, he repeated, "I told you a lie." He paused, squinting, searching for a formulation, and then, with assurance, he said, "Now I have to tell you the truth. I don't believe the Pope has any desire that the Jews get hurt. But the business of the Faith—of the Church—is to save souls. The business of the Pope is to keep the Church in business. As from London, Chamberlain—ignorant—appeased the Germans, the Pope—who *knows*—appeases them in Rome."

I didn't understand him then, but the words were fixed in my mind, to be remembered when I would.

Then Enrico, his flash of temper dissipated, turned to Annamaria. "I'm not afraid of execution." He took her hand, as if a minute before he hadn't shouted at her, and with as little inhibition as they'd shown in letting me hear the sounds of their passion, he said, "I'm not afraid of the bullets that kill, but of the bullets that paralyze. One that will take my manhood away. I want you to promise. If I'm not of use as a man, kill me yourself."

"Shh!" she answered. "Stop."

"But I don't want to die without having left a child. If I die when he's small, I don't mind—he'll remember his father was good, and he won't discover my faults. But I want you to promise if I lose my manhood . . ."

"Shh, *carissimo,* shh," she repeated. Rotating her hand, so that it was clasped in his, she said in a rush, "Nothing will happen—you're unnerved—but yes, if that's what you'd want, I would." Then, seconds later, as he seemed to relax, she said with a smile, "Ruth, give him your leaf. It's lucky, Enrico."

"Women's jewelry?" he said. "Where is your head?"

He wouldn't take it, but he seemed reassured, and toward me he showed a remarkable change. He was finally letting me into the secrets of all he was part of. He was one of a group of five, ordered to place explosives at enemy headquarters, steal weapons, attack transports, and exchange information with Partisans out in the country.

June 5, in Rome, was the turning point. The Germans retreated, the Allies took the city, and the front moved north. The next day, Partisan posters were out on the walls of Florence, calling on anti-Fascists to act, openly, finally, to follow Allied orders issued to the Partisan commanders. A day later, a British general, in a radio broadcast, called on all Italians to rebel against the occupiers, cut communication lines, destroy the bridges and railways.

The Germans answered. There were new arrests of Partisans, horrendous torture, executions, and punitive measures against us all. In a city that had hardly any food, they now cut off the gas supply, reduced the flow of water, and ended the telephone service, but Partisan action only increased.

One evening, Enrico came home from a day in the hills and said, "Draw me some pictures. Draw me your brothers in Rome."

I didn't ask why. I started with a full-face sketch of Nathan, but he stopped me.

"Enough! Now the other one."

"The other one in Rome's my cousin, not my brother."

I started a sketch of Theo, and again he stopped me. "The brother you said is a Partisan."

I started on Aaron's. When I got to his ears, Enrico said, "It's him! Orecchio Rotto." Broken Ear. I looked up. "A code name!" he said. "They say he's a crazy Frenchman not afraid of anything. Finished in Rome, wiggled through the German lines, and now he's here. I met him."

"Here?"

He pointed toward the eastern hills. "There. When there's fighting in the streets of Florence, he'll be here."

"Did he come with a girl?"

"He *says* it's a girl—it looks like a boy. All bones and nose."

My head was whirling. Aaron! But Ondine? Though her nose was aquiline, it was much too small to deserve his remark. My hands flew over the page as I drew her in profile.

"Is this the girl?"

"Too much hair. The less hair, the more nose." I erased almost all of the hair. "See?" he said.

Excited, I asked, "Did you tell them I'm with you?"

"There are thousands of Partisans! I hadn't seen the picture—how could I know who he was?"

We were into July. We could hear from the south the sound of the cannons, and in the city and surrounding countryside the air raids with their hellish noise appeared incessant. People were staying indoors when they could, but my own imprisonment ended when searching for food was more than Annamaria could do by herself.

We would roam the streets, separately, looking for an open shop where they might have a bit to sell—anything however old, moldy, rancid—or looking for a peasant who had braved the shell-pocked roads to the city with a cart on which he had some wilted vegetables. If we were lucky he would have some meat from animals he'd badly needed but had slaughtered, rather than let the Germans take them away for themselves.

And now that I was going out, I started to do what Enrico had thought I would do. The intelligence he gathered was for transfer to the Allies, and he assigned illustrations to me—meticulous sketches in color. Groups of vehicles, signs on buildings to be targeted, anything at all, even drawing simple markings on a truck, filled me with a joy that let me for a while forget my hunger.

Early on, the Fascist official who lived in the building saw me, looked me over, and then went on.

Then, on a day near the end of July, Signora Pietranera came for me. An illness had broken out in parts of the city, a form of cholera, she said, and Imma had caught it.

I didn't have time to discover my feelings were mixed.

"Hurry up," she said. "I sent you away. I don't want it on my conscience that she died without you."

Annamaria moved between us. "Are you sure it's cholera? And she *sent* for her?"

"I'm sure. And no, she didn't send."

"But you want it on your conscience if *this* one dies?"

"This one is young. If she catches it, she'll live."

I turned to Annamaria.

"You're fourteen," she said. "Decide for yourself."

Pacified, conciliatory, Signora Pietranera asked her, "Do you really like this girl? Then if you're not afraid of the sickness you're welcome to come to the house."

"Maybe I will," she said, "if I go to my mother's."

I asked her if her mother lived near the signora.

"Yes. If we cross the river because of the bombing, or if they send us across on a mission, Enrico and I will go to my mother's."

"Then *arrivederci,*" I said. "And, Annamaria . . ." I wanted to add to it—something affectionate or grateful—but I didn't know what, and I stopped.

When we had crossed the river, Signora Pietranera said, "She started getting sick this morning, but she doesn't know it's cholera, and neither does your mother, so don't say anything yet."

"Signora," I asked, "why don't you like me?"

Abruptly, she stopped, and, throwing back her head, she clapped the palms of her hands together. Then, without a word of answer, she resumed her walk.

"Does Padre Cipriano come?" I asked.

"He's been arrested."

"And?"

"And what? Do the Fascists let me into their secrets?"

"Have you heard from the Leonis?"

"Through my niece."

"How is my little brother?"

"Growing. Making noise."

"Crying?"

"Why would he cry? He has everything. They even moved."

"Moved?"

"Away from the *centro,* to the other side of the river. That way," pointing north.

The Arno was south. North, near Via Bolognese, where the Villa Triste was, was water Enrico had called a canal.

"The Mugnone?" I asked. "But why?"

"Neighbors, that's why."

"I know that place. What street?"

"Would he tell? He was afraid of a chain of arrests—your mother and grandma, then me. You think I'm a saint? So then all of them, him and his wife and the boy."

I was silent, but she, reading my mind, asked, "What's the matter? You think the professor would kidnap a child?"

But in thinking that Imma was close to her death, the signora was wrong. The illness was still in an early stage, and though cholera might have progressed to the point of disaster, Imma was sleeping, saving her strength. My mother, astonished to see me, seized me in her arms, sobbing with guilt and relief, entirely out of control.

"Aaron is safe," I said. "He and Ondine."

My mother shook Imma awake and told her.

Both, excitedly, "How do you know?"

"The people I lived with—they saw them."

I didn't go into detail, and Imma, afraid that if we let ourselves be optimistic we would bring bad luck, wouldn't allow my mother to press me. All they asked was how we had gotten our water and food.

None of us spoke of Daniel at all, as if that might be unlucky as well.

The next day, translating, I read them the Fascist paper. It said that the German Command, because of compassion for Florence, had declared it an open city. The Allies, however, it said, refusing to recognize this, might attack us or bomb the bridges spanning the Arno. To limit the number of casualties, the Germans had issued an order. People along the river, and in other places of strategic interest, which they listed, must leave their homes by the following day. Now we expected war in the streets.

Imma turned to my mother and asked, "What is an open city?"

Before she could answer, I said, "It means it has nothing for war, so you shouldn't bomb it." My mother nodded. "But there *are* war things here," I said. "There are guns—theirs—all along the north side of the river, and near the Mugnone, and up in the hills. It's the *Germans* that mined the bridges, and the *Germans*'ll blow them up."

Imma looked annoyed. I thought she'd say she had asked my mother, not me—that again the eggs were teaching the hens.

Defensively, I said, "I lived with Partisans! I know! I carried messages. I made all kinds of drawings for them."

In the silence, I heard the sounds of my own regret. I had come back willingly, for Imma's sake and mine, but I missed what I had been doing.

"Partisans?" my mother asked.

"That's how I know about Ondine and Aaron. They're in the hills, where Vittorio and Eva are." Carried away, and wanting to add to my glamour, I added, "Maybe the drawings I made were for them."

They stared in disbelief, and then with understanding, and at last with clear acceptance of another kind. I recognized it. I had seen it in the way my mother looked at Eva in St. Martin, when Eva became my mother's peer.

That evening, I spoke of Enrico and Annamaria, answering questions, happy to have my mother's and Imma's esteem.

The next day, Annamaria came to the attic. Though the house she lived in was not exactly a riverside one, she had decided to leave it and go to her mother's. For now, Enrico had stayed.

The Germans, she said, had retreated toward us, destroying crops and stealing cattle, horses, donkeys, and pigs. Now in the city, and continuing north, they were leaving their snipers behind to stay on the rooftops and fire at the incoming Allies. The Partisans, from both Florence and the countryside, had taken positions between them. They'd act as a buffer, receiving the fire from the snipers and forming a line beyond which the German patrols couldn't go back.

She, on the north side of the river, was joining a group of

couriers, all of them women, learning about the position of enemy headquarters, tanks, batteries, troops—to give to the Allies—just as we'd done in the past.

Before I could offer to draw, she glanced at Imma and said, "Not this time. You have plenty to do." She gave me a fragment of paper, adding, "Here's where I'll be if you need me."

My mother moved closer, ready to speak, but Annamaria drew me aside.

"How good is her Italian?"

"Not bad," I said.

Softly, with hardly any movement of her lips, she said, "Your brother's arrived."

"I know. I knew it the second you said there were Partisans here from the country."

"He found your sister's boyfriend, and, through him, your sister, and then Enrico told him you and your mother and grandma are here."

I restrained the impulse to hug her. "Which side of the river?"

"Today, the other side, like Enrico. Tomorrow, who knows?"

"They're taking the sniping."

"But giving it too. Decide if your mother should know."

"She'd worry. Where is his girl?"

"In the hills, with your sister. She's been vomiting, maybe she's pregnant."

"Might she have cholera?"

Louder, a victim of the months-long tension, she answered, "No! Only vomiting. Do I have to tell you what cholera is?"

Abruptly she left, and when she had gone, my mother wanted to know what had made her so angry.

"She's nervous," I said, "like everyone else."

"Who has cholera?"

"No one. That's why she got so annoyed."

"She said 'Enrico.' Where is Enrico?"

"The other side of the river."

Now, with an accusing tone, "I didn't thank her—you didn't introduce us."

"I didn't think of it. Next time I will."

Another day passed, and then another, each of them harder than the one before. Imma's fever was high, and Signora Pietranera hovered over her, putting her hand to her forehead every half hour. From loss of fluid Imma seemed shrunken, but bad as she looked, her mind was untouched.

One day, Signora Pietranera said, "A miracle! They say Padre Cipriano's back."

There was no gas, no coal, no electricity. Signora Pietranera cooked our food—moldy flour mixed with water—on fires she made of the branches and twigs that she, my mother, and I had found in the streets. Nor was there any running water. There were wells in the courtyards of some of the houses, and we went to the closest of them, my mother and I, to stand in a line of women, holding straw-covered bottles—four of them fastened by cord at their neck—in each of our hands a cluster of flasks.

Then, on August 3, a new proclamation appeared, signed by the Commander of the City of Florence and plastered on the walls:

It is now forbidden to walk in the streets.
All doors and windows must be closed.
The people are to gather in the inside rooms
of public buildings.
Patrols of the German forces are ordered to
fire on anyone seen at a window
or found in the streets.

When we told the signora, she said that the notice had just been posted—she couldn't have seen it—and, without explanation, she left. When she came back, she had in her pocket a bottle of medicine.

"From Padre Cipriano," she said. "Also a hug."

During that night, the city shook with terrible roars as the

Germans exploded the mines on the Arno's bridges. They left the Ponte Vecchio, blocked by the ruins of the buildings near it. Shortly afterward they mined the synagogue, but most of it stayed intact. That it had survived, Signora Pietranera later said, was another miracle.

We stayed in the attic. Several days went by, and women started ignoring the order not to go out. It was impossible to do without some water or give up the search for food. Perhaps out of fear of open rebellion, the Germans revoked the order. Women could leave the houses—but only women and only during specified hours.

In the streets, there were Partisans now, not in uniform but armed, and openly moving about. Serving as a kind of uniform were their distinctive neckerchiefs, which identified their group. On the day Enrico had told me of finding Aaron, I hadn't remembered to ask for the name of his group, and now, with no clue, I looked for his face.

Then, on August 11, we heard that the Allies had taken control south of the river. There were Americans, English, Canadians, the Jewish Brigade from Palestine, and more. They were bringing in water in trucks and giving it out, and equally wonderful, they were giving out bread. It had been baked from American flour—not from the mixture of substances used in the bread we had gotten, when we could get it—and it yielded a wonderful bread, as white as milk.

"If only Daniel were there," my mother said, "instead of up north."

It was the first mention of Daniel since I'd been back.

That night, we were rousted out of our bed by a terrible noise. German soldiers had plunged unexpectedly into the house. They were banging on the doors with rifle butts, and we, sure they had found us—*now,* so close to liberation—were rooted in place. All they were doing, however, was sending us out to the public buildings they said would be safe. They didn't force us to go, so rather than leave, we went to the cellar, Imma's weakened body upright, her chin on her chest and her arms on my mother's shoulders and mine as we walked her down.

In the cellar, some of the tenants already had gathered and crowded together. They sat or lay on the grimy pavement, their dazed, undernourished children pressed against them, suffering from the August heat but wrapped in blankets against whatever debris might fall when the bombing resumed.

No one seemed curious. Nobody cared that my mother and Imma were speaking in Polish. Hours went by, filled with tension, until a horrendous rumbling shook the building, shattered the windows, and delivered a shower of plaster onto our heads.

Children started to scream, and Imma, for the first time, got hysterical. Signora Pietranera, apparently unmoved by the suffering of children, panicked at Imma's despair, grabbed me by the collar of my shirt, and ordered me up to her kitchen. In the commotion, she had forgotten the medicine.

As I tried to stand up, my mother seized me. "*I* will go."

I shoved her away. "Papa said!" Then, apologetic, I added, "Mama, they've forgotten us. Besides, I'm not going out."

I cautiously went upstairs. The windows had lost their glass, and in the outside walls there were gashes wide enough to see through. At the window of Signora Pietranera's kitchen, a pair of German soldiers were stationed, shooting down into the street. I prayed that Aaron was nowhere around. One of the Germans saw me, stopped shooting, and with nothing more than curiosity, watched me come into the room.

"*Mi scusi,*" I said.

The signora had told me where on her shelves to look, and after a minute or two I left.

Hours went by, and the soldier came down to ask for some water. He stayed for a while to play with the children, lifting them out of their torpor, and Imma, in spite of his presence, was calm. My mother was sure she was better. I, however, was now infected—not with physical illness, but with the signora's conviction that Imma was finally dying.

The next day, in a tone implying the days when she might have been able to stop me were past, I told my mother to go for the water without me. I was going to San Marco to see if my father and Joel were alive, and to ask for a doctor for Imma.

It was the hour when we could be out on the streets, but on Via Cavour there was no one. Far ahead, things were scattered about on the ground, and when I got closer, I saw what they were. For the first time, I was seeing a scene such as this.

There were bodies, three of them, one of them fully extended, the other ones bent into different positions. Now I knew why no one was out. There were snipers up in the buildings just as there were in ours, and whoever had seen the bodies had fled.

I turned and ran, intent on escaping the snipers, but it suddenly didn't seem right that I had to escape. *They,* after all, had told us that women could be in the streets, and I was entitled to go to San Marco, I thought, just as I'd planned. But—to avoid the scene ahead of me—I'd go by a different route. And then even that didn't seem to be right. Someone should see if the men were wounded and bring back a doctor for them, as I had been planning to do at San Marco for Imma.

Now the thoughts I had put from my mind forced themselves through. The men on the pavement were dead, or they would not have been left by their friends. And then I was sure—in the way that Imma would say she was sure—that one of the corpses was Aaron's. Now, though my dread was greater than ever, I had to go nearer and see.

I went forward, as slowly, I think, as I'd ever walked, close to the buildings despite my conviction that then, at that hour of day, a woman wouldn't be shot. The closer I got to the men, the more I dreaded the sight. And even if none of the men was my brother, I wondered, how would I know for certain if someone was dead? I edged closer, as frightened as months before on the riverside road, when Joachim the German had taken my coat.

Two of the men were in rivers of blood so wide that I was

convinced without even looking that neither could still be alive. And since neither was built like Aaron, I turned from them quickly, avoiding the sight of their faces, their clothes, or their wounds.

The third one was slim but entirely too short to be Aaron. And yet I stopped—I recognized the neckerchief. Slowly I went to the man. I stood over him, behind him. He was lying on his side, his face directed away, his legs apart and bent, his left arm extended, under his head, as if he were swimming the side-stroke.

I knelt down and, with a shudder, pulled the body onto its back. Enrico looked up at me, dead, his eyes wide open in surprise, his mouth wide open too, as if he were saying, "Answer me," out of a pool of blood.

I stood up and fled. When I reached the corner I stopped, thinking I had to go back, that I'd made a mistake. Of all the Partisans in Florence, how could one of so very few have been Enrico? And yet it was, I knew it, and, having found him, I had no idea of what I should do. Again I started to run.

When I reached San Marco, the man in the booth was again condescending, speaking as if to a child, but he wasn't impatient. He seemed sympathetic, in fact, and his sympathy frightened me. *Something,* I thought, has happened to Joel.

"Padre Cipriano," I said, and went to sit down, praying he'd come to me soon, giving me time to get back before I was shot. It was August, but I was shivering.

When Padre Cipriano saw me, he smiled—his hearty, toothy, reassuring smile—and now I could ask, "My brother?"

"Better!" he said. "Much better, thank God."

"And my father?"

His eyes widened, and, with a moment's hesitation, as if he were telling me less than the truth, he answered, "Fine!"

I didn't insist. It was a principle, almost ingrained, not to think of the past, to think of the future only as much as we had to, and to stop thinking when we knew we must. Enrico and Imma were more than enough for the moment.

"My grandmother's sick," I said. "Cholera. Could you get her a doctor?"

He returned in minutes, beside him a man with a Red Cross band on his arm and a medical bag. The doctor addressed me in Polish, asking me why I believed that Imma had cholera. Then, in Yiddish, he added, "Papa sends you his love."

We started to walk toward the door, the doctor and I, and Padre Cipriano walked beside us. As we reached the door, I turned to him, putting a hand on his arm to stop him.

"Padre, they're in the buildings shooting down."

"Yes, of course."

"But maybe they'll shoot you."

"They're letting the women go out," he said. "Shouldn't they do the same for a priest?"

I didn't know whether he meant they did or they should, but I knew how much his being there would mean to Imma, so I merely said, "Please go without me. Tell them I went to Annamaria's."

I really didn't expect to find her at home and didn't know what I would do if she weren't there, but she was, and she flung the door wide—most likely in hope of seeing Enrico.

She listened, flinched, but said nothing. She sat down for a minute. Then she hurried through the streets with me, and when we reached him, she knelt beside him. Slowly, she lowered his arm to his side. She straightened his neckerchief, and gently, as if she could hurt him, she closed his eyes and, cradling his face in her hands, she covered his open mouth with her own, and kissed his face and eyes and the hair on his nose again and again, and lay across his chest, her face at his neck. When she was back on her knees she was covered with blood, and I put my arms around her and held her, as if I had always loved her.

After a minute, she said, "Go back. Here you'll be shot."

"You come too."

"Soon."

"I'll send Padre Cipriano."

"No."

"Then whom should I tell?"

"No one. Just go home before you get shot."

I stood up, slowly, but before I could leave, she put her hand on my foot to detain me.

"I'm carrying his child," she said, "and he knew."

Padre Cipriano and the doctor had already left. Imma was not getting worse, the doctor had said, she would only get better. Though people were calling this cholera, he didn't believe that it was. In Signora Pietranera's eyes, the man was a fool, not a doctor, but Imma was not only calm, she was happy.

"Our angel is back," she told me. "He didn't forget us."

He'd been seized by the Fascists and taken from Florence. Now he'd assured her that Joel was well, that my father, good though he was, was stubborn, and that Matilde had been caught but then released from prison. Released by whom? I asked. A police official, she said, but we mustn't tell.

We later learned it was Vincenzo Attanasio. He had been watching for a time when he'd be able to, then he had opened the door and let her walk out. It was as simple as that.

Imma's eyes were shining. "Aren't we lucky?" she asked.

When she fell asleep, exhausted, we watched her in silence. Around us the others were quiet.

Softly, my mother said, "A year ago you were a child. Now you tell me nothing."

"What am I not telling you?"

"What did Padre Cipriano say?"

"About what?"

"Papa."

"Just that he's fine, that's all."

"And you believe him?"

"I don't know."

She put her arms around me. "Papa left San Marco. Joel got better, so he felt he'd done as much as he'd promised."

I asked where he'd gone.

"Nobody knows. Perhaps to the hills, or to Don Casini."

"You're angry at him?"

"No. If only he lives, I'll *never* be angry at him. I've even been praying Luciana is safe, that we'll see her, soon."

Gently, I pulled myself free of her arms, and now, instead of her holding *me,* I was holding *her.* She seemed in a way even younger than I, as innocent as long ago in Warsaw, before she'd been changed by the hardships in France.

I couldn't reveal what I thought. When Enrico had gone to the country to meet with the Partisans, Annamaria had prayed he'd be safe and probably felt she'd never get angry again if only he'd live. Later, when he got home and provoked her, she did. Now he was dead. Maybe with death, anger would end. I thought this idea had never occurred to my mother.

"Ruthie?" she asked. "Why did you go to Annamaria's?"

I decided to tell her. "Something terrible happened. I found some Partisans. Dead. And one was Enrico."

"Oh, my God," she moaned. "My God, these suffering children. I never even thanked him." After a while, she said, "And where is Aaron?"

Imma stirred, and my mother got quiet. Minutes went by, and then, calmly, she said, "You haven't asked about Daniel."

"The signora told me he's out of the *centro,* beyond the Mugnone."

"Are you worried?"

"Yes."

"I'm not," she said. "I refuse. We've been afraid of a chain of arrests. We have to have faith in a chain of trust."

That night, we went back to the attic, and after the cellar the attic looked good.

The next day, Allied infantry crossed the Arno and entered the *centro*, Partisans having preceded them. Corpses lay in the streets, rotting in the August sun. Again I told my mother to go for water without me and went instead to Annamaria's.

She didn't speak of Enrico at all. "Your brother's brigade has gone through," she said. "He's probably near the Mugnone by now."

"But where are the Allies?"

"The Partisans lead, the Allies will follow. It's as it should be. Florence is ours, not theirs."

"Do you think my brother's alive?"

"Why not? More are alive than dead."

Then, on the 16th, a tidal wave swept through our street. Liberation! Everyone—old, young, widowed, orphaned, strong, half-starved, pale and shrunken from illness—plunged outdoors from apartments and cellars, desperate to see our liberators, finally—Americans, Canadians, Partisans. Desperate to touch them, to take from their hands that white American bread, to look at their jeeps—that vehicle which we'd been told could climb the mountains—to show our love, to laugh for them, to cry, to hold.

Shots rang out from a nearby roof, and an answering volley of shots arose from our midst, but nobody ran. It was finally over. We were free. What was a sniper or two after all we had seen?

And yet, if it was joy we felt, that joy was mixed. I think of it now as the finest day of my life, but as a day not only of joy but of rage, of memories of fear suppressed, of images of those whose fate we didn't know. I felt myself crying their names. Daniel! Nathan! Luciana! But Imma was beside me, standing between my mother and me, a sweet reminder of almost incredible luck.

A laughing Partisan leapt from the crowd and seized my hand. "Why so serious, sweetheart, why so serious? Come! Come with me!"

I didn't move. As if I were three years old, he lifted me up in his arms, and, holding me firmly with one, he circled my wrist with the hand that was free. He carried me out to a jeep and thrust my hand at a grinning American soldier, a boy with lemon-colored hair and dirty cheeks. My hand was a fist, defending itself, trying to wrench itself free.

"What are you doing?" the Partisan asked me. "What are you doing? He's giving you chocolate!"

He accepted the chocolate for me, slipped it into the top of my shirt, and carried me back to the side of the street, where I stood immobile, stunned, between terror and euphoria.

My mother, holding some bread, having no reason to think of the day of the truck, and not having heard of the day Joachim had stopped me, was carried to earlier, innocent days, and as if she were mad, she laughed.

And yet she didn't laugh for long.

"Go for Joel," she pleaded. "Go for Joel."

I ran to San Marco for Joel, while he and the doctor as guide came running toward us through a different route. By the time I got back, my mother was up in the attic pacing the minuscule floor, looking at Joel every few seconds but worried for Daniel at last. As the Germans had blown the Arno's bridges, they also had blown the Mugnone's, and the battle, she knew, would be moving toward him.

Her mind was made up. There was now a bridge on the Arno, quickly built by the Allies, and food would arrive. That was enough. We wouldn't go back to the villa. We would wait for Daniel—right here—no matter how long it took the Allies to cross the Mugnone. She had turned superstitious, exactly as Imma had been in Paris, certain that letting herself have comfort would bring discomfort or death to her child.

Joel and I, understanding, exchanged a glance and a shrug, but trying to go beyond it, I discovered we'd grown apart. He had known my obsession with hands, and the reason is clear: we had listened together to Aaron reporting the day of the truck. We'd seen the effect of the day on Eva, had seen my mother watching her during the night. But Joel had been in his room at San Marco when I was on Via Cavour, finding Enrico, holding Annamaria, pressing her face to mine, and sharing his blood.

Joel talked of the books he had read, of the life the Dominicans led at the convent, and then he listened, entranced, when I told of the months with Enrico and Annamaria.

But Enrico, to him, was only a name. I loved Joel, would always love him, but now it was Aaron I longed for, more than for Daniel, more than for Nathan or my father. Aaron would know—would feel—how I felt when I heard myself saying "Enrico." This change, this separation, from Joel above all, had happened in seven months.

What, I wondered, would seven months have done to Daniel, who, when he left us, was less than three years old? If my mother was wondering too, she didn't admit it to me.

She had said she would wait in the attic, but instead she was out in the streets, keeping track of where the Allies were, where the Partisans were—how close to the Mugnone, how many days from Daniel they were, as if she could possibly know. She was distraught when the Germans would counterattack, and the streets in the hands of the Allies or Partisans once again would fall into theirs.

But the Allies had built the bridge on the Arno, and the family, crossing it, started to gather—first my father, who went back to San Marco to learn at last where we were. He had agreed with Padre Cipriano that until the Liberation he should not be told. Ondine and Eva came next. They had heard where we were from Aaron, who'd in turn been informed by Enrico. Each one's arrival was happy, of course, but Ondine's had something additional, cheering my mother a little. As Annamaria had guessed, Ondine would be having a child.

Signora Pietranera took her in, not to the attic, but into her own apartment, with Imma, Joel, and me, leaving my mother and father alone. Only Eva left, to go to the villa and wait for Vittorio.

When Imma and Joel had fallen asleep, Ondine and I were able to talk. I was wearing the leaf on my shirt, and Ondine took hers from a packet of clothes.

"Don't you wear it?" I asked.

"Sometimes."

"I always do."

"You like it so much?"

"It made me feel as if you and Aaron never had left."

"I never really was gone from you. Here, take the other one. You and I don't need them. Not to connect us. Give one to somebody else."

"I really don't want to."

"But you and I are together, and not just through Aaron."

"Through the baby?"

"Through what's happened. I'm a Jew. I've picked my stool."

I had forgotten what Aaron had said in Entraque, and I didn't have any idea what she meant.

"It's something I learned from Theo," she said. "You'll hear when I tell your parents, maybe tomorrow."

I accepted the leaf, saying I didn't know what I would do with it.

"Keep it," she said. "Someday you will."

Nicole came next, bringing her baby. She had gone to Viale Michelangelo, to the address she had taken from Nathan, and had found the Bellinis. They had returned to the villa the day the Germans retreated. Eva was with them. She now recrossed the Arno, bringing Nicole and the child to us.

The caves near the Appian way had been opened in June, more than three months after the Via Rasella attack and the German reprisal.

Somewhere on the heaps of bodies rotting there were those of both our brothers, Theo and Nathan.

XIII

THE MUGNONE WAS A DRY RIVERBED IN AUGUST, ITS banks steep, and now—with the Germans making a stand in the distance beyond it—its bridges in ruins. As soon as the Allies had crossed it, my parents and I would go there to wait, with others, on the south bank, watching the far side, hearing the guns in the area north of it. The rest of the family now had gone to the villa, the women to rest and Joel to help the Bellinis however he could.

Along the north bank, too far for us to recognize faces, people were standing about, looking toward us, and we, the lucky free ones, waved, almost wildly, with more apparent joy than some of us felt. We wanted to help with encouragement, poor though the gift might be. They had shared our hunger and fear—they were "ours"—but we hoped that one or more was *specifically* ours, our Leonis, our Daniel, who by some miracle would see us. More than once my parents were sure they were seeing a child and that it was he.

On the 22nd, most of the area close to the river fell to the Allies, and in hours there were Partisans down in the riverbed, their red neckerchiefs bright in a background of brown. They were carrying ladders, setting them against the banks, helping the old, the weak, the children to cross to the *centro*. Nowhere did we see a group of three, a little boy among them. My mother started to panic, my father tried to calm her, and I—who, unlike my father, had met the Leonis—was almost convinced I couldn't remember them.

Late on the 23rd, when my mother was close to prostration, we saw him—Professor Leoni. He was thin, like so many others, but to us who had seen him with Daniel, he wasn't like anyone else. Regaining our strength, we ran to the ladder.

He was tired, solemn. "Daniel is fine."

As before, on the day I'd come back to the attic, my mother started to cry. She had seemed to be strong when Nicole had arrived—had hidden her anguish—but now she was crying for Nathan in grief, and for Daniel in joy. We walked away from the ladder and sat on the ground, Professor Leoni facing us.

"Please," he said, "we have to discuss this. We aren't prepared. We moved, the neighbors think he's our child, he calls us Papa and Mama. You have to allow us some time."

My mother's face went blank. "For what?"

"It's a terrible thing to admit: we didn't believe you would still be here. That you hadn't been taken away."

"You could have come! You'd have known!"

"Yes, at some risk, and to what end? We couldn't have saved you. And now, it's as if he were ours—we have to have time to adjust."

"Adjust?"

"You'll see how healthy he is, you'll know how hard we've . . ." He couldn't go on.

"I can't," my mother said. "I can't. I have to have him today. You'll see him whenever you like. I'll never forget my debt. I'll find a way to repay you." He was shaking his head. "I have to go back with you now," my mother insisted, "I have to go back."

"Please," he begged. "We'll bring him tomorrow."

My father moved close to my mother, put his arm about her, and in Polish he told her the man was suffering.

"And we?" she said.

There was a brief exchange in Polish—from my father some words about gratitude, trust; from my mother an answer: losing a child. But my mother relented. She told the professor that *she* would agree to waiting a day if *he* would agree to tell his address. Relieved, he did, and recrossed the riverbed.

In the morning, when Signora Pietranera left for food, we waited in her living room. At ten, they arrived, all three, the Leonis with a taller, healthy Daniel between them, holding them each by the hand, standing in the kitchen doorway, silent. It was I who had opened the door, and I backed away to let them come in.

Daniel looked up at me, then at my parents. He didn't move forward to any of us, and we, confused, stayed where we were.

"Daniel," my parents said, their voices together.

He looked inquiringly up at Signora Leoni.

"Daniele," she said, sorrowful but obviously puzzled, "but this is your mama. Your papa."

He turned his back to my mother, releasing Professor Leoni's hand, and looking up at Signora Leoni with a patient smile, he said in Italian, "*You* are my mama," in a tone that told her *everyone* knew she was teasing.

My mother moved close and knelt on the floor. Disbelieving, and in a rush, she said, "Daniel, this is Mama, this is Papa, this is Ruth."

He stood back, staring at my mother, still holding Signora Leoni's hand. "Let's go home," he said.

My mother, horrified, searching Signora Leoni's face and seeming to lose for a moment even her broken Italian: "What have you done to him?"

"*Done* to him?" She wasn't angry—she was appalled. "Would I have done *anything* to him?"

"No, no," my father assured her, "come in, signora. Come into the living room. Please. We didn't expect this—that's all."

"Nor did I! I told him nothing—I meant to surprise him. I thought he would *run* to you—why do you think I needed some time?"

"I'm sorry," my father said. "This is nothing. So young. Only three. A shock. Twice. He'll remember. Magda, stand up. Please, signora, come in and sit down. Sit down, Professore. Ruth, give Daniel the chocolate you saved."

I ran for the chocolate, my mother stood up, and we went to the living room, where Daniel, wide-eyed if not exactly worried, leaned on the edge of the sofa, pressing against the signora's knee.

He accepted the chocolate politely, adding, in Italian, "The Americans brought it?"

I answered in French, "Yes. Soldiers in a funny car."

He looked at me carefully. "What?"

My mother nudged me. "Remind him of the horse."

In French, I said, "Remember the day the signori took you away in a carriage? Remember the little black horse?"

Smiling, embarrassed, he looked at Signora Leoni. "What did she say?"

Signora Leoni repeated some of my words in Italian.

"Cavallino?" he asked.

Both horse and French were forgotten.

"Ruth," my father ordered, "take him and draw him some pictures."

"Go, Daniele, go, darling," Signora Leoni urged.

I took him into the kitchen and sat at the table beside him, hearing the talk in the other room.

There, they took it for granted, it seemed, that soon he'd remember. The Leonis were asking my parents to settle in Florence, where Jews were respected, admired, before Mussolini had bartered with Hitler; to take an apartment somewhere near theirs, where Daniel would find himself fully at home in both.

I turned my attention entirely to him. I drew him a picture of Joel, the first I had done of him. "Joel?" I said.

"I'll draw too," he answered.

I gave him a pencil and paper, and as he scribbled I drew him a picture of Nathan and told him his name. In Italian, I added, "Blond."

I did Eva next, describing her in words, and then Imma, and even Aaron with his broken ear, the brother I couldn't expect him to know. Half an hour or so went by, and the others came into the kitchen to watch.

The day went badly. He was tired of my pictures and talk. He sat on Signora Leoni's lap and waited to leave. She delayed, and after some hours he was tired but wouldn't lie down. He wanted his bed. My mother agreed to their leaving, arranging that they would come back the following day.

And on that day, my father saw that nothing had changed. He was solemn, embittered. "I don't know," he said, "how any of this could have happened—that madman in Germany, the death of our son, or why our baby forgot us so fast. Because of grief? Fear? Bitterness toward *us?* I don't know. But somebody will, somewhere."

He walked away and stood for a while, his back toward us, while my mother, as if paralyzed with fear of what he might suggest, watched him.

He turned around and faced the Leonis. "He loves you," he said, "and I see why he does. But he loved us too, and we can't allow him to do this. My wife has told me he cried when you took him. He'll cry when you go, but he might as well cry today as tomorrow. Please."

And yet, he hadn't understood. The Leonis, who had heard Daniel screaming then—before they had loved him—now couldn't bear to witness his grief. That evening, with my parents' permission, they stayed, and they held his hand as he lay in the bed, until he was fast asleep.

The following day he was quiet, sad, uninterested in us. And the next as well. And the next. And each evening, the Leonis crossed the Mugnone and sat at the bedside, each of them holding his hand.

At the end of a week, we went back to the villa, having told the Leonis we'd see them as soon as we could.

During one of the nights in the early part of that week, Aaron, with a companion, carrying explosives, went to a German encampment out in the northern hills. They placed the explosives under some trucks that were loaded with fuel, and, now unencumbered, started back to the city. They hadn't gone far when the other young Partisan stepped on a mine and was killed. Aaron fell too, but stood up, and looking down at his arm, saw his hand, severed almost through, dangling from his wrist.

On September 1st, five years to the day since Germany had marched on Poland, Florence and its countryside were free. At the Fortezza da Basso, which the Partisans captured right at the start of the battle and never surrendered, three thousand Partisans marched in a formal parade reviewed by a British commander. Among them were Vittorio and Aaron.

The following day, separately, each of them went toward the villa.

We could count our losses for now. We still didn't know that Luciana had not survived, nor had the Hartmans, nor my father's sisters and their families, nor Imma's cousin Abner and his family, nor my mother's parents, nor Rudy, Liesel, and their children, nor even the Pole my father had trusted—Marek's mother, who had kept my grandparents hidden for months, and then, through a treacherous neighbor, had been caught. We learned of them later, after the war, after the records were found.

We now had Ondine, Nicole, and Nicole's little year-old girl, dimpled, hazel-eyes, fair-haired, but otherwise strongly resembling the father lost from her memory.

Her name was Emilia. She was Daniel's friend and toy. She sat on his lap, if not quite willingly, then with resignation. More often they'd be on the floor, on all fours, while he pressed his nose to hers in a game he had played with Professor Leoni, a game of rubbing noses together, with Daniel repeating again and again the names of Renaissance painters—meaningless words, of course, to them both, but Emilia was bringing him back to the family.

When six weeks had passed since Nicole had come with the news about Nathan and Theo, my parents began to emerge from mourning, from exhaustion, from constant fear, from despair over Daniel. Aaron was well, learning to live with the loss of a hand. The war in Europe hadn't yet come to an end, nor would it be ending for months, but everyone talked of a future, as if certain it would and that only the Allies could win.

In late September, a little more than a year since we'd crossed into Italy, my father asked the Bellinis for yet an additional favor. He wanted a Sabbath dinner with all of the family we could be sure of at least for the present. Food was becoming available now, and they said they were glad to oblige.

There were twenty of us, two-thirds the number who'd been at our Passover seders in Warsaw. They were our combined families—Bellinis and Levys—as well as Don Casini, who had again been released from prison, Padre Cipriano, Signora Pietranera, the Leonis, and Annamaria. Matilde, only weeks before the Allies had reached us, had crossed into Switzerland.

When the Leonis arrived, Daniel flew to their arms and asked them if later, when they went home together, the three of them, they also could take Emilia. Kissing him, stroking his hair, they told him that neither could come except to visit—anytime, always. He argued, but briefly, and then went back to Emilia.

At the table, somebody—probably Joel, since he was the one who'd been least subjected to danger—had raised the question of fear. There were answers, but the ones I remember were Annamaria's and Don Casini's. Annamaria insisted she never had feared for herself. Nor, she said, had she really been worried for me, except, perhaps, once. It was only, always, for Enrico.

Hesitant, Joel asked, "And what about Enrico?"

She thought for a long time and said, "Enrico was never afraid."

"I was," Don Casini said.

"Of what?" she asked. "*You* were convinced that a heaven was waiting. Of what?"

"Not of death," he said. "What is death? But of a foolish image, an imaginary fate. Foolish, no doubt, but to me it was real: a barbed-wire noose."

My father was hardly paying attention. He kept looking at Daniel and then at Emilia. He signaled to Daniel to come, and when he did, he gave him some bread and told him, "To share with Emilia."

It was then that I knew a day would arrive, when Daniel was seven, when my father would say that he, Daniel, for as long as he lived, would be responsible for her, Nicole's child, as I, I already knew, would always be, had already chosen to be, for Annamaria's.

I stared at Ondine until she looked over at me, meeting my gaze. I nodded, and as she watched, I walked to Annamaria and gave her the leaf.

EPILOGUE

RABBI CASSUTO DIED AT AUSCHWITZ. SO TOO DID HIS sister's husband, Saul Campagnano, who had been arrested in Piazza della Signoria. And so too did Mario Finzi.

Anna Cassuto, condemned to Auschwitz as well, survived. Her youngest child, forty days old, died. Her sister-in-law, Hulda Campagnano, entrusted the other three, together with her own two children, to Catholics, who sheltered them until the Liberation, and later took them to Jerusalem, where, in 1945, Anna Cassuto joined them. She was one of seventy Hadassah Hospital workers killed in the ambush by Arabs on April 13, 1948.

Raffaele Cantoni, on the way to meet the cattle car waiting in

Verona, jumped from the moving train and survived the fall. He died on June 24, 1971.

Padre Cipriano Ricotti, elected by his Dominican brothers, became the prior of the San Marco monastery. He lived until January 4, 1989.

Don Leto Casini is now Monsignor Casini, eighty-eight years old, much honored and loved in Florence, as is Matilde Cassin Vardi, much younger, in Jerusalem.

Palo Alto, California, July 9, 1990